BLACK DOUGAL

Also by David Walker

The Storm and the Silence
Geordie
The Pillar
Digby
Harry Black
Where the High Winds Blow
Storms of Our Journey and Other Stories
Winter of Madness
Mallabec
Come Back, Geordie
Cab-Intersec
The Lord's Pink Ocean

FOR YOUNG PEOPLE

Sandy Was a Soldier's Boy
Dragon Hill
Pirate Rock
Big Ben

BLACK DOUGAL

DAVID WALKER

HOUGHTON MIFFLIN COMPANY BOSTON

1974

FIRST PRINTING   C

Library of Congress Cataloging in Publication Data

Walker, David Harry, 1911–
   Black Dougal.
     I. Title.
PZ3.W14666B13   [PR6045.A275]   813'.5'4   73–14769
ISBN 0–395–17128–8

Printed in the United States of America

BLACK DOUGAL

⚜ 1 ⚜

"I MUST BE GOING," he said at last, but another twenty minutes of *the facts are inescapable* and *we must face the facts* and *the fact is, Dougal* elapsed before I was permitted to escort Jasper Pilgrim to his handsome Rover, just the car for an eminent solicitor and tweedy Writer to the Signet. He looked at me in a kindly way, said: "The ultimate decision must be yours," and drove down the potholed drive of Drin.

The ultimate decision was not mine. It was being forced upon me by inescapable facts that I could not quite bring myself to face.

"Damnation," I said. "Come on, Bernardo." He settled to walk beside me, my hand on his noble brow, wide as a soup plate. Bernardo knew that I felt doom and gloom. In untroubled times he never deigned to keep close company, but would amble after interesting smells. That afternoon he stayed with me through the beeches and up the Den, and all the way to the Fall of Drin where we sat together on a rock. Thanks, or no thanks, to disease and Danish nets, not a single salmon climbed the Fall while we were there.

It was a cascade rather than a waterfall, after the first high jump quite an easy stepladder for a fish as it neared the end of its spawning journey. An early flash of memory, still vivid, was of Grandfather bringing me to watch the salmon try and fall back and try again. Grandfather said something in his jokey voice about me having to keep on trying like the salmon.

One's childhood memories are isolated pebbles on a dusty path. It was winter the next time at the Fall of Drin. I see icicles. I hear Grandfather say: *I have something bad to tell you, Dougal.* Then he told me of my father's death in February 1945 when I was eight. I cried and soon forgot, but always did remember.

"Well now, Bernardo," I said to my friend, who cocked his head and then lay down to hear me out. Only a nearby listener could have heard me out below the loud Fall of Drin, but there was no other listener. "The situation is that we have one lowground farm in hand, and that barely pays its way. We have two hill farms which do not. We have woods valuable to the timber merchant, but then no woods. We have an excellent small salmon river with few salmon in it. We have grouse disease. We have a decrepit nursery garden down in Surrey. We have Drin, an Adam house of modest size, quite charming in appearance. We have some five thousand pounds, death duties all paid up. These are our assets. Our liabilities, Bernardo, are first that the charming Adam mansion is newly discovered to be riddled with dry rot, estimated cost of extirpation: ten thousand, which makes us minus five. Our gravest liability, Bernardo, is the new laird, Sir Dougal Trocher, still of Drin, who is an incorrigible vacillator.

"I know that I lack drive. I have no business skills. I flounder in accounts. I know that at thirty-four I am already a pedantic bachelor. Plant life is the one single thing of which I am a cognoscente, yet the nursery makes a pittance. So we have got to sell."

There was a stir in the dark surface of the pool, a trout come up. It could be a grim place in grim weather; a lovely place as now, the sun on ferns that clung to rock, the rainbows in the spray, wet boulders in white water. My trouble was that I loved the place. Perhaps few human beings are any longer blessed and burdened with one particular place to love from early childhood, and through youth, and to come back to. You can call that sentimental, and it is. Nostalgia must be sentimental.

2

Bernardo leaned his head against me, and I said: "I kept the worst thing to last. Worse than losing the hill, than losing the Fall of Drin, than losing the Den, than losing the people, than losing the house and losing the parks and losing a chance to make a garden to end all gardens — worse than any of these is that I am going to lose what I can never dare to try to win. I am going to lose Tirene." Tie-reeny, she is called.

Bernardo growled. It was a long low rumble from his boots, the first growl that I had ever heard him utter in four patrician years. Bernardo spoke his mind for a very human reciprocal reason. *That disobedient bum,* she called him. *That slothful moron.* "I quite agree with you, Bernardo, and yet I love her. And what is love? What is truth? asked Pontius Pilate." I emitted something of a caustic chuckle. "Let's go home."

Bernardo deserted me forthwith to go bumbling down the Den. It was a small wilderness astride the river which ran fast and shallow, with no salmon lies. Hence, the banks had never been kept clear for fishing. It made a natural shrub garden, the path meandering above lively water, but in Grandfather's late years had become a tangled jungle. And here I was, how typical of me, tearing out the old Ponticum, the dreary laurels (in that I could be ruthless), here I was, thinking of the new Den I would fashion. I glimpsed his white and brown through undergrowth. "Heel, Bernardo!" But he ignored me. Something else merited attention, and he crashed through bushes at a burly gallop.

"If I could only go where I am going," I remarked. "And damn the obstructions and the consequences." I was surprised to meet my friend and neighbor round a corner. "Oh, hullo," I said. "Was talking to myself."

"Hullo, Dougal. That's enough, Bernardo, you amiable oaf." But Tarquie Duncatto said it with affection, scratching him in a popular place between ear and brow. "I do a lot of mumblin' to myself. They say it's mad. I say who isn't?"

If anyone was less mad than most, it was Duncatto, that redoubtable Laird and Lord. "On my way home from

Crummock," he said in his clipped way. "I thought perhaps a quick one. Ida Peebles said you started up the Den."

We walked on down, Bernardo now faithfully at heel. Duncatto had that effect on people. "They're far better than ours," he said about the giant beeches. "How old are they, Dougal?"

"Two hundred and sixty or so."

"They look sound too," he said.

I did not comment about that, knowing that he meant the timber merchant. I also guessed that he had met Jasper Pilgrim, and had come this evening not primarily for a quick one but to help me at last to make my mind up. Tarquie is the most plain-spoken, forthright fellow, full of guile.

I left him in the library with whisky, and went to get Bernardo's supper. "I tellt His Lordship you was away up the Den," said Ida Peebles. "I thought His Lordship's company would be a nice change after the gas-gas of yon lawyer gentleman. Did I do right, Dougal?"

"Yes, thank you, Ida." She was my nanny, and I escaped her.

"I met Jasper Pilgrim in the High Street, sorry to hear about the dry rot. Bad, eh?"

"At this end of the house." The library paneling looked healthy, but the surveyor sleuth had removed sections, now cunningly replaced. "Riddled with it. Ten thousand is the estimate, and you know what that means, more like twenty." I helped myself to whisky.

"Bad luck," he said. "We had it at Duncatto too, but in the disused kitchen regions." He looked at me. "I suppose that means the final kibosh, Dougal?"

"I suppose it does," I said. "I know it does. But still . . ."

Tarquie Duncatto was the third executor of Grandfather's estate, and knew about my financial woes, but he knew or understood much more than that because we were the same kind of animal, if of different degree in titles and possessions, Duncatto of Duncatto, Trocher of Drin. Yet it would be hard

4

to find two more dissimilar same animals than us drinking whisky in the rotten library at Drin.

"You would need a cool hundred thousand capital to make this place a going proposition," he said patiently, too patiently. "You can't beg it. You can't borrow it. You're much too decent a milksop chap to steal it." He paused. "Take my own case now. Thanks to Lois having a bit to help us out, I manage to struggle along with a colossal overdraft. But by God, Dougal, if I was as rich as Croesus, I wouldn't lend you a single brass penny to bungle with and be taken for a sucker with. You cherish a notion that you could work the farms. Well, in the first place, you're far too nice a cluck to sack your manager and your grieve who have been at Drin for thirty years. In the second place, can you imagine yourself being midwife to a cow?"

I shuddered. "To be honest with you, no."

"Honest," he said. "That's another thing. You're too damned honest."

It seemed to me that one is either honest or dishonest, not too damned honest, but I was afraid of Tarquie on the warpath, in fact quite enjoyed getting the rough edge of his tongue. Bernardo scratched at the door, so I let him in, and he subsided with a clump on the hardwood floor. It sounded hollow, more hidden rot, no doubt. "What else?" I asked mildly.

"You're sorry for yourself, is one thing. Another is that you should be telling me to take a running jump."

"Why bother when everything you say is true."

He grunted. One never quite got to the bottom of Tarquie's grunts. "It isn't as if you lack a beast at bottom. We all know what you did at Aden."

"That was only bullets. What are bullets?"

"Bloody fool," he said, quite pleased with me, and helped himself to a modest top-up. "I know, Dougal," he said. "I know. I know." He was a wonderfully good friend, fifteen years older, ageless really. "I was talking about Lois helping us out. It isn't much, but a healthy *dot* to tip the balance, clothes her, travels her, keeps that vulgar Rolls. What I mean is, Dougal . . ." He was now ill at ease. "What I mean is that some of the likes of us have been able to keep body and soul and place together by snaffling rich females from across the water." He looked me full in the eye, and said: "I suppose that isn't on?"

I shook my head. You see, the wayward, adorable Tirene was his daughter.

He went over to the window. "Not bad-lookin' beasts," he said about my fat black bullocks in the park below the house. "Y'know, flash-alecky go-getter types, I never had much time for them. But at least they do something. At least they don't step backwards, apologizin' for their existence."

"Meaning me?"

"Meaning you," he confirmed. "Far and away the best heavyweight of your time at Cambridge, but you gave up boxing, not because you couldn't take punishment, because you couldn't bear to dish it out. True, eh?"

"True," I said. "If there's one thing I loathe, it's violence. Don't you?"

"Until it comes to the point," said Tarquie Duncatto, a gentleman in the true meaning, a killer too. "You haven't decided yet, and I know damned well you won't decide. You will sit here moping, sorry for yourself, while the floors buckle, the walls fall in, the whole place goes to pot, and finally the people who work for you are out of jobs at the age of sixty. And all why? All because, as that pettifogging Pilgrim says, you will not face facts. In other words, you won't meet life head-on."

"Is it meeting life head-on to give up without a struggle everything your family has had for X hundred years?"

"It can be," he said. "And in this case I am very sorry, Dougal, but it is. Well, Adolf Hitler wanted to take the place down with him. Does Dougal Trocher?"

"That's too much," I said.

"I know," he said. "I've been trying to provoke you. I've

6

been doing my stupid best to provoke you into being the man you are, or could be." Another grunt. "A rich wife is out. Which leaves one last impossible solution. If you had some oomph, you would embark upon a life of crime.

"Well, you can't, you won't, you never could, you haven't got it in you. If you pulled off the Great Train Robbery alone, your melting heart would require you to give half the loot to the guard whose jaw you bashed, and in retrospect, it hurt you more than it ever hurt him, poor chap; and the other half you would hand over to the Chancellor of the Exchequer because you had a guilty conscience." He glared at me. "Prissy poop," he said. "Well, I must go home to face the women."

Women. Plural woman. Could it be? My temper had been rising, but now it was my heart that thumped. "Women?" I rapped it out in Tarquie fashion.

"M'daughter's home. Arrived at lunchtime with a Californian communist author in an Aston Martin. Well, he ate and drank us out of house and home, uttered not one word except to condescend how rewarding it had been to catch a glimpse of our way of life, and drove away, thank God. But no thanks to the Deity for what ensued."

"What did ensue?" I asked as we walked to his scarlet souped-up Mini, a grave Bernardo in attendance.

"The usual, only more so. M'wife got on to the company m'daughter kept, and from that to the girl's appearance, especially the hair, I must say it is absolutely ghastly, *looking like some ropy slut, how dare you!* was m'wife's conclusion. Lois can dish it out, as I know to my cost, but she meets her match in young Tirene."

Bernardo growled. It was a long low rumble from his boots. "That's a funny thing," I said. "I never heard him growl before this afternoon, and the other time was when I chanced to mention Tirene's name."

"Sage hound," said Tarquie, giving Bernardo the kind of haymaker pat he understood. "I wish you'd bite the blue jeans off her shapely backside." He guffawed at his tasteless joke, thanked me for whisky, and departed.

7

I ate my lonely dinner, and carried the dishes out to Ida Peebles.

"His Lordship was saying Miss Tirene's home."

"So I understand, Ida."

"And His Lordship was saying Miss Tirene's appearance leaves much to be desired. *Tirene looks like Bernardo's dinner,* was what His Lordship said." Ida Peebles cackled. "He's a caution, is His Lordship."

The sage hound was out of earshot in the library. ". . . Sorry, Ida, I didn't hear that last saying of His Lordship's?"

"It wasn't His Lordship, it was me. But I was mentioning His Lordship, and I was saying if there was more grand jocks like what His Lordship is, we wouldn't be hearing yon daft blether about Wumman's Lib like Miss Tirene."

"How come, Ida?"

"Because there's no sic a thing as a braw laddie any more. Why would a self-respectin' lassie be accepting lesser wages than some softie in currlers not worth takin' to her bed? Yon's what Wumman's Lib is all about."

"Is that so, Ida?"

"Ay, that's so, Dougal." She stacked the dishes. I was not allowed to dry. "Like what His Lordship was telling me about courting Her Ladyship in Boston in America, shilly-shally, dilly-dally until His Lordship was fair desperate, until His Lordship had to rape her future Ladyship pure and simple more or less, His Lordship's very words." Ida emitted an ample chuckle.

"I don't find rape particularly funny."

"Nor me neither, nor His Lordship. It was a figure of speech His Lordship was making, mebbe like a comparison."

"With what?"

"With what once used to be, but His Lordship never said it. And His Lordship never said a word to me about what him and the fancy lawyer gentleman are trying to persuade you, Dougal. It wouldn't be right to speak to me in my position. But I ken fine what's in their minds — that you're to sell the

8

place, that you'll do better for yourself and for the likes of us, and for the land by selling now."

Ida Peebles hung up the dishtowel and turned to look at me for the first time in this one-sided conversation. "I'm just an old body, Dougal," she said. "But I was your nanny from the month, and I'm taking the right to say: Don't do it. We can manage."

"We can't, though, Ida. They're right. We can't."

"*We can't.* Was yon what Dougal Trocher of Drin said in fourteen hundred and seventy-six when he and his men and the women and the bairns starved through a long winter's siege in the old castle on this very spot? Did he surrender?"

"No," I said. "In the springtime, the pretty little ring time, he broke out and laid the County of Crummock to waste — pillage, murder, theft and rape. He even personally raped the Lady of Duncatto. What would His Lordship say to that?"

She chuckled again. "If I ken His Lordship, it wouldn't be what His Lordship would be after saying."

"What should I do, then? Lay Crummock to waste etcetera for the sake of Drin?"

"When you were a wee boy, Dougal — it was that summer after your poor dad was killed, and it was a rare hot day and you had a swim at the Fall of Drin, and I was at my knitting and I never saw until you were standing on top of the rock twenty feet up and more, and I cried: *No, Dougal, you're not to do it!* And you said: *It's what I'm to do,* and down into the deep black water Dougal jumped. What's happened to Black Dougal?"

⚏ 2 ⚏

THE OWL HAS a mixed reputation in my family. There was the propitious owl that hooted every winter's night of fourteen hundred and seventy-six, and then, broad-winged specter flitting through the forest in the moon, showed Dougal Trocher of Drin a way to lead his starving men between his sleeping enemies. Once through the investing lines, they turned, slaughtered every living soul, and feasted.

But all through our waning history, there have been owls that hoot in daytime, invariably foretelling doom. *To-whit-to-woo when the sun is high, Trocher of Drin will surely die.*

I had been wrestling yet again with the estate accounts, trying to think of some honorable stratagem that might pull us through. But it was hopeless, the more so because certain insults festered in my mind: *Too decent a milksop chap; sit here moping, sorry for yourself; you prissy poop. What's happened to Black Dougal?*

I think it fair to say that few prissy poops could be slower to anger than myself, but it grew in me. And yet Ida Peebles, bless her, had spoken stoutly against selling out. That was why I had tried again, a last vain time.

Bernardo and I went for our bedtime dander through the hay that now marked the sweeping lawns of Drin, and to the arboretum, a treasure of exotic trees, many valuable to the timber merchant.

The witching hour was near upon us, but night never falls in our part of Scotland at the end of June.

We had turned for home when an owl hooted in my great-great-grandfather's *Sequoia gigantea*, a prize specimen. It was neither sunlit day nor moonlit night. It was the gloaming. To which school of Trocher legend did this owl belong?

Being in rare seething mood, I did not care a dam, cupped my hands in the ancient way, and blew a veritable owl. We exchanged hoots while Bernardo sat watching me, his head cocked to one side in some perplexity. He had never heard me be an owl before. Then he raised his broad muzzle to the sky where only Venus shone. Bernardo howled. It was a doleful dirge, and it put a stop to hoots.

"I know why you howled," I said at his kennel outside the house. "You howled for everything, and so could I." Two hardtack biscuits and a hug. "Good night, Big Boy." I closed the door of his sleeping quarters, and went to mine.

The face in the looking glass was doggily lugubrious, and too damned honest. It was true that I could not tell a lie. Everything they said was true about me. And yet what could be more dishonest than running away from an inevitable truth?

"You bogus philosopher, shut up," I said to my image, and went to bed. I had strange dreams that night.

They were not the usual quiet dreams of a horticulturist and landscape gardener, but a kaleidoscope of brood and vicious action — chop his head off with the broadsword, not very fair, he was asleep — an interlude of tawny owl, the enigmatic ghost, unblinking — now concupiscence too, blood hot to rape the Lady of Duncatto, but the pale limbs beside the Shalimar, they went away — and now Black Dougal at the Fall of Drin, a mammoth splash of Dougal in black water . . . There is a storm, the lightning stabs, the thunder crashes, ripples down and down to far away to the Royal Bank of Scotland in the Royal borough: *Stick 'em up, it is I, Trocher of Drin behind my mask. A hundred thousand, Janet, if you please. — What would you like it in, Sir Dougal?* — *Fivers, Janet, English notes, and stir yer stumps, wee Janet.* — *It's market day, Sir Dougal, but I'll do my very best.* — *Your very best is not quite good enough,* I said, and I shot Janet in the Crummock Branch of the Royal Bank of Scotland. She was a bonny wee teller, and I woke up with a fearful yell.

Or did I yell? But I think so, because Bernardo wowfed once below my western window, on the arboretum side. A blackbird sang for breaking dawn. There was no sound inside the House of Drin. *You can't, you won't, you never could. You haven't got it in you.*

"We'll see about that," I said, and slept like an infant until Ida Peebles brought my morning cup of tea.

"Fine day fer it, Dougal."

"Fine day fer it, Ida," I replied in Scotch.

"What are ye wantin' tae yer breakfast?"

"There's finnan haddie?"

"Ay, there's finnan haddie."

"Stir yer stumps fer finnan haddie, Ida Peebles."

"Stir yer stumps, the very idea at my time of life!"

"Well, get a move on," I said in English. "I don't want to have to shoot you too." I remembered that part very well.

Ida stared, drew in breath to speak, thought better of it and went away. I quite liked the face in the shaving mirror, black mop, square jaw, the pale eyes gleamed.

Duncatto is an early bird, so I telephoned him before breakfast. "Duncatto here," his invariable opener.

"Hullo, Tarquie. You'll be relieved to know that I've made my mind up. But I could do with some advice. Would you happen to be at home this morning?"

"Might happen," he said. "Good news about the mind up, well, I mean, bad news but can't be helped."

"And Lois too, if she chances to be about the place?"

"Might chance," he said. "I'll ask the woman. Want to stay for lunch?"

"I'd like to, thanks. See you about eleven, then."

"Do you usually go to lunch with people at eleven?"

"Not always," I said. The unprecedented euphoria of decision-making had not yet worn off. "Good-bye, Tarquie."

Salted porridge and cream, finnan haddock with two poached eggs on top, it was a smashing breakfast, and I told her so.

"Your appetite's back," she said. "Well, that's something." But Ida was a little guarded with me.

"I'm out for lunch. Going to Duncatto."

At that, she looked me over, head to brogues and back again, a sniff, no other comment.

"Ida, would you say it's possible to be too damned honest?"

"I would that," she said. "And you should know."

How shaggily beautiful Drin looked that morning as I went my rounds of kennels, farm and vegetable garden. How cheerful was my mood after four downward months to gloom, and the faithful few responded to it.

There were two vehicles in the motor house, the one my Morris van, the other Grandfather's ancient motor bicycle and sidecar. One of my few successes in these dim times had been to get it going again, a handy and economical means of transport on the rough roads of the estate. Bernardo loved it, and he leaped aboard the sidecar now without waiting for permission. Yesterday I would not have dreamed of risking Constable McIntoon, that puristical pest. This morning — well, why not? The die was cast, the air was balmy, and the sun was shining.

We were a good combination, being of approximately equal weight, a help in such a tippy vehicle. To Bernardo, riding the sidecar was purest bliss. He sat with episcopal dignity beside me, entirely motionless but for the twitching of his coal black nose.

There is a fast way to Duncatto, but I took sequestered sideroads on that fateful morning, chugging at twenty along the winding lanes of our native Crummock, which is both a highland and a lowland county, and we rode steep byways where the one merged with the other.

I was happy, at last a future to grapple with. That was it, to grapple with. I stopped at a vantage point, whence to spy for McIntoon. It was the mating time, the growing time, the scented time. A few white clouds were sailing, and their few dark shadows sailed across bare hills up there, across the fields and woods down here. Nearby in a larch a pigeon cooed, *coo-coo*, flew out and up with a clap of wings, glided and went back to coo, to woo, the cushy-doo. No McIntoon in sight, I mounted the bike, gave her a kick, stowed my kilt decently, and rode on to Duncatto.

The Baltigg gate was open, as always when the Duncattos are in residence. I stopped on the drive because Tarquie and Lois had come to meet us with the Labrador, Garry, a good friend of Bernardo's.

"I haven't seen that thing for ages — your grandfather's scoutcar, wasn't it?"

"You look so cute together," Lois said.

"Thank you, Lois." I never see the Duncattos without thinking what a marvelous pair, point and counterpoint, the gruff rough baron, his slinky baroness, the square and the slim of it, and they made Tirene.

The dogs played in the park, where we walked the bank of the River Tigg. "So you've made your mind up," Tarquie said. "Well done you."

"Don't be so heartless, Tarquie. I think it's the saddest thing I've ever heard. No sooner do we have Dougal back at Drin than he has to leave. And you only say: *Well done.*"

"Dougal knows quite well what I mean." Lois took my arm, and I thought how funny-strange it was that I should feel perfectly at ease with Mother, not tongue-tied, nor impelled to sermonize, not ill at ease, uncouth.

"We're going to miss you terribly," she said.

"I'll be away a month. I hope a month will do it."

"That's sensible," Tarquie said. "Then you won't feel honor-bound to lead prospective buyers to your dry rot. Let 'em find it."

"Couldn't you please stop being sarcastic?" Lois said.

"You've formed the wrong conclusion. I'm not selling Drin. That's what I want your advice about."

The effect upon my friends and neighbors was indeed electric. "Not selling, Dougal? Have you had some lovely windfall?"

"Have you gone off your bloody rocker?"

"No windfall," I said. "And probably off my rocker. If so, it's your fault for provoking me."

"I told you not to bully him. I told you that in poor Dougal's present state of mind, you would only drive him to a nervous breakdown, but would you listen? Will you ever listen?"

"Shock tactics. Cruel to be kind, y'know. Last resort, I thought it might work."

"It did work," I said. "I'm ready to embark, but how and what and where, I need some help."

"Ready to embark what on?"

"A life of crime. *You can't, you won't, you never could. You haven't got it in you,* Lord Duncatto's very words. Well, I can, I will, and I think I have, don't ask me how, entirely thanks to you."

"Oh, I say."

"*Oh, I say,*" she mimicked him. They bickered quite a lot.

We walked beside the Tigg, a placid river here. Larks were soaring, singing. Where is she? I wondered about Tirene. Sweet one at Heaven's gate, where is she? ". . . Sorry, didn't hear."

"You mean: Hold up the bank in Crummock, sort of thing?"

"Tarquie, don't be idiotic. That's cops and robbers stuff."

"I dreamed it actually, a fearful nightmare, had to shoot wee Janet, and I woke up yelling. That was when I decided. But not the bank, for various reasons."

"What reasons?" He looked closely at me.

"First, even on market day I would get only a modest haul. Second, however disguised, they would recognize my shape. Third, I would be taking mostly the hard-won earnings of the poor, and that is against my principles. So a preliminary thought is that it must be further afield, outside Scotland probably."

"H'mm," Tarquie said. "What about pickin' off the Burlington Arcade?"

"That's old hat," said Lois. "Barred now too. But there's always Cartier's."

"No, there isn't, not a hope in hell. I've cased that joint myself."

"When?" I inquired, ever new depths to be sounded in this peer of the realm.

"Hanging about while Lois looks at what she can't afford. A mental exercise to pass the time. Could I crack this one? Decided against it."

"I can't think properly when I'm walking," Lois said. So we sat on warm grass above the River Tigg.

"There goes a fish." He had a phenomenal eye for the shadow of a salmon, moving or at rest.

"Concentrate, Tarquie."

"I am," he said. "All shocked attention. By a life of crime, do you mean make a steady job of it?"

"Certainly not. I mean devote one month wholeheartedly to this project, whatever it may be, that's why I need your advice — then invest the proceeds wisely and nurse Drin back to health, very simple really."

"And the proceeds — how much did you have in mind?"

"A hundred thousand minimum, that was the figure you suggested."

"A hundred thousand pounds, but Dougal dear, that's quite a pile of lolly to pick up in one month."

"Well, what about those hijacker chaps who jump with a cool million dollars, one day's work? There is a difficulty, though, two in fact. First, I wouldn't dare to parachute. Second, I don't fancy holding guns to people's heads, nor them to mine."

"If you can shoot a pretty little teller in a dream, would you stop at shootin' a pretty little hostess in the flesh? What's the difference?"

"Oh, shut up, Tarquie. Can't you see that Dougal is in deadly earnest?"

"Are you?" he demanded.

"Never more so, Tarquie."

"H'mm," he said. "Let's get down to it, then. The object is to clobber a lot of riches quickly, and when you've got it, get away with it — far more than half the problem. That means you can't frig about with lesser jobs. One big coup would be the best of all. Your inexperience is a liability. Your inability to tell an honest whopper is another, although it mightn't be entirely in a one-shot operation, in fact, manifest integrity could help a lot. Your turn, Lois."

"Well, I agree with Tarquie that it must be big. And if it's going to be big, it has to be where the money is. So that makes me think of across the ocean. And I agree that his integrity could be a terrific asset, I mean his looks and lineage and everything, all are on the credit side. He's clever too in his rather pedantic, I mean deliberate sort of way. But, Dougal dear, if we're going to help you, we have to know some negative things — for instance, where you draw the line?"

"I've been thinking about that. Holdups are against my principles. Bleeding the poor is against my principles. Soaking the rich is quite another matter. In fact, soak-the-rich is the key to the enterprise as I see it."

"A splendid sentiment," said Tarquie. "But how to soak 'em? There's the rub. Blackmail is not to be ruled out, provided the victim is unsavory enough to soothe your well-known conscience. Kidnap is a possibility, even if limited violence is implicit there. And then there is plain theft."

At this point, Garry and Bernardo, who had been cavorting near us, spotted a hare across the Tigg, yelped like puppies, plunged in, swam over and took off. "Garry, come back, Garry, damn you!"

Whistles and shouts, to which I contributed to no avail. They departed in full cry, far behind the agile hare.

"You have no more control over that dog than I have over our . . ."

"Over our what?"

"Over our daughter, idiot."

"Where is Tirene?" I could ask it casually.

"Don't ask me."

Tarquie touched her hand, and she turned hers to his. Then he stood to blow another whistle blast, no dogs in sight. "Plain theft," he said again. "What about that one, Dougal?"

"It's clean," I said. "I like it. A weekend party sort of thing, I was turning over in my mind."

"It has merit. A few bank presidents with fat wives showing off their rocks to one another, you might net a fortune that way."

"Stupid," Lois said. "If they're showing off their rocks to one another, how do you remove the rocks without a gun's persuasion?"

"It occurred to me that they can't wear them all the time, not swimming, surely, not working in the garden, for example. It's just a guess, I haven't thought it through."

"For someone who never in his life has strayed from the path of virtue, you're not doing too badly, I would think." Tarquie looked at me with baffled respect. "Dougal, my boy, what's got into you?"

"Despair," I said. "The breaking point. I jumped. It's a great feeling, even if I don't quite understand myself."

"Remarkable," he said.

"Dougal, do you have any contacts in the States or Canada, the right kind of people?"

"There's a professor at the University of New Hampshire, writes to me about hybrid rhododendrons, a delightful chap, he sounds."

"But perhaps not quite the right kind of people I was meaning."

"Not another soul I know of in the USA. I do have a third cousin once removed in Montreal. I believe he's head of something called Algonquin Steel."

"Algonquin Steel, but that's enormous, sounds much more like the right kind of people."

"Claud Merriwell by name. I've never met the man, although he wrote after Grandfather died. And there was a letter from him among Grandfather's papers, office of the president, type-like printing, cordially yours, and all that. He sounded a most frightful snob."

"One's transatlantic kith and kin, they tend to be."

"He could be a super contact. *Allow me the honor of presenting you to the Chief of Clan Trocher.*"

"But, Lois, I don't want to go like that, and perhaps get caught and drag our name in the mud. I thought of a false passport."

"Do you know what a decent false passport costs?"

"No, I don't."

"Nor do I. Now, wait a minute, let me think." Lois put her elegant hands to her face, one hand with a very elegant solitaire diamond on it, and was lost in thought. The dogs straggled back from their fruitless chase, tails down. Tarquie cursed Garry, I cursed Bernardo. They shook their wet coats, and lay down panting at respectful distance.

"I've got it now. A false passport is very noble, Dougal, but it's the wrong way absolutely. Also, if you were caught, Interpol would soon find out who you really were — wouldn't they, Tarquie? — and that would make you twice the criminal, not once. And don't forget that the cause is noble too. If you don't believe that, you shouldn't be going."

"In this case, young fella, the end indubitably justifies the means, within proper reason, that is, of course." Far from dissuading me, my neighbors were proving to be most enthusiastic advocates of my venture into crime.

"What do you suggest, then, Lois?"

"I suggest that you go with kilt swinging, bagpipes squealing, escutcheon flying, figuratively, I mean. In other words, you put on optimum dog. But you go as more than a common baronet. You go as Sir Dougal Trocher Bart, the eminent horticulturist and landscape architect, which you are, just far

19

too modest. So you draw them two ways, and both spell S-N-O-B. Gardening is an ultimate status symbol. It's a natural, isn't it, Tarquums darling?"

"Brilliant, my love, entirely worthy of your genius." But he frowned. "There's one snag, as I see it. Supposin' you've got them all clustered round you at the kidney-shaped pool, or hangin' on your every word at the shrub border in sensible gardening clothes, how do you manage to snaffle the diamonds, rubies, emeralds and whatnot from the boudoir?"

"That is a very real difficulty. I shall have to think."

"And I'm cook today, so I shall have to cook. Let's talk later. But, Dougal, I think it's a super idea, and what I wouldn't give to be your moll, stealing from one bedroom to another where the action is, but I don't think my stuffy old Lord would quite approve."

Lois walked off to the house. At forty-five or so, she still moved with the loose-limbed flow of a girl. I shook my head to shake away a snatch of dream remembered, pale limbs beside the Shalimar, the River Tigg. One's subconscious can be the very devil, pushing up dreams one never thought of, quite appalling.

"And what a moll that one would make," said Tarquie. "Now, Dougal, you can talk freely to us, and you have, a great compliment. But if I were you, I wouldn't breathe a word to anyone else, not a soul, not Tirene, for instance." He glanced anxiously at me and away.

"Less than likely," I said.

"Life is full of troubles, and one of mine is trying to keep the peace between m'wife and daughter. If it isn't one thing, it's another. At the moment it's two things mostly: It's the personal appearance, which is awful, especially those Medusa locks . . ."

"Medusa. Was that snakes for hair?"

"It was, and Lois told her so, another screaming match, like fishwives. And then it's the fount of all wisdom, Chairman Mao. Personally, I couldn't care less if people want to be communists as long as they don't bother me in my commune,

20

which is a hell of a lot more communistic than any commune Chairman Mao or Comrade Brezhnev live in. Well, isn't it?"

"Well, I don't know quite, Tarquie. Depends just what you mean."

"Lois takes a very different view. I have to keep reminding myself that she's American, and a communist to an American is like a whisky bottle to a temperance fanatic. So more screaming matches. But it's mostly Tirene's fault. Look at that dreadful chap she produced yesterday, patronizing phony. She did it on purpose to infuriate her mother. Love and hate, what's it all about? Well, all I can say is thank God I'm not a passionate woman."

We had a bit of a laugh about that.

"You and Tirene used to be great buddies."

"Yes," I said. "When she was a child." And I thought: Safe with Tirene, the enchanting child. Safe with Lois now. *Safe.* It was my fearful trouble. "Will Tirene be at lunch?"

"Dunno," he said. "All I ask for is a bit of peace, and all I get is a bit of stick." Tarquie sorry for himself was not unfunny. "A bit of stick," he said thoughtfully. "I wish you . . . H'mm."

"I'll fetch the motorbike."

"Okay. See you at the house."

Bernardo came with me. I had a few words with him about his bad behavior, but my mind was not in it. Where was she? What was she doing? Would I either be speechless or make her speeches. Would I see her alone?

We climbed aboard. We rode up the winding drive to Duncatto, which was an Adam house much like our own, but in sound condition. I parked Grandfather's combination in the shade, switched off, and sat a moment. So much had changed. So much was going to happen. "It could be called dishonest," I muttered to myself. "But how can a noble cause be called dishonest?"

⊠ 3 ⊠

Two TREES BORDERED the front lawn at Duncatto, one a cedar of Lebanon, in whose shade I had stopped, the other a European elm, a fine specimen of that species, with one great horizontal bough half as thick as the trunk.

I told Bernardo to stay in the sidecar, and my shoes crunched on gravel as I walked toward the house, no sign of Tirene. Then I heard a voice, the words indistinguishable, and my heart gave its mammoth jump.

That voice came from the elm direction. I moved round to see her reclining against the tree, her knees drawn up, bare legs below the tattered blue jeans above the ropey sandals, and on her knees a small red book. She wore a pink vest-sweater effect, not uniformly pink but shot with gray corruptive smudges, you may know the mode called The Dirty Look, no doubt a perfectly clean garment. The nose and brow were pure Grecian with the faintest tilt of tip. The rest of her features were obscured by long black locks with smoky red hints or tints in them, the loveliest hair in all the world, but look at it.

"Hullo," I said.

"Oh, hullo," she said, not very nicely. The gulf between ten and twenty-three, perhaps that very difference had let us be the best of pals imaginable. Such was not the case between twenty-one and thirty-four.

"Don't you know you shouldn't sit under elm trees?"

"I'll sit under what I want to, but why not on earth?"

"Why not on earth because that branch could come down without the slightest warning on your head. That's what they do."

"It seems to have stayed up for a century or two." But she stood, the book closed on one finger, and moved a little. Her mother's comment about Medusa locks had been near the mark, alas.

"What are you reading, Tirene?" I said it rather more loudly than I meant.

Bernardo growled, the same deep rumble, for the third time now. "What's he growling at?"

"I'm afraid it's at the mention of your name, seems to be a new thing with him."

"Big softy," she said. "I didn't think he had it in him."

"Careful!" The intrepid girl was walking straight over to the sidecar, Bernardo's property, his face impassive. There were patches on her blue jeans, a smaller black one on the left of backside, a larger red one on the right, but they faced me, not Bernardo.

"Say hullo," she said.

Bernardo shook his head from side to side in a jowled way that might be menacing, but then he wowfed: *Hullo!* basso profundo, a sure sign of approval accorded to few people, most mysterious, and a relief.

Tirene scratched his ear. She had her father's love for dogs. It was perhaps Bernardo's phlegmatic disposition linked to mine that made her a little intolerant of him.

"I used to love riding in that thing," she said, coming away. "You were quite human then."

Ten or twelve years ago, I was quite human then. And all this morning I had felt quite human almost at last again until I met my former friend. "We could go for a ride now if you like, just down the drive and back, a little one, it's such a glorious day and not lunchtime yet, we don't get many days like this in Scotland, dreadful climate, would you like to?"

She looked at me with a certain kindness. "You do sound sort of queer," she said. "Are you all right?"

"I'm fine, thank you very much, Tirene. Out you get, Bernardo, out!"

Bernardo had been sitting up. He now lay down, a tight fit, a contented grunt. "I'm afraid he won't. But there's a pillion seat, Tirene."

"The dog in the sidecar, the little woman on the pillion seat, how typical!"

"You drive it, then."

"Gosh, could I?" She was so mercurial. "Here, take this."

I put her book in my jacket pocket, explained controls, kicked the starter, climbed on behind, and we started down the drive. All went smoothly until she essayed a change of gear for higher speed. "Steady!" I said, nearly jerked off. "Nothing to hang on to."

"Hang on to me, silly." I put a hand on each side of her waist for greater security. There were no more jerks, for Tirene was a quick learner, a gifted driver of anything, but she did love speed. It was something of a relief, and yet much too soon, when we slowed to a stop, my thumbs meeting behind her back, my second fingers touching in front, waist encompassed, I had to try it, and I did it.

"That was fun," she said, not moving, nothing moving, the noisy engine quiet. There was a gap between her tangled locks, and in that gap was the valley of her neck. If I dared, if only I dared to put my lips to that pale valley of her neck. She was held captive from behind by much superior strength. For the first time in her adult life I had Tirene where I did not dare to have her, and I did not dare. "Tirene," I said. She was still my captive, and she had not stirred within my grasp. "Would you do me a favor?"

"Oh," she said, and she did not stir. "Well, what?"

"Would you comb your hair?"

She leapt from my grasp and from the machine. "Would I comb my hair? You're all the same. Appearances! What are appearances but hypocrisy? That's what I've just been

24

reading. Do you think Chinese women tart themselves up to be men's playthings? No, they don't. They wear plain smocks; they use no cosmetics; they get equal pay for equal work. And us! What are we but slaves? Now, gimme that book, and just listen to Chairman Mao:

> "Men and women must receive equal pay for equal work in production. Genuine equality between the sexes can only be realized in the process of the socialist transformation of society as a whole."

"Surely true communists do not seek the filthy lucre of reward, Tirene."

"Are you being sarcastic?" It was the danger look.

"No, no, Tirene. But every politician says the same about equality for women. It's hardly the soul of originality."

"But Chairman Mao is putting it to effect. He isn't a paper tiger of capitalism, and that's what you are."

"A fair description," I said. "But I feel sure that Chairman Mao makes them comb their hair."

"He doesn't *make* them. Women in China are truly emancipated."

"They still comb it, don't they?"

"Oh dear, I'm so muddled," Tirene said, her anger mysteriously abated. "In London everything makes sense. In London there's involvement, people care. In London things are relevant. But what relevance is there here? What *is* there here but crummy bourgeois feudalism? All I can say is thank God I'm going South tonight. Bonny Scotland, you can have it, even if my feelings are ambivalent." Tirene sighed at her birthplace in the summer of her discontent. "It's your way of life that's so intolerable. *Verra good, M'Lord. Och ay, Sir Dougal.*" And she giggled, but briefly. "The real live suffering world means nothing to you."

"I lived ten years in the South, and that real live suffering world meant nothing to me." I spoke with some asperity. "The world isn't only people, Tirene."

"But it is," she said. "That's the terrible truth you funny old

25

rustics are hiding from in your never-never land where the faithful peasants touch their forelocks."

"Do they touch their forelocks to Chairman Mao?"

Tirene frowned, considering that. "They worship him, but that isn't touching forelocks."

"Do they disagree with him?"

"I don't think so, not very much. I mean he's so wise, how could they?"

"Do the peasants here disagree with your father?"

"Well, sometimes, I suppose, when he's more impossible than usual."

"He said this morning that his commune is a helluva lot more communistic than any commune Chairman Mao lives in."

Tirene laughed. "Daddy's hopeless."

"He also said that all he wants is a bit of peace, and all he gets is a bit of stick."

"Who from?"

I answered that with silence.

"You're not like yourself today. You seem almost bloody-minded sometimes."

"You find this bourgeois feudalism intolerable. Well, I need a change from it too. I'm going away."

"It's none of my business, I mean, well . . ." Tirene hesitated. "But are you selling Drin?"

"Not for the moment. I think I shall go to Canada and see how things work out."

"Canada? That's worse plutobourgeois. Do you know people there?"

"I have a cousin, head of a company named Algonquin Steel, a proper capitalist, I daresay, no paper tiger."

"You're twisting things in a cynical way."

"Just joking," I said. "You used to like jokes. You were quite human then."

"Then isn't now," she said. "Then isn't now in any way at all."

Bernardo was fast asleep, tired from his abortive hare hunt. I started the engine. "Will you drive us again?"

Tirene drove off, and I held on, permitted to clasp the waist of this bewitching creature whom I loved and feared so much. She drove more slowly and yet more slowly the second time, stopping at last in the shade of the cedar of Lebanon. And I said: "Her countenance is as Lebanon, excellent as the cedars."

"What did you say?" Tirene had not moved, and nor had I.

I misquoted the Song of Solomon again, adding: "Thy neck is as a tower of ivory." Not lifeless cold ivory, but soft warm skin before my eyes.

Tirene shivered. As I felt the shiver tingle in her spine, I chanced to see her father at the window, and that took my poltroon hands away. His red face vanished, and I said: "Now, would you do that favor for me?"

I took the comb from my sporran pocket. It was of tortoiseshell, gold-backed, a small heirloom bearing our coat of arms, once carried in some Trocher woman's reticule, removed this morning from its present home, a glass-topped table in the smaller drawing room at Drin. I thrust it at Tirene. "Please!" I said.

Tirene yielded, but all the time she drew that comb through that matchless hair with many a tangled tug, her bosom heaving, and I watched the bosom, and I watched the hair until it fell in glossiness, smooth order, black touched with smoky tints of deepest red, it was so beautiful, she was so beautiful — all the time she glared at me, not with contempt so much as blue-eyed hate, her bosom free beneath the pink chemise or sweater thing. She threw the comb at me. "Male chauvinist!"

"Your hair is so beautiful. Don't you like it to look nice?"

"Look nice! That isn't me for my own sake, what I'm really like. That's phony, and so is every nice thing you stand for, you reactionary dodo!"

Tirene ran into the house and slammed the door. But

Tarquie appeared. "Welcome to our happy home," he said. We went into his study. There were two decanters of sherry, dark and pale. I took the former and expressed approval.

"It's South African, better than anything except what costs the earth. But I have to hide the bottles when m'daughter's home. She knows damned well where it comes from too. What the eye doesn't see and so on, and I don't begrudge the girl her pleasures, you reactionary dodo, I couldn't help hearing through the window." He laughed shortly. "The fact is I'm worried about the child. What caused that outburst, if not a rude question?"

"I asked Tirene to comb her hair."

"When I tried, you should have heard what I got. Did she?"

"Yes, and then that broadside. It's genuine, Tarquie. She does hate sham."

"I know," he said. "They do. That's the saving grace about them, but . . . Oh, here she comes."

Not only was Tirene's hair as sleek as might be imaginable, but she wore a brief skirt of Duncatto tweed, a green jersey, nylons. "I'm sorry I was rude," she said to me with that enchanting smile, so rarely seen in recent times, and helped herself to South African amontillado. "Are you going to Canada for long?"

"About a month, I think. A month should be enough for the job I have in mind." Looking back on it now, in the wisdom, one might say, of after the event, I remain astonished at my confidence about the job I hardly yet had in mind.

"Oh, it's business. Shrubs and things?"

"Shrubs and things, Tirene."

"But surely that climate is so different from the one you know about."

"There are indeed differences, Tirene, deriving in the main from such variants as latitude, continental mass, oceanic influence, organic structure and precipitation, but these are marginal, lying, as I like to think of it, at each end of botany's vast spectrum."

"Oh, God," she said, refilling her glass.

"Stated otherwise, the fundamental laws apply as much at Duncatto as Peking."

"Very funny." Her sunny mood had been of short duration.

"I was practicing, Tirene. My plan, still in embryo form, and expressed in the simplest terms, is to reap honorable reward by giving gardening instruction to the sort of people who can afford to pay my price."

"Quite a high price to pay, I would think, if that was a sample."

Duncatto chuckled. "All square," he said. "I bet old Dougal soaks 'em too."

"But he hasn't got it in him to soak anybody."

"I happen to be here in person. I am not *he* or *him* or *old Dougal,* a dodo specimen to be dissected."

"Quite right, my boy. I apologize."

"I don't," Tirene said. But then she did address me personally: "You're different. You're not a bit like yourself today. You and Daddy are up to something in cahoots. What *is* all this in aid of?"

But Lois bounded in. Mother and daughter either bounded gracefully, or they flowed with indolence. "Lunch is ready, such as it is." Then she catalogued Tirene's appearance from top to toe, a cool appraisal. "Well, well," she said. "Wonders will never cease," and turned to lead the way, not bounding this time, into the dining room.

"No damned sense," Tarquie muttered. "Now the fur will fly."

Luncheon, such as it was, proved to be no less delicious than one would expect from an incomparable cook like Lois on the couple's day out. For more than one reason I had lost my hunger, but could marvel at the young lady's appetite.

"You eat like a horse, Tirene, good to see. Makin' up for London, eh?"

"Yes, Daddy." And she attacked her second lot of Eggs Benedict. "The hollandaise is a little lumpy."

"It would be less lumpy if the cook hadn't had to set the table too."

"I forgot," Tirene said, and scowled.

"You're going down tonight, Tirene?" My contribution.

"Yes. I'm on the job tomorrow morning."

"But you gave up your job in May, thirty quid a week. I wish I could afford to give up thirty quid a week."

"I couldn't, Daddy," she said blandly. "That's why I have a new one."

"Wouldn't it have occurred to you to tell us?"

"Wouldn't it have occurred to you to ask me, Mother?"

"*I am asking you,*" Duncatto said.

"Well, I'm reading novel manuscripts, I'm a so-called editor, if you want to know."

"Who for?"

"Radclyffe and Christoferson."

"H'mm, they have some reputation."

"They have some reputation for pornography. Was that creep yesterday one of theirs?"

"Yes, Mother. That creep just happens to be the most brilliant younger author on our list. He's making a study of fuddy-duddy British ways. That's why I brought him."

Now the expected fur did fly. "You brought him here to make a study of your own parents, like specimens on slabs. How dare you!"

"That was precisely my complaint, Lois, before luncheon. They were dissecting me in the third person, discussing the specimen on the slab." The Duncatto women glowered, but I, in my ponderous way, had cooled the atmosphere.

This ponderous way of mine, so infuriating a bad joke to Tirene, perhaps merits a brief interpolation. You may recall that I was eight at the time of my father's death. I had lived with my grandparents all the war while he fought in North Africa and Italy, and my mother drove a staff car in the South. After Father was killed, she soon married one of her wartime lovers, and was as soon divorced. I met my wretched mother once. She was (and possibly still is) an insatiable man-devourer, from Manhattan to another bed to Acapulco.

And so I was the lone apple of grandparental eyes, the

distaff Irish, comfortable amusing Granny, but she died when I was twelve. Thus, I came home each holidays from Winchester to the company of my grandfather, a bon vivant, a bibliophile, a gardener of repute, a hopeless man of business. He was also what Ida Peebles called *a caution*, droll.

Undoubtedly I caught my ponderous archaic way from Grandfather. One could hear him speak again as one read his diaries (which I had been looking through since his death), written in a convoluted style and with an elegance reminiscent of, and yet distinct from, that of the distinguished American author, James Gould Cozzens.

Grandfather fuddied and duddied and let Drin fade away in his last years, not only because he was a haphazard manager but also because his stock market speculations had left little means with which to manage.

Poor old Grandfather, one might say. And yet, early in the Second War, it was Grandfather who rode his motor bicycle and sidecar (*my Combopede*, he called it) all over the County of Crummock, recruiting, training, inspiring, driving every man past military age, welding them into the finest Home Guard in the whole United Kingdom. Fair weather or foul, he rode his combination velocipede to repel the invasion that never came. I hope that my dear grandmother never learned what grew to be common knowledge, much approved — that the old rip found time on his tireless rounds to comfort two widely separated grass widows.

At the time of the luncheon at Duncatto of which I write, I still took a strait-laced view of that particular aspect of my grandfather, Sir Dougal Trocher of Drin, eleventh baronet and dilettante, leader of men to arms, of women to comfort.

". . . If you're going out to dinner," Tirene was saying, "I could take the Mini and leave it at Crummock Station to pick up on your way home, Daddy."

"You know perfectly well, Tirene, that your father is incapable of going out to dinner without drinking too much for his own good and for the breathalyzer."

31

"Lord Lieutenant gets thirty days, no option," Tirene said. "At least someone's human in the family."

They were as human a family as could be, but not that day, and the fault . . . But who is to say that fault lies in one corner?

"Carmichael will take you to the train." Carmichael was the pigman/chauffeur.

"He can't. The big sow's due to farrow any minute."

"I could take you, Tirene, if you like."

"On the motorbike — gosh, could you?"

"Not on the motorbike, I'm afraid. That would be too big a risk."

"Why a risk?"

"Because its license expired in nineteen forty-two."

"But that McIntoon! Do you mean to say . . . ?" She stared at me in disbelief.

"We have more byways than we have Constable McIntoons, Tirene." I almost added wittily that I had broken the law more for the sake of Bernardo than bravado, but that would have annoyed her again. As it was, Tirene regarded me with perplexity, even a curious respect.

"You certainly have suffered a sea change," she said. "Well, at eight, then, if you're really sure. Shall I make the coffee, Mother?"

"Oh, would you, Tirene, thank you so much," Lois said politely, too politely, ever an edge between them.

After coffee, Tarquie went off to mark a young plantation for thinning. He was, and is, a first-class forester in theory and practice. "I must go and read that creep's manuscript," Tirene said. "It is a bit creepy too, not the kind of honest self-respecting fornication I enjoy. See you later, Dougal." She bounded out.

"Well, really!"

I also was shocked by Tirene's remark, but . . . "Well, don't you?" I said. One did not need to be clairvoyant to opine that Tarquie and Lois enjoyed a form of physical engagement in which, at that time, I was almost totally unversed.

Lois giggled. "You've made me blush. Think of blushing at forty-six. But now to business. I jotted down some jumbled notes while I was getting lunch."

I have kept those notes, written in Lois's dashing hand because they, as it were, codified, began the reduction to systematic order, of an amorphous concept. We discussed them at some length.

Passport. Up to date? *Sir* D. U.S. Visa? If not, get.
Dollars. Have lots of ready. Do quiet swop.
Air ticket. First class, *invariably*.
Telephone tycoon cousin. Montreal 10 A.M., here 3 P.M.
Sure to ask stay. Don't accept.
Go first to best hotel, Ritz. Suite.
How soon leave? Suggest one week.
Publicity, opt. Put on dog, opt. Practice same.
Pave horticulture way. Mighty build-up.
Man/woman Friday. Think vital. Worst headaches, that and swag conversion.
Keep in mind Harry Zee.

". . . It's all I can think of for the moment, Dougal."

"Thank you, Lois. How can I thank you?"

"Don't," she said. "It's wickedness, clean fun to plot and plan, but with a great big BUT. How clean is the fun when the sordid action starts? That's what Tarquie said in the kitchen. He said: *What are we going to think of ourselves if we've egged on that outsized lamb to five years in some penitentiary, or worse?*"

"Or worse, Lois?" A small cloud of apprehension.

"Whatever worse it is that happens to lambs," she said, and kissed me on both cheeks. "See you tomorrow."

Bernardo was wide awake on our journey home. I kept a watchful eye for the ubiquitous McIntoon, but he must have been seeking crime elsewhere.

Lesser crime, lesser criminals, I thought, turning in at the broken gates of Drin. *Tarquie says: Plan the basics, but not the details, keep a free hand, and mum's the word,* were my instructions, and I would obey them. But far more important — I was going to drive my lovely crosspatch, my divinity, to Crummock Station.

"Tell me something, Bernardo," I said, now approaching our ancestral seat. He turned, much interested. "Tell me why it is that you growl in your boots at the mention of her name, and yet say: *Hullo!* to her with warm affection?"

He shook his head. It was neither a growl, nor was it a wowf. It was a double grumble of perplexity. It was *"Dunno."*

⚇ 4 ⚇

MY NAME PRESENTS difficulties outside my native land. I am
Trocker to the English, sometimes *Trotcher,* even *Trosher.* I am
Troché to the old alliance. Properly, I am *Trocher* as in *Loch,*
expectorant primeval *Och.* And if we speak in the broad
language, the short *o* changes to the longer *au,* thus: *Traucher,*
but not quite. Think of vulgar spit-collection, and you have at
least the theory. I write this not to belabor importance, but in
the cause of a euphony precious only to my personal ear.

"This is Sir Dougal Trocher, speaking from Scotland."

The call had taken about five minutes to put through. It did
not take that secretary five seconds. "Sir Dougal Trocher. Oh,
yes. I remember very well. Good morning, Sir Dougal, or it's
good afternoon with you. Mr. Merriwell is at a board meeting,
but I'm sure . . ."

A brief interval, and the president was speaking — vibrant,
cordial, reserved. I had been somewhat apprehensive of this
conversation. But he evinced sincere pleasure, no surprise at
all, asked me to stay, did not press the matter.

*Engage a small suite? . . . Arrange for you to visit some of
our fine gardens? Why, certainly, of course.*

It was my first experience of a new world of formidable
competence, command, all roads made easy. The auguries
were encouraging, even if it did occur to me that the safe in
the office of this particular president (third cousin once

35

removed on my wretched mother's side) might not be the easiest safe to crack.

I went to ask Ida Peebles about early dinner. "I'm taking Tirene to the station."

"Away down London, I suppose, poor lassie."

"Yes, Ida."

"How does Miss Tirene seem?"

"Unsettled, Ida, not very happy in herself."

"It isn't in herself that happiness could be."

"How do you mean, Ida?"

"Och." That was life with Ida Peebles, sooner or later the pregnant *Och*.

"Och to yersel," I said, and the old girl smiled, continuing to sew. I went to the door of her sitting room. "I shall be flying to Canada next week, and possibly the United States. I expect to be away a month. But we can talk about that later. There are things to do." I left before question time.

One thing was to wash the van, eleven thousand miles into the second round of its speedometer, a venerable stout machine. I cleaned it inside and out to please Tirene, but how difficult to please her, and how impossible to give thought to my odyssey when, two hours from now, she would be sitting in the car beside me.

I had a bath, but perhaps she would prefer me dirty. I put on my better kilt, but perhaps she would prefer me scruffy. I read some quotations from Chairman Mao (who had remained in my pocket since our second bicycle ride) so that I might seem less of a reactionary dodo. I had a drink. I had my lonely dinner on a tray, which I took to Ida.

She said not a word about impending travels, playing two-can-play-at-that-game possibly. "Here's a wee pin cushion for Miss Tirene, just finished, it's from you, Dougal."

"From you, Ida, not from me." She wrapped it in tissue paper, and tied a ribbon.

"Couldn't you give the bairn a present?"

"But it wouldn't be my present."

"Och," she said, inspecting me from top to toe and round

about. "You're a braw figure of a man," she said, a first compliment about my current self since I had come back to Drin three months ago, but Ida qualified it: "In the looks I'm meaning."

I arrived at Duncatto on the dot of eight, went inside and called.

"Oh, hi! Just coming." Tirene in her clothes for London was just coming.

But round the angle of the stairs there came progressively the sandals, the blue jeans and the smudgy vest, a haversack dangling from one shoulder, a gas mask satchel from the other, perhaps relics of her father's war. But the hair was tidy, silken sheen, at least that concession to something or other. "Hi!" she said again, quite nicely said it for me alone, my longing terrible.

"Gotta suitcase I can fetch?"

"No thanks, I'm complete," and she patted her field equipment. "Just my waterproof to get." She bounded into the cloakroom for an army groundsheet, strolled back and to the car. The warm day had softened, cooled. It was high summer, but without the heaviness of English summer. "Smutty old London, what a thought," Tirene said, and we drove away.

Ida's present was on the seat between us. "She finished it for you this evening."

Tirene made fast work of ribbon and tissue paper, but then she turned the small pin cushion, turned it slowly, turned it back. "It's exquisite," she said. "Just look at the stitching and the leaf design. I love it. Oh, why would Ida Peebles bother?"

It was indeed exquisite, but more precise, more minute in form and execution than I would have expected Tirene to admire. "Ida is fond of you. She always has been."

"I can't imagine how anyone could be fond of a crummy mess like me."

"The crumminess could help," I said, and we laughed together like ten years ago.

37

"So you're off to Canada," she said as I turned out of the gate.

"For a month or so."

"When do you leave?"

"A week today. I booked myself from Prestwick."

"Oh, what airline?"

"Global."

"H'mm," she said, and was silent for a little. "Did you say Global?"

"Yes, I did, Tirene."

"Surely they're jam-packed in summer, or did you book some time ago?"

"This afternoon," I said. "There is usually plenty of room first class."

"*First class* — that costs the earth."

"It is expensive, yes," I said. "But as Chairman Mao has told us, the true communist does not reach his destination by riding the paper tiger's spindly rump."

"Very funny. Terribly amusing."

I had incurred Tirene's displeasure, but was putting a stop to questions. "Here is the book. You know, Tirene, I think that the Chairman is a wise old man, in many ways profoundly right. He would weld the masses into a noble instrument of truth."

She muttered something close to me, beside me, with me, far from me.

"Were one to find oneself at the wrong end of the barrel of the Chairman's gun, one would have only oneself to blame. In fact, there must not be a oneself at all."

"That's true," she said. "But you're being facetious."

"On the contrary, I am in deadly earnest. To Mao Tse-tung, as to all authoritarians, whether of the left or right, the real danger is neither the capitalist nor the rebellious prole — these are blatant enemies to be as blatantly expunged — the real danger is that snake-in-the-grass, the liberal in lower case, myself, Tirene."

"Couldn't you please for God's sake stop pontificating?"

"Sorry, Tirene." Inexplicably, or for the most obvious reason under the evening sun, my eyes became blurred, and I had to drive more slowly. We came to the main road where the big trucks thundered. Poor human beings, hell-bent for their bread and butter, how I hated it. "I'm afraid of you," I said.

"Me, too," Tirene said. She did not say whether of herself or me. But she put her hand over to touch my hand on the steering wheel and took her hand away. "Still friends in a sort of a way," she said. "Sometimes."

"Do you like your new job?"

"I thought I would, but I don't know. I don't know anything nowadays. Like this bastard's novel." She patted the haversack on the floor. "How can you judge something properly when you hate the puking perversion even if it is well written? How can you vote to turn it down when you know his last one sold a hundred thousand hardback copies? Editorial hack, her problem."

"If you are spared to be a centenarian, Miss Duncatto, you will never be a hack."

She smiled at me. "That's what I am, or I lose my job. But there are compensations."

I am so indifferent a scribe that I cannot indicate the needle-sharpness, the fickle artistry of Tirene's mind. "Compensations, you said?"

"Oh, like finding something good, like helping occasionally, like mostly being able to work at home, or sleep off a hangover when needs be."

"Do you still have a flat?" I asked the question casually, orgiastic visions flashing. One of the times she had been up, in May, Tirene's passionate hobbyhorse had been Free Love, and I had been rendered not wordy but speechless, knowing all too well that she would never preach passionately what she did not practice. But perhaps the austerities of Chairman Mao had reduced the flow of lovers. I groaned. ". . . Sorry, Tirene, I didn't hear."

"You never listen."

"It isn't so easy." Nor was it, even if the prime reason for my inattention was other than the behemoths that roared and snarled and blasted past little us and one another. But we turned off at the by-pass, and things were quieter. "About your flat?"

"I said I've been sharing with another girl but she has to leave, which is such a pity, as she's madly amusing, and brilliant too, and does she love to whoop it up. We've had some super parties at the flat."

"So then you'll be alone?" Ah, the dangerous improbability of Tirene ever being long alone, now confirmed.

"Well, there's a nice boy at the office who seems keen to share."

We were approaching Crummock Station, and I was thinking of the shocking change in morals that this demented age had brought about. In my Cambridge days, and as part of an educative process, I had made one or two sordid explorations up to London, and found them distasteful. And then I ran timorously from rapacious women, possibly mindful of my wretched mother. What might be called Oedipus Reverso.

And then I had watched my childhood friend grow to womanhood and to estrangement, and now I wanted her; I lusted for her with pure passion. But how far away her world from mine. Suppose I were to cast away the whole Canadian adventure, and say to Tirene: *Let me be the nice boy to share your flat with you?* Her reply: *What, share my flat with a bloody old reactionary dodo? Are you crazy?* I groaned.

"You seem to groan a lot this evening. So you're leaving next week. I hope you have a lovely time giving nature lessons to the plutocrats."

"I have to earn my living," I said stiffly.

"I know, Dougal. I'm sorry I said that." Tirene leaned over and gave me the softest, the lightest of kisses on the cheek. "Thank you for bringing me, and Good Luck. Perhaps you might learn as well as teach in Canada."

"I'm sure I shall. But how do you mean, Tirene?"

"Oh, well, you know, live and learn, live it up a bit."

We had arrived, and I accompanied her into the station where she bought her ticket. It was nicely timed, for that no sooner done than the London train rolled in.

"Which sleeper are you in, Tirene?" The dread moment here.

"I haven't got one. I'm sitting up, of course."

"But why on earth?"

"Because sleepers are phony bourgeois, that's why."

This stirred me into instant and uncontrollable vexation, and I looked down at the bewitchingly beautiful Tirene, and I said: "Perhaps sleepers are phony bourgeois, whatever that may mean, but is it not just possibly equally phony or false deliberately to garb yourself, in your father's words, to look like Bernardo's dinner, and then sit up all night being a phony member of the masses?"

"Oh, fuck off, you stuffy old fucking prig!" Tirene bounded into a second-class carriage, and I sought along the windows to see her in a packed compartment, weeping, weeping as the London train drew out.

Tirene wept for rage and insult. Only that day I had said to her father: *She does hate sham.* That had been true of Tirene all her life. But now I had attributed sham to her, and I would never be forgiven. So it was good-bye forever to my angel. I walked back along the platform. The rude verb and adjective I quote above had almost never passed my lips. But now I reviled myself loudly with Tirene's parting words, somewhat to the surprise of others present.

⊠ 5 ⊠

LATE THAT EVENING I wrote a penitent note to Tirene, care of those publishers, saying only that my loss of temper at Crummock Station had been quite disgraceful, that the last human frailty or sin I would ever attribute to her was hypocrisy, and that my deplorable outburst had been caused simply by dismay that she should espouse the cause of truth sitting all through the long night in a crowded compartment, no doubt rendered sleepless by squawling infants, and would she forgive me? Love, Dougal.

It was the best I could do, and it would avail me nothing. Duncattos do not forgive lightly, and Tirene, despite many differences from her father, was every lovely inch one of them. No reply came during the ensuing week.

That vain hope ever in mind, I busied myself with preparations. I obtained a new titled passport, the old one having expired a year before. I made arrangements for an adequate supply of dollars, a delicate matter upon which I need not here dwell. And, with the loyal help of my friends, other ways were paved.

There was also much work to be done at Drin to keep the old hulk afloat in my absence. As a result of all these things, the five thousand pounds aforementioned dwindled alarmingly.

I say alarmingly, but in truth I was not at all alarmed. I did not understand the metamorphosis in myself, nor bother to understand it. To employ a vulgar expression: I was going for bust in no uncertain terms. When my conscience troubled me, as indeed it did from time to time, I had, as it were, my watchword ready: *For the sake of Drin.* Since the dawn of history, after all, soldiers have had resort to subterfuge to win their honorable battles.

On the eve of departure I made the rounds with Bernardo, whom I would sorely miss. Everyone speeded, or sped, the parting laird — my farm manager, grieve, keeper and stalker, head gardener (he had one neophyte assistant), shepherds and their wives. Only Tarquie and Lois had the smallest inkling of my intent, but rural Scotland is both a sensitive barometer and a secret society, and I have no doubt that the word had gone round: *Dougal's up to summat, high time too.* Their farewells varied from: "Have a grand holiday, Sir Dougal," to the parting words of Lachlan, the shepherd, a sly fellow. He regarded the craggy summit of Ben Drin, remarking gravely: "There's a new light in the laird's eye, I'm thinking. May it burrn bright as Lucifer to guide Sir Dougal on his road." Lachlan employed the third person either when displeased with me or when making comment of import.

Last, there was Bernardo. Ida said that he would be unhappy in the house, and would mope even more at the Drin kennels. So I took him over to stay with his friend Garry.

"Good-bye, Big Boy," I said, giving him a kiss on that noble brow. He lay down, head flat between paws, and would not look at me. "Be good."

"Some hope," Tarquie said. "Those two together are a bloody menace."

"Dougal dear, wouldn't you please change your mind and wear your kilt tomorrow? It could work such wonders on arrival."

"Look, Lois, I don't even wear the kilt in Edinburgh, so I positively decline to wear it in a jet. But special occasions might be another matter, so the thing is packed. Don't you agree, Tarquie?"

"I do indeed, my boy. Those airborne chieftains make me ill. See you at nine, then."

I was to be accorded the signal honor of being driven to Prestwick by Lord and Lady Duncatto in person.

And so the time came to bid farewell to Ida Peebles. She gave me and my tweed suit the usual overall inspection and seemed satisfied, but worry creased her brow. "I hear tell them American wummen are fair daft for men. They'd rape you as soon as look at you, Dougal, so just you watch out."

"Ida, you seem to have rape on your mind a bit."

"It was a figure of speech, Dougal. I was just meaning they'd fair tear the pants off ye."

"Such a liberty I would certainly not permit."

The old girl cackled. She called herself an *auld body,* but in fact was not so old, fifty-eight at that time, the same age to me ever since I could remember. Now she thrust something at me. "It's a wee present for luck to put on your key chain."

It was a silver Saint Christopher which I, being touched, slipped round and onto my key chain with some difficulty. "Well, thank you, Ida, thank you."

"Good-bye, my wee Dougal, and may God bring you back safe and sound to Drin."

So we embraced. I think that I may say, with or without sentimentality, that Ida and I truly loved one another. Ah, the tears of love, the tears of joy, the tears of sorrow, the tears of parting.

I waited alone on the front steps of Drin. The pigeons were cooing in the woods. The peewits wheeled in haphazard flight above the park. The oystercatchers called along the river. But let us not paint only beauty where horror also must reside. A rabbit in the late stages of that disgusting myxomatosis blundered blindly across the drive, and so I took a stick and killed it, my last act before the beginning of my journey. It made me unhappy.

Punctually at nine o'clock the Lord and the Lady arrived in the Lady's maroon Rolls-Royce. My suitcases stowed, I said: "I'll sit in the back."

"No, me," Tarquie said. "I'm safer there if Lois piles up this damned barouche."

There was little likelihood of Lois piling up the damned barouche, for she was a faultless driver, never taking a risk on the long and tortuous and traffic-ridden drive across Scotland. We were soon on the main commercial artery from Carlisle and Glasgow to Aberdeen, a nightmare road, the narrow stretches, the brief miles of completed motorway, and here was one, and she drew out and passed twenty or thirty juggernauts, who ceased their road race for this while, yielding to the power they saw in their mirrors, yielding to the square nose that ghosted past them at ninety-five. I think that all professional drivers admire quality of machine. But not all peers. This one grumbled: "Cool it, woman. You're showing off."

"Oh, shut up, Tarquie," she said to him. "You should do up your seat belt," she said to me.

"You're so good, I won't bother," I said to her.

"Butter-up and bloody butter," from behind. "Watch out, Canada."

During the drive, we discussed my plans, which were developing almost entirely through the acumen, the enthusiasm and the influence of my friends.

"I told you I'm a sort of Honorary President of the International Institute of Horticulture. Well, they're lined up. Stick it to them, Trocher."

"And, Dougal dear, you're such a humble person, but you must change that. Always remember to be the grandee. And another thing: you're too soft-hearted; you must be tough. And, Dougal, sometimes you do tend to seem a little ponderous and long-winded. Lighten it up as much as you can."

"Hear, hear," said Tarquie. "I've laid on the Highland Society too. You could do them a sword dance, even sing a bit."

"You have such a nice heathery baritone, Dougal."

"Many thanks," I said.

45

"And don't forget to talk Scotch at times. They'll adore that, particularly after your la-di-da."

"Background stuff," said Tarquie. "The image. But my guess is that you should pin your hopes of swag to the gardening aspect. By the way, I dropped a word to International News."

"Oh, and I telephoned Harry Zee Gilpin. He says they would be delighted to have you stay at Camber Island off the coast of Maine. Harry Zanzibar was our tenant one mad winter when you were in the South, but perhaps you heard, Dougal."

"I did hear rumors," I said carefully. I had, indeed.

"It was we, I mean us it was who brought Harry and his little Gloria together, wasn't it, Tarquums?"

"You could say so."

"So could you. Well, the thing is, Dougal dear, that Harry Zee is loaded beyond the dreams of man, and he has contacts everywhere about everything, so he could be an invaluable ally over small complications like transferring funds and so on. But there's one promise I want you to make me, Dougal."

"Any promise you ask, Lois, that I will make."

"It's a very simple one, really — not to fleece or plunder the Gilpins. You see, he festoons that little bitch Gloria like a Christmas tree with jewels of untold worth. For instance, there is one pendant with a diamond called the Koala, worth what, Tarquie?"

"A cool two million or thereabouts."

"And at the drop of a hat or the absence of a bra, it dangles in the valley of her lovely bosom. It is a lovely bosom, don't you think so, darling?"

"Used to be pretty decent. Don't know about lately."

"And you had better not know, Tarquin." When Lois called him by his proper name, danger loomed.

Ever the peacemaker, I quoted from Solomon, of which I am something of a scholar: "Thy two breasts are like two young roes that are twins, which cherish little Gloria's Koala."

46

This remark was such a success that Lois had to draw into a lay-by to recover. "Darling Dougal," she said. "You can be madly funny."

We slipped through the streets of Kilmarnock to admiring, envious, hostile glances. Grumbles from the back: "People keep starin' in at me as if I was some bloody plutocrat. God, I loathe this car except the way it goes."

"Never mind, my darling seedy Lord," she said, and kindly.

It was cloudy weather as we neared the coast. "We've done our best," Tarquie said, "but failed totally in one thing — to find you a reliable accomplice. And that's essential, don't you think so, Lois?"

"Yes, I do," she said. "But please be careful, Dougal, who you choose. You're so inexperienced, and I'm afraid there may not be much honor between old thieves and new ones. So I would say: Bide your time."

"Sound advice," said Tarquie. The control tower was in sight, the Atlantic out there. "I think they'll be rolling down the carpet a bit. I telephoned."

"He is a most extraordinary codger. He won't lift a finger for himself, can't bear to. But just watch him go into action in Sir Dougal's cause."

"I know," I said. "And thank you both. I won't say it again."

The trunk opened itself by some magic, Grandfather's suitcases were removed, and Lois went to park the car. The red carpet in the shape of Mr. Williamson the Global Airport manager awaited us at the door.

"I'm Duncatto, and this is Sir Dougal Trocher."

"On behalf of Global Airlines, I would like to say what a great pleasure it is to have you fly with us today, Sir Dougal. Happily, flight conditions are excellent all the way across. Now, if you would let me have your ticket, we can be rid of the preliminaries."

Because of gardening books and so on, I was thirty pounds over my sixty-six, but nobody seemed to notice that, and the stout, battered cowhide bags ran away on the moving carpet.

"Lois, this is Mr. Williamson m'wife," Tarquie rattled off, awkward at that sort of thing.

"Hardly, darling," she said, which broke the ice in a quite charming way. But she spoke and she looked, she spoke and she looked so like Tirene, the insouciant Tirene for that moment that I could not quite endure it or anything.

"What's wrong, Dougal?" Lois asked.

"I was just thinking."

"Dear Dougal," she said. "I know. I know." Lois took my arm and we went to the sanctum of Global VIPs, and to gin and tonics. I had never flown the Atlantic before, and viewed the prospect with some doubt, but a second healthy nip laid that to rest.

"Your flight has just landed from London, Sir Dougal, so perhaps you would like to come now."

The four of us stood at the door of the departure lounge, but through it and toward us there hurried a Global stewardess, papers in hand. No male eye could fail to notice the fair-haired girl in her scarlet uniform. She embraced us all with an enchanting smile. "Mr. Williamson?"

"Yes," he said.

"There's some tiny stupid thing wrong in the manifest. It won't take a sec if you could come with me."

Mr. Williamson bade me good-bye. "Holy Moses," Tarquie said. "That going with you? What I couldn't do to her."

"Lecherous old beast."

But the time had come. Lois and I kissed one another. "Dear Dougal," she said to one ear. "I don't need to say it," she said to the other.

"Good boy," said Tarquie, tough, square, indomitable friend. We never shake hands.

They walked away, and I took my new passport for its virgin stamping.

✕ 6 ✕

HALF AN HOUR LATER, my ears were popping, we were in cloud, and I was having a first cigarette. The purser, darkly saturnine, spoke a word to the other two first-class passengers, and came back to me. "I hope you're quite comfortable."

"Very, thank you. Is this what they call a Jumbo?"

"No, sir, this is not one of those elephants. This is a super DC–8, a very fine aircraft. We are full in economy today, a hundred and ninety-two passengers. So now, excuse me. Your stewardess will be here at once." He moved aft through the curtain to the common people.

My stewardess was that same astonishingly decorative girl. "Would you like a drink, Sir Dougal?" She asked me in a friendly way, without a trace of coquetry.

"I would, but no hurry. Why don't you ask the others?" My companions were plump men in shiny suits, and asked for whisky as if there were a flirtatious aspect in asking for whisky.

Then the captain came on, about altitude and flight time to Gander, Newfoundland, and so on. He was a taciturn-sounding captain, welcoming us aboard the Apollo Service of Global Airlines like Tarquie Duncatto barking the Lord Lieutenant's duty welcome to Prince Rainier.

The stewardess came back, above her left bosom a small golden plaque: Diana Arden. "Have you decided?"

"I had gin and tonic at the airport. But I don't know." It was the old Trocher back, vacillating over triviality.

49

"Do you like Campari?"

"Yes, very much."

"Then I'll make you a Negroni."

We came through to sunlight, and in a minute now the tone of the hum changed for level flight at 35,000 feet, and below us was the white plowed-land of cloud, or the mountain range of cloud. I was looking out when she brought my drink, and she said: "It's so tranquil, I always think, far above the world."

Which expressed my thought for me. "Do you fly the Atlantic often?"

"Not the Atlantic, Sir Dougal, but it's rather complicated. I'll explain. Now, would you like to see the menu?" Doing her job, but quite unhurriedly, tranquil as the clouds below, whatever storms they hid. My fellow plutocrats were asking for their third large whiskies, feeling irresistibly attractive.

To employ a hackneyed phrase, the menu staggered the imagination. "I've never had a lunch like this in all my life." There I went, *too damned honest*. I had much to learn.

She smiled at me. "You're just being nice, Sir Dougal."

"I shall content myself with a cold Lucullan feast, to wit: caviar, quails in aspic, Brie, and peaches and cream. I like the cheese first."

"So do I," she said. "The French way. And champagne?"

"You wouldn't have Löwenbräu?"

"Of course, Sir Dougal."

"Hey, honey, stop talkin' to that guy. We want attention. That's what we're paying for."

"Their companies are paying," Diana Arden murmured. "I'll get them stinko, then peace will descend." Her eyes were brown, and they laughed at me, sober chums together.

First-class luncheon on the Apollo Service was served on a tray but not in the usual packaged fashion. Napkin of linen, cutlery of shining silverplate, the large pot of beluga proffered by Miss Arden's assistant. And so it continued through a magnificent cold meal as we whispered serenely toward Newfoundland. It was what Tarquie would call life on the pig's back, entirely new, not quite believable.

50

The two girls served three men, myself at the back, the others across the aisle from one another, not yet quite stinko, but loud and obstreperous, the one an American, the other, I regret to say, a Scotsman. He was the worse of the two, and after luncheon as Miss Arden happened to be passing, he grabbed her by the wrist.

"Please, sir!" she said, unruffled, but the hostess-smile was absent.

"Bonny lassie. What's the hurry, bonny lassie?" Now he held on with both hands and was drawing her toward him.

Perforce, I went to the rescue. "Let go," I said.

"Who the hell do you think you are?" he inquired belligerently.

I am of fair dimension and fair speed in action, so I took him by the collar, gave him a little shake, showed him my other hand, and said: "Would you like to find out?"

It seemed not, and peace reigned in the first-class cabin. The other girl brought them large mugs of something, and in a while Miss Arden came along. "I've put enough Irish in their Irish coffee to send them to the Land of Nod. Would you like a modest Irish coffee? It's delicious."

I did not know Irish coffee from Indian tea but said: "Yes, please." Miss Arden brought it. "This is our quiet time," she said. "May I sit with you a while, Sir Dougal?" and did not wait for my permission.

I sipped the creamy stuff, too rich for my liking, but it was potent, the sensation balmily agreeable.

What seemed so good about this girl was her sisterly way, reminding me suddenly and sweetly of Tirene long ago. And I closed my eyes, remembering the child happy in the sidecar.

"You sighed, Sir Dougal."

"Yes, I was remembering." There is an intimacy in high travel. "You said you would explain — about the routes you fly, I think."

"Well, you see, our flight crews in Global are based at London or at Montreal. The London crews fly the Hong Kong–Australia route, which is the one I've been on for a year.

The Montreal crews fly the Atlantic route and the Tokyo route. The only complication is why I'm on this aircraft, and that's because I'm being transferred to the Tokyo run. Actually, it suits me quite well. You see, Sir Dougal, I grew up all over the place, but some of my teens were in Montreal."

Her voice had different traces from what we rather arrogantly call our standard English, but surely not North American. "Are you Canadian, then?"

"No. My father is Danish, and my mother is half French from France and half Australian. So I'm a bit of a bastard."

"I'm three quarters Scotch, one quarter Irish, so it might be said that we both enjoy bastardom."

She laughed. It was a merry peal of laughter above the snores of my fellow passengers. Miss Arden had certainly put them to the Land of Nod, and I thought what a strange life it must be for girls like this. Aged what? Aged twenty-four perhaps, flying across the world, time lost or time forgotten, enduring the likes of those in front, but perhaps there were compensations. "Do you get many drunks?" I asked.

"Quite often. It's partly the altitude which can do odd things, and sometimes people who are afraid of flying, sometimes just getting pie-eyed on the expense account. But they hardly ever make actual passes at you." The soft brown eyes changed to hard anger. "Rich fat porkers, how I hate them!"

"Small wonder," I said.

We sat in silence for a while until she said, her voice gentle again, musical, with that hint of accent. "The purser was saying that you have huge estates in Scotland, Sir Dougal."

"Not huge," I said. In fact, Drin was modest in Highland terms, but I must remember my instructions. "Not so big," I said. "Fourteen thousand acres, actually."

"Not big, Sir Dougal! But that's enormous."

Let it go, Trocher. Let this friendly, simple girl think fourteen thousand acres, mostly hill, enormous.

"You said that you lived in Montreal."

"For five years. Daddy was Danish Consul General, but

when I was seventeen, I took off. He was posted to Hamburg after that. But I haven't seen my parents for ages." She glanced at me with a hint of defiance or mischief or something. "Our relations are not of the very best." Or was it sadness? They were extraordinarily expressive eyes.

"Do you like the idea of the Tokyo run?"

"Well, so so. A change is always better than it seems at first. But I love London, and Mummy's family are in Sydney. And then there's Hong Kong. Hong Kong can be most rewarding," she said thoughtfully, looking at the back of her hand, ringless, as slender as the legs. "Most rewarding," she said again, and did not enlarge, and I did not ask.

"Have you been long with the airline?"

"Almost two years now."

"I read somewhere that the spinster expectancy of air hostesses is rather less than that."

"So it is," she said, "and what fools they are. Marriage is the end of all things."

The saturnine purser came from astern. I could not say that I wanted to be herded back there with a hundred and ninety-two people, and I could not deny that I liked it here in unprecedented luxury seven miles above the Atlantic, but I knew that, were I not a new-found madman on my way to Newfoundland, I would be in my proper station — Economy. Still, I had paid my own way for my golden purpose. But he was speaking. "Many thanks, Sir Dougal," he said with a nod of his head to the recumbent gentlemen, and went forward.

"Have you always lived in Scotland?"

I explained about being born there, growing up there, schools in England, and then the nursery garden down in Surrey. "But since my grandfather died, I have been at Drin again. It's the only home I ever had."

"To have a home, that must be wonderful," she said smiling, but with melancholy. "I never did. We were always moving when I was young, and I suppose it got in my blood, and at seventeen I just took off, drifted to here and there and India and everywhere, learning nothing much unless the seamy side

53

is learning. Well, after two or three years, I got bored with that, and took a secretarial course in London. I'm pretty quick at things — too quick perhaps," she said, confiding. "And then I landed a super job with a man who ran his own import-export firm. He was quite brilliant, and he was just teaching me the ropes of dealing when he wheeled and dealed a little too brilliantly for once, and so he went to prison, and I came to the airline." She looked at me again, a light of amusement, a depth of gravity. "That's all about boring me. Is this your first visit to Canada, Sir Dougal?"

"Yes, I plan to stay about a month, giving some lectures, that sort of thing."

"So it's not just a holiday?"

"Far from it," I said.

"My month is. I have four weeks leave coming to me before I join the Tokyo run. I suppose I'll just lie about and swim. But I'm not very good at being hedonist on holiday. Fortunately, I know some interesting people in Montreal — new left types, revolutionaries, even one queer lot of anarchists."

She looked at her watch. "About an hour to go. I must get those customs forms." But Diana Arden made no move. "It's been lovely talking to you." She hesitated, and said quite shyly: "I thought Scottish people were mostly sandy-headed, but your hair is black, really almost black."

"It's the Celtic, I suppose. They call us Black Scotsmen. In fact, my name means that: *Dougal* in the Gaelic is *dark stranger.*"

"Dark stranger," she said, and she went away.

It was the purser again. "Captain Harvey's compliments, sir, and would you care to visit the flight deck?"

"I would be delighted." I followed him to be introduced. The three of them seemed quite pleased to see me. Captain Harvey was a girt man of fifty or more, his neck seamed like a laborer's from wind and weather. "Have a seat. Ashtray on the left. Ask any questions. I'm not busy for a while." He rapped all that out very much in the Tarquie manner. I sat behind him and had the cigarette and asked simple questions about height and speed, the battleground of instruments being totally incomprehensible. It was enjoyable up there with those calm competent men, next to the astronauts, I suppose the most highly trained men extant.

Harvey looked back at me. "I hear you saved us a spot of bother. Thanks. You a boxer?"

"Once upon a time I was. But I gave it up. I didn't much like bashing people." One found oneself saying things that down below one would never say to an acquaintance of five minutes, and it was not the Irish coffee, long worn off.

"Funny thing," he said. "I was the same. You'd be a heavy. I fought welter in the Raff."

The first officer, who had earphones on, spoke across.

"Okay," he said, and to me he said: "We're starting down now, time for work. It's against the rules, but no inspectors aboard today. You can stay for the landing if you like."

There was a faint change of sound, and the needle began to unwind to confirm what my ears were telling me. The captain pointed to the weather radar. "A bit of turbulence ahead. Tighten your belt." He spoke into his microphone.

She jostled and shook in the gray wet world of cloud, but soon we were through that, running off the height until one could see the white tops of wind on water, and here was the coast. A sound of flaps, an intestinal rumble as the landing gear came down, the runway ahead. We sank to meet the very end of it, to touch at last with a trundle of wheels. "You take her in, Joe," said the captain, and to me he said: "First stop, Gander, Newfoundland."

"Thank you," I said. "I enjoyed it immensely. In fact, I've enjoyed the whole flight." And I added with a little care: "That's a remarkable girl, that stewardess, quite apart from the looks, in spite of the looks, one might say. I mean sensible, intelligent, been everywhere, done everything. Surely you can't have many like her."

55

"No," he said. "We don't. She flew a few times with me when I was on the Far East route last year. The boys used to say she should be running the whole damned airline, not dispensing cocktails. Dumb as a whip, is our Diana."

⚹ 7 ⚹

I WENT BACK to my seat. Miss Arden was making the ritual speech, "On behalf of Captain Harvey and the crew . . . Remain seated until the aircraft has come to a complete stop . . . All personal baggage for customs examination." She said it in English, in impeccable French, in German which sounded equally fluent. So that was three languages.

The Scotsman and the American were wide awake and sober, if puce-faced. It was remarkable, and amnesia permitted the former to greet me affably, with then a shadow of some doubt.

Gander was warm and overcast, and its best friend could not call it beautiful. Inside, we went through Immigration, and we waited: The ancients and the infants, the plain and the voluptuous, the high-booted and the barefooted, the black and the white and shades between. Beside me was a young man wearing a pink vest-sweater effect, not uniformly pink but shot with gray corruptive smudges, the double of Tirene's. She was nearer to me than ever, far away. I simply must put Tirene from my mind, and to that end I engaged the youth in conversation. He was bearded and beaded and looked quite dreadful and turned out to be a most engaging fellow who had ridden a ten-speed bike from Istanbul. "You go first," he said. "He'll take me apart. They always do."

"Are you visiting us, sir?" the man asked, and chalked my three cases through. "Have a nice holiday." But I looked back to see that the cordial welcomer had changed to a lynx-eyed sleuth, and the contents of the young man's duffel bag were examined minutely piece by piece.

Now that I was headed for a life of crime, I gave careful thought to matters not before considered, and it occurred to me that if I wanted to smuggle fifty pounds of heroin, I would eschew the beard and beads, and would present myself as squarely as Dougal Trocher. I mention this self-evident thought to indicate my ridiculous innocence at that time. Still, I think that customs people are simple-minded, wasting energy and their taxpayers' money in the hunt for an odd reefer.

"Global Airlines Flight Eight-five-seven Apollo Service is now boarding for Montreal." As I crossed the tarmac someone handed me a sheaf of cables, which I put into my pocket, and — it shows what a muddle I was in — forgot all about until we were at cruising altitude.

"Will you have a drink, Sir Dougal?" asked my by now old friend, Diana Arden. *Dumb as a whip*, the captain said. And what did he mean by that?

"May I have whisky and a lot of water, please?"

"One gets so dehydrated, flying. I'll bring a big glass."

The first cable or telegram looked forward to meeting me at Montreal Airport, cordially, Claud Merriwell, my third cousin. That was kind of him. But as I read the second, the third and fourth, horror mounted. "Oh, my God," I said to my window, the weather clearing, those white specks icebergs possibly.

"Not bad news, I hope, Sir Dougal."

"Catastrophic," I said, added water, gulped whisky. "Just read them."

The Highland Society — a true Highland welcome at the airport. *Yoch slaint n va.* The Institute of Horticulture, an informal delegation, perhaps not so bad. International News, a press conference arranged for arrival. "Oh, damn their eyes," meaning Tarquie and Lois.

"Whose eyes, Sir Dougal?"

"Theirs, everyone's, not yours." But it was my own fault for giving the Duncattos unbridled rein.

"They're all so glad to see you. Isn't that rather wonderful?"

"But I've never held a press conference in my life. All I am is a so-called Scottish laird, and a landscape gardener."

"Well, I think you're a terrific man." She gazed at me with warm admiration. "Not to worry, Sir Dougal. Perhaps I could think of some things to say." She stood again. "We serve a light dinner, but you could have anything you like."

"Perhaps the simple life after that delicious luncheon. Would scrambled eggs and bacon be possible?"

"Lovely," she said. "And I'll get you more whisky first."

The prospect of the press conference still loomed horrible, but somehow or other this girl had made it seem less terrifying. I felt safe with her, didn't I? As safe and platonic as I felt with Lois. No such thing with so young and so feminine a creature had happened to me before. But then nothing like any of this had happened to me before. But I said to myself: It is not what will happen to you. It is what you are going to make happen. Take the initiative, grasp the nettle danger. They were musings with whisky, nonetheless valid for that.

The scrambled eggs were buttery, like Ida Peebles's scrambled eggs, good old Ida. I looked out of my window again. The blueness of the sky was dark above us, but the infinite sea was blue, and land crept to us soon, and Diana Arden took my tray away. "Will you have time to talk again?"

"Back in a minute," she said, and she was.

"Do you enjoy this job?" I asked her.

"Sometimes," she said. "A flight like today in first class is a rest cure. But the girls back there are being run off their feet. They call it glamorous, and I suppose it is, meeting new people all the time. But in a way that makes you more alone, flying on and on and round and round and always alone, do you see what I mean?"

"Yes," I said. "Some lines from a poem have been tantalizing me since Prestwick, and now you make me remember them:

> *"It is so hard to be alone*
> *Continually, watching the great stars march*
> *Their circular unending route . . ."*

"Could you say it again for me?"

So I said it again, and she said: "Yes."

"Is this the estuary now?"

"The Saint Lawrence leads us into Canada. Are you still worried about the press and all that?"

"I've never done it, and I'm sure I'll make a mess of it."

"Not if you're confident in yourself."

"But that's the whole trouble. I'm not." Now where was the bold buccaneer, Sir Dougal?

"Stand away, then. Look at them from somewhere else. Look at them from home in Scotland. Then it will be easy."

"I see what you mean. How do you know these things?"

She looked at me, and perhaps there was a glisten in her eyes. "I don't know much. But I've been up and down and in and out and around and around the goddam mulberry bush. Excuse me, I didn't mean to be impertinent, Sir Dougal."

That made me laugh and made me wonder how much my leg had been pulled in the past few hours.

"Now about what to say," she went on briskly. "The first thing is how wonderful it is to be in Canada. That's a sure winner. The next thing is something nice and sentimental about your fellow Scotsmen. Next is how much you look forward to seeing Canadian gardens. That's the main object of your visit, isn't it, Sir Dougal?" The glance was quizzical. I was beginning to think that Diana Arden, Chief Stewardess, regarded me as a good joke.

But that reminded me again of being regarded as a bad joke. "One of my difficulties is that when I'm nervous of people, afraid of people, I become long-winded and pontificate."

"Do you?" she said. "I noticed you talk in rather an old-fashioned way, that's not pontificating."

60

"No fears have haunted me today," I said, and nor they had, and she laughed.

"Anyway," she said, "I don't think it matters a bit if you sound a little archaic. In fact, they'll like that. Just put in a few of your pawky quips. Do you speak French?"

"Yes, I do," I replied in that language. "My grandfather and I always spoke French at meals."

"En Ecosse?" she said with some astonishment. *"Ce pays barbare?"*

"H'mm," I said, having no riposte but a sardonic smile to that in French or anything.

"Your accent is perfect."

"For many years, so I understand, my grandfather used to make excursions to Paris to improve his French with sundry distinguished ladies of the aristocracy, and so it may be said that my accent is Parisian at Grandfather's secondhand."

"Your grandfather sounds marvelous. But now, don't just talk French in a set speech way, you're quite good enough to jump from one language to the other and back again. That's all I have to suggest, Sir Dougal."

"It sounds splendid advice. I just wish I thought I could live up to it." The unknown lay heavy before me, the awkward, the unexpected. "What do I say if they ask me what I think about French Canada and Separatism, that kind of thing?"

"Avoid it at all costs. Plead ignorance, or slide round it with a joke, like saying you're not *le grand* Sir Charles but only *le petit* Sir Dougal. And talking of *grand*, in your modest way you do have rather a grand air. Please never lose it." Which was precisely what the Duncattos had advised.

"I wish I had more confidence, Miss Arden."

"Diana," she said. "But I wonder. Would it help if I came along, just in case you got stuck or something?"

"Enormously, but it would be far too much to ask."

"I think you've forgotten," she said, pointing forward. They were boozy again, quiet boozy, too boozy to hear. "Or perhaps you don't know what would have happened. That yahoo would have pulled me onto his stinking lap, and then I would have chopped him slightly." She held her hand out sideways, flat, too slender a hand to chop, one might think, but one decidedly might not know. "And then Global Airlines would have had a *cause célèbre*, I mean it, Sir Dougal. That's why we're grateful."

"I only threatened the little man."

"Yes, but you did the threatening, not us. Well, I'm off duty as of the moment we arrive. I wonder if the captain would let me . . . I'll go and ask him."

I was left alone to think. Diana Arden liked me, she clearly liked me in that charming you're-my-elder-brother way. She was starting a month's leave, and she did not enjoy having nothing to do. Were it only a secretary that I wanted, needed, must have. But that was not all I wanted, needed, must have. And yet she had made a remark about Hong Kong, and had repeated it: *Most rewarding,* a cryptic remark in the way it had been made. And she had said other things. She was the wrong person. She would not do it, and I did not know her, and could not trust her. *Bide your time,* Lois said seven or eight hours ago, and we would be landing at four o'clock Montreal time, nine o'clock in the time I had left behind to come along with me.

We had begun our descent to Montreal. The narrow fields stretched away from the river. "That's quite all right," she said. "I have my night bag with me, and the captain says I can make a lightning, last-moment change. He says it's the least we can do to help you, Sir Dougal. That's a terrific compliment from him. Captain Harvey loathes passengers. He calls them the scum of the air. Shall I get you a little whisky *pour encourager les Hollandais?*"

She did, and I drank it as we flew over the city of Montreal with its tall buildings and its noble river. "Here I come, Canada," I said for the self-assurance so sorely needed. The determination was not lacking, but the confidence. *For the sake of Drin* was my watchword, and I added to it. "Oh, Canada, here comes Trocher for the sake of Drin," I said to my window as we circled Dorval Airport.

⚹ 8 ⚹

Diana Arden beckoned to me. I took down my Burberry, and picked up Grandfather's briefcase from below the seat. It was a handsome object with *Sir Dougal Trocher Bt.* in prominent letters, a relic of days when baronets let the fact be known. If Grandfather traveled, it was in style. Indeed, Grandfather's style was in large measure responsible for my predicament.

Her lightning change had been into a blue cotton dress, entirely plain but for a narrow piping of red. "It's unheard of, Sir Dougal, but Captain Harvey wants to say good-bye."

"Good luck," he said. "I hope you don't have to bash 'em at the press conference. And if you get stuck, Diana will help. See to that, Diana."

"Yes, Captain, Sir," she said.

He went back to his flight deck, and we walked into a corridor and down to the gate. I braced myself for the Highland Society and so on, but one man came forward. He stood out among the motley throng not like a sore thumb, but an indubitable president.

We introduced ourselves. "This is Mr. Merriwell — Miss Arden of Global Airlines. The captain asked her to help me with a press conference, but I don't see any sign of that."

"You will," he said. "I hope you don't mind the publicity. It's none of my doing."

It was a long walk into the airport, not on a common floor,

but on a moving carpet, along which we also strode, thus making handy progress. I considered my distant cousin, our leader. It was easy to place him as successful and agreeable. And it was easy to place him as a dressy chap, with his striped seersucker suit, his plum velvet waistcoat, gold buttons and a watch-chain, his black suede shoes, I rather draw the line at black suede shoes. It might be less easy to place him as a human being. He looked about forty-five, gray-haired, spare and athletic, brown of face.

We came to the hall where baggage emerged, and our flight number, 857, was already up at one carousel. "My chauffeur, Grenier, will collect your bags. Do you have the checks?"

I produced those, explaining to Monsieur Grenier that they were ancient and cumbersome, with my name printed on them, and would be unmistakable amid sensible modern luggage.

"We take this elevator," Merriwell said, after more walking. My nervousness must have betrayed itself because my personal stewardess murmured: "Not to worry."

Outside the lift there awaited us a Pipe Major in full dress. He saluted with the quivering perfection of a regular. "Pipe Major Donald McBain, Sir Dougal, late Pipe Major of the Firrst Battalion, now with The Black Watch of Canada."

"How d'you do, Pipe Major."

His moustaches were waxed to needle points, and he looked quite splendid in Royal Stewart, green doublet and the rest of it. "I'm to play your own slow march, Sir Dougal, 'Trocher of Drin,' and then 'Highland Laddie,' if that meets your pleasure."

"Fine, Pipe Major." No such dignitary had ever before played Dougal Trocher into any form of an assemblage.

He filled his lungs and blew and spanked, and was playing that melancholy tune of ours. I slow-marched behind him, feeling ridiculous, but then lost in the haunt of it. This was a superb piper, his grace notes throbbing. As we neared the end of a long hall, he broke into the wild flood of "Highland Laddie." As always, it sent a shiver up my back and down my legs and up again, hovering sweet and bitter in the hairs of my neck.

It was a sizable room, and there were three groups of people in it, and cameras were flashing. The Pipe Major led me to the left, halted, turned about, gathered his pipes with that hollow clunk.

"Thank you, Pipe Major," I said, shaking hands.

The first group were the Highland Society, half of them in kilts. I was made a short speech of welcome, but was too confused to hear it, and I was given envelopes. Diana Arden took them from me, and she murmured: "Shake hands all round. Speak later."

Having met some twenty Highlanders, none affluent in appearance, I moved on to the Institute of Horticulture. They were a much more mixed bag, some weather-beaten like gardeners, some pale like professors, some polished and prosperous, and two rich-looking women. The wrist beyond one hand that I grasped bore an emerald bracelet worth a small fortune, if genuine. More envelopes were taken by Miss Arden. In the airplane she had been the friendly stewardess. Now she was the earnest secretary, attentive shadow. "You speak from the dais."

There were three microphones, two with letters on them, so I would be broadcast to somewhere, or tape-recorded. "Make it quite short," she said, coming up to stand behind me.

Look at them from home in Scotland. Then it will be easy. And I could do that. I was looking at them from the rock above the loud Fall of Drin, and I said:

"Ladies and gentlemen, I have come a long way today, first driving across my native land, which is also the native land of some of you. And then I flew over the Atlantic, not thinking back," first lie, "but thinking forward to your wonderful Canada. That word has a magic sound, perhaps particularly to Scotsmen, so many of whom have crossed the ocean to this promised land.

"It was Shelley who wrote:
> *"From the forests and highlands*
> *We come, we come;*

65

> *From the river-girt islands*
> *Where loud waves are dumb."*

I waited for the clapping to die down. "Marvelous," said Diana Arden.

"And as we were losing height over Montreal, I looked at the tall buildings by the noble river, thinking how beautiful your city is, thinking how peaceful it seemed on this fine afternoon. I knew that my thought was illusory, for in this age, every city in the world is troubled. But I was reminded as I made my small wish for you, I was reminded of Verlaine:

> *"Mon Dieu, mon Dieu, la vie est là*
> *Simple et tranquille*
> *Cette paisible rumeur là*
> *Vient de la ville."*

This was a second untruth, I had just thought of it, and the applause was thunderous. "How could you ever worry?"

"Now lastly, I have not come to Canada only for a holiday. My occupation is that of landscape gardener, on this continent usually called landscape architect.

"But *architekton* in the Greek was a master builder, and I have never attempted the formal landscaping, the creation of new shape and form which is so essential a part of urban landscape architecture. I have tried always to do a much simpler thing, to follow the way, to stress the curve, to point to the beauty of God's own hand. And where could there be more for me to learn about that than here in Canada?

"Now, ladies and gentlemen of the press, I would be pleased to answer, or to try to answer, any questions you may have, but please not too many, for I have had quite a long hard day of it. As we say in Scotland: *It's aye a lang road tae the bonniest glen.*"

I was coming on. The day had been long, but positively steeped in luxury. And as for the road to the bonniest glen, that was Dougal Trocher's own specious and impromptu aphorism.

They asked me how long I was going to stay — three weeks

in Canada, perhaps a week in the United States. They asked about economic conditions in the United Kingdom, and I spoke badly and ponderously of an inflationary trend throughout the free world. They asked for my views about Britain joining the Common Market, but I pleaded lack of knowledge. I was floundering, pinned here by them, not standing away as she had told me.

A French reporter said that he did not mean the question rudely, but how had I come to speak such excellent French. Had I been educated in France? No, I had not been; but then my mind went totally blank. "Grandfather," she prompted.

"My grandfather taught me. We always spoke French at meals. You see, Grandfather made many an expedition to Paris to perfect his French in the nicest possible way." Loud laughter. "So it may be said that my accent is Parisian at Grandfather's secondhand." This also was a success.

Then someone asked: "You lived with your grandfather, then?"

"Yes," I said. "My father was killed in the Second War." I spoke bluntly, the only way I can speak of that.

A sympathetic murmur, then some sensible reporter brought up the lighter controversial: my views about women's lib. Thanks to Chairman Mao and Miss Duncatto, I was briefed on that one and I roundly extolled equality for women.

It was a woman who asked the loaded question, a girl with a pale fanatical gleam. "Sir Trocher, do you have sympathy for the aspirations of the French-Canadian people? Will you look with favor upon the free and independent nation of Quebec?"

"As I have said, this is my first visit to Quebec and to Canada, but there is an ancient alliance, an alliance that goes back many centuries between Scotland and France. And so, when I come to New France, I am in a very real sense coming home." But I was laboring. I was stuck.

"*Le grand Charles,*" she whispered.

"Let me say with sincerity: *Vive le Quebec.* And let me add: *Je ne suis pas le grand Sir Charles. Je ne suis que le petit Sir Dougal.*"

Diana Arden's words took a few seconds to penetrate; then there was tumultuous laughter.

"Sir Dougal, you were absolutely super."

"You saved me twice," I said. "I can't tell you how grateful I am."

"And I can't tell you how grateful *I* am," she said with gravity, handing me the letters. I glanced through them: invitations to judge Highland dancing, to attend a banquet in my honor, to visit the Botanical Garden, to lecture to the Institute, to appear on "Meet the Celebrities."

"That's only the start of it," she said. "And it'll be your own fault, Sir Dougal, for being such a smashing success." She smiled, and was going to say more, but seemed hesitant.

"Go on, Diana."

"I told you I'm on leave. And I told you I can't stand slothful holidays. You'll have oodles of letters to write and calls to make. Couldn't I please help, Sir Dougal, please?"

"Would you really like to?"

"I'd adore to. Will you have a sitting room I can work in?"

"Yes, I think it is a small suite — at the Ritz."

"Would ten o'clock tomorrow morning be all right? Now I'm going to disappear, Sir Dougal." She blessed me with that delightful sisterly smile, and was gone.

I came down from the dais, and people clustered to talk, but Claud Merriwell dealt with that, the air of courteous command about him. "I'm afraid we must rush," he said. "Or Sir Dougal will be late for his next appointment."

He shepherded me out, and down in the lift, and out to a dark green Cadillac. "Fabricated appointment," he said. "I thought I should rescue you. To the Ritz, please, Grenier."

It was a vast machine, and we cruised silently to Montreal. "The air conditioning is on," he said. "But you might rather breathe fresh air. I usually do after a long flight."

I thought that a good idea, and pressed my window button. The air was warm, no warmer than we sometimes had in Scotland.

"I thought you handled that in masterly fashion."

68

"If so, it was thanks to the Global Airlines girl. She has razor wits."

"And looks to match," Claud Merriwell said, and continued: "Since we're cousins, even if remote, may I waive formality and call you Dougal?"

"I wish you would," I said, thinking that there was a certain smoothness about Cousin Claud.

"We're almost there," he said. "This is Sherbrooke Street, a few good shops on the right."

"What a fine city it is."

"Yes," he said. "Even if we have our share of problems."

The great green car stopped at the Ritz-Carlton Hotel.

⚜ 9 ⚜

You may remember that on the eve of decision my nightmares were violent and intensely vivid. But since then sleep had been almost dreamless. Not so on a first night in Canada. It was a potpourri of travel, of Lois ghosting past a column of jumbo jets, of holding a press conference at the Fall of Drin, of *Vive le Quebec libre,* but I never said that, did I? *Je ne suis pas le grand Sir Dougal. Je ne suis que le petit Sir Charles.* Of drunken sailors in first class. Of the captain barking: *You land her, Dougal. Bash 'er in. — But Captain, I don't even know how to put the wheels down. — On her belly then, you scum.* I woke up sweating from that horrendous belly flop. It was after five, and daylight showed at the edge of curtains.

I slept again with a kindly dream, of Tirene in the sidecar, laughing, not the Tirene of long ago, the Tirene of nowadays with smudgy garb and tangled hair, but laughing, dear Tirene. And then she was fishing the river down. I watched her cast a long line, mend it with a skillful flick, let it swing, take in, step down and cast again. This time the line checked, and she waited and waited to set the hook. *I'm into a fish, Dougal,* she called to me, softly and happily she called, it was a lovely reality until the telephone clamored to tell me that it had been a dream. "Your call, sir, eight o'clock." I had slept twelve hours, some troubled and some peaceful to a pain of truth that it had not happened with Tirene.

But I was rested out, ready for breakfast and the day.

70

A morning paper, the *Gazette*, arrived. There was quite a flattering photograph of me marching behind the broad Pipe Major.

SIR DOUGAL TROCHER, SCOTTISH LAIRD AND
FAMED LANDSCAPE GARDENER, IN CITY.

It went on to say nice things about my appearance, urbanity, professional dedication, dry wit, and mastery of French and the reason therefor.

I felt some embarrassment at my own vulgarity in speaking thus of Grandfather. They were a most devoted couple, and I am sure that Grandmother knew nothing of his little wanderings. He kept his diary locked in the safe, and wrote it up after travel. He wrote about horti- and numerous other cultural matters at length in his orotund style, but guardedly thus: *Took tea with A de la R, civilized converse.* From an earlier entry, recording a first meeting, one might guess this to be Amelie, Marquise de la Roche, bedtime toast of Paris in the thirties.

At five to ten the telephone rang. "This is the reception desk, Sir Dougal. Your secretary is here."

I left the outer door ajar, and waited for my secretary. There was a knock. "Come in."

She carried a typewriter case in one hand, a folder in the other, a large purse or handbag slung from her shoulder. She wore another plain summer dress, of compromise mini length. Her clothes had an expensive look about them.

"I hope you slept well, Sir Dougal."

"Yes, except for some wild dreams."

"I was just the same," she said. "But I feel quite human again. I had my hair done early." She took off her only bright item of attire, a large silk head scarf, tiger-striped, shook her fair hair, and became businesslike. "I brought my portable electric, and carbons and things."

"The invitations are on the desk," I said. "Another one just came by hand, from some Country Garden Club, inviting me to judge their annual competition."

Diana Arden read them through. "Perhaps the first thing to

71

do is to establish priorities, or shall we start the other way round — what don't you want to do at all?"

"I can't judge Highland dancing. I'm not good enough."

"Then you much regret that your very busy program . . . What about the Highland Society Banquet in your honor?"

"I shall have to accept that. It means a speech, I suppose."

"It certainly does. Daddy used to say that everything in Canada means speeches. But a short one would do. The Institute of Horticulture, though, that's a lecture. The other thing is: Would you like to do the formal engagements early in your visit or spread them over the three weeks? Except for the TV people and the press, who want you now, they ask you to suggest dates."

"I think earlier rather than later, Diana. Then my hands would be free for things like the Country Garden Club, if they're big enough to be worthwhile."

"I expect they are," she said, glancing at me and away. "Only the stinking have real country gardens around here, and some of them are lovely too."

The telephone rang. "Sir Dougal Trocher's office . . ." She raised her eyebrows in question and I shook my head. "Sir Dougal has stepped out for a moment, but I will ask him and call you back. At six-forty for make-up, you say?"

"That's 'Meet the Celebrities' tonight at seven, prime TV time, Sir Dougal, a ten minute interview."

"Oh, Lord."

"It's much easier than a press conference and you'll be madly photogenic on color TV with your rugged brown face, and your black black hair." But she bit her lip, and said with apparent haste, "I suppose you have color sets at home, Sir Dougal?"

"Good heavens, no. They cost the earth." Think, Trocher, think! I enjoined myself in my rich sitting room at the Ritz.

But she did not seem to notice, sitting upright in the chair, notepad at the ready, knees together and legs flowing down. "Shall I say yes about the TV?"

"Okay, I suppose." But that was the telephone again.

". . . Dinner on Saturday but how very kind of you, Mr. Farrow, I will ask Sir Dougal as soon as he comes in. Good-bye."

"I can't stand much of this," I said, going to the window. I felt trapped, as always in cities in city buildings, trapped worse than ever by the utter absurdity of this venture.

"Don't worry, Sir Dougal." How kindly her voice was behind me. "Why don't you take a little walk? Turn left on Sherbrooke and go along to Guy. There are some nice shops to look at. And in the meanwhile I'll make phone calls about dates and so on, and work out a tentative schedule. I could even draft letters for your approval. Do you write Dear Mr. So and So, and Yours sincerely, or the other way round, or just Sincerely, and how do you do the date, Sir Dougal?"

"I put figure One ST April nineteen hundred and what-not April Fool's day in brackets. Dear Miss Arden, Yours sincerely, Dougal Trocher."

Diana Arden giggled. "You're so quick sometimes. It takes me by surprise."

"That does not surprise me. By the way, I'm having lunch with Claud Merriwell at his club. It's opposite, he says."

"Perhaps Mr. Merriwell's secretary would have the lowdown about the Country Garden Club. I'll call him or her."

"It's a her, I think. Do you like sherry, Diana?"

"I love it. Very dry, but you shouldn't bother."

"No bother. *A bientôt.*"

"Toodle-oo. Have a nice walk, Sir Dougal." Most respectful, and yet so friendly. She was dialing as I went out. It was apparent already that this girl could be a paragon secretary. And what were paragon secretaries paid in Montreal?

"My name is Trocher," I said at the head porter's desk.

"Oh yes, Sir Dougal, glad to have you with us. I hope you're quite comfortable."

"Very, thank you. I wanted to order some sherry and things. Perhaps I should have called room service for that."

"No, sir, I can easily arrange it, if you'll just tell me what you would like."

I told him. "In an hour would be plenty of time. I'm going out for a walk."

"In that case, I suppose you wouldn't like to buy it yourself. It would be much cheaper for you, and there's a liquor store quite near us on Mountain Street, the next one west."

I thanked him, and said that I would do that.

"Oh, and here's a strong shopping bag, much easier to carry, and it looks less like cradling bottled babies."

There and then began my attachment to the Ritz and the people who worked there. It was to grow during my stay, nothing too much trouble, no hand ever held out for tips.

It was much hotter today, ninety-one degrees on the thermometer at the door, but I walked briskly in my tropical suit, stopping to look at some smart windows, and back and down to the queue in the liquor store where surly gentlemen took your money and dispensed their bottles with dispatch and latent hostility. I did not understand it, and was relieved to be out of there, my booze discreetly in shopping bag, and so back to *le petit* Sir Dougal's suite. I did feel rather small and lost.

"Oh, hullo," she said, her fingers flying.

I put the whisky and the gin on a table, the Dry Sack and the Tio Pepe in the freezer. Grandfather used to chill his sherry in warm weather, another small quirk of his. Perhaps few other people in Scotland did that until his grandson did it too. It is odd, I thought, having stowed them for rapid coolth, while Miss Arden typed like a muted machine gun. It is odd that in so many ways, habits, mannerisms, I should have taken after Grandfather, and yet in one way am so different, feel such distaste for the libidinous in him.

"I've roughed out a possible program, Sir Dougal, but nothing is settled except the telly this evening; and with all the phone calls, I haven't had time yet to draft any letters."

She gave me the list. "What I tried to do was to get the first formal engagements into about a week, and I've checked with them all, and they're amenable. TV today, Tuesday the fourth. Tomorrow morning, the Montreal *Star* wants an exclusive interview. All tomorrow afternoon at the Botanical Garden. Thursday there's *La Presse* at any time you want, if you do want, and I would advise it for the sake of French-Canadian relations. Friday evening, lecture to the Institute of Horticulture, Saturday, dinner with the Jonathan Farrows, he's king of the Country Garden Club, Sunday free, Monday the Highland Society Banquet. That's all so far, but they keep rolling in."

"It looks splendid, Diana. How on earth did you manage all that in an hour?"

"I do work fast," she said, looking troubled. "Sometimes too fast, as I told you in the plane. Oh, and by the way, I spoke to Mr. Merriwell's secretary, and she knows about that garden club. It's very exclusive, with only thirty members or so, all most prominent and influential people. But Mr. Merriwell himself is not a gardener."

"That's good," I said, having experienced some unease at the thought of expropriating the jewelry of my cousin's wife, however rich. It hardly seemed cricket.

"Why good, Sir Dougal?"

"Oh well, a garden is a lovesome thing, God wot, but if all were gifted gardeners, my job would go to pot." The indifferent best I could do on the spur.

Diana giggled. "That's the quick Sir Dougal again."

"Half-past twelve, and he's picking me up in a quarter of an hour. Time for that sherry."

"Frosty cold," she said. "How delicious. I bet not many secretaries get this treatment." But her mind was still on business. "Mr. Farrow hummed and hawed, and inquired delicately about your fee, and I said would he care to make a suggestion? He thought that two weeks' work might be involved, and he wondered whether you would consider two thousand dollars an adequate honorarium. I think you could easily stick them up for more — I gather they're all absolutely rolling."

To accept two thousand dollars from the very people whom

you intended to rob was another case of decidedly-not-cricket, not even French cricket. I paced the wall-to-wall in some agitation. "I can't possibly take an honorarium."

"But, Sir Dougal, have you gone altogether crazy? You're not on holiday, *far from it*, you told me yourself. And don't you know what an honor it is for them to reap the fruits of your knowledge? There could be only one reason that would justify your not taking a fee . . ."

"Yes, Diana?"

"That you're so rich that money is just so many marbles."

I had twelve hundred pounds of invested capital remaining, and a gross underestimate for the extirpation of dry rot was ten thousand pounds, and I was so rich that money was just so many marbles. "Not quite, Diana, I shall have to think."

"Couldn't you please let me negotiate? You're so unmercenary and diffident. If you'll just agree to leave this little problem in my hands, I will get you five thousand dollars, not a miserable two, and the garden people will be ecstatic, still more so when they know you. Please, Sir Dougal!"

Diana Arden had me in a cleft stick. If I declined, she would be suspicious. Indeed, I had already wondered whether suspicion might not be dawning in that agile mind. Five thousand dollars was or were so many marbles compared with the sum to which I aspired, but it would be limited insurance against defeat. Typical hypocrisy, I thought about myself. "Have it your own way," I grumbled.

"Please don't be cross with me, Sir Dougal."

"I am anything but cross with you, Diana. A little sherry?"

"Love some." She sipped at her second glass of it and said: "Tio Pepe is dry nectar, if that's possible."

"This talk of my honorarium reminds me of a more important matter, Diana, and that is your salary. Already you are being a tremendous help to me, but I don't know your plans. Would you be prepared to accept employment for, say, a week or two?"

"Would I ever, Sir Dougal!"

"Then you must tell me what a fair amount would be. As you can understand, I am wholly inexperienced about Canadian salary scales. I suppose I could ask Claud Merriwell."

"Oh, please don't, Sir Dougal. But I always say business is business, so we must certainly agree on a fair amount. Still, it is a little difficult because I'm getting full pay for my month's leave, and a chief stewardess with Global packs down a whopping salary. And I told you how I hate idle vacations, bumming it around. So this is just really keeping busy working for a lovely man." Once more she frowned and bit her lip, perhaps with doubt about the lovely, and hastened on: "Would a dollar an hour be too much to ask?"

A dollar an hour, eight bob, forty new pence. "But, Diana, that's a mere pittance for your talents."

"No, honestly, it's much more like fun for me than work. But I tell you what, if we go into more than eight hours a day, I'll charge you double for overtime, and keep a faithful record, that I promise." Her face lit up with the endearing smile. "Shall we call it a deal?"

"It's not nearly enough," I said. "But, oh well, a deal and many thanks. I can't think what I would do without you."

"I shall probably make the most hopeless boo-boos. Just one afterthought, Sir Dougal. Would you mind paying me in cash, so we won't have to bother with income tax and all that kind of nonsense?"

"Gladly," I said, as the telephone rang.

"Sir Dougal Trocher's office. Oh, hullo, Mr. Merriwell. You'll wait in the lobby? Yes, I'll tell him."

"By the way, he offered his car for a drive this afternoon. Would you like to add guiding to your secretarial duties?"

"Guiding is free fun," she said. "So I'll make it up in the evening without overtime. Could I order myself a sandwich?"

"Of course. But why not go down and have a proper lunch?"

"Too busy," she said. "Now brush your hair and off you go. It would never do to keep your tycoon cousin waiting."

Now brush your hair and off you go, reminiscent of Ida Peebles. I obeyed orders, cogitating. A dollar an hour was slave labor veritably. But the heart was so good, the tongue so persuasive, the will so steely that one found oneself bedizened into yielding.

⚹ 10 ⚹

DRINKING SHERRY WHILE he had Dubonnet Blonde I soon got over my endemic constraint about Christian names with strangers, and managed Claud to his Dougal to the manner born. Everyone passing greeted him, and all were introduced to *my cousin, Sir Dougal Trocher,* so our preprandial libation was a jack-in-the-box affair. But how reticently courteous they were, how much more concerned with their fellow man than the weary ex-imperial British. One felt a warmth, and one responded to it.

At luncheon we sat alone. He asked me about that notorious clan through which we were related. I could answer only vaguely. We Trochers had feuded with them and then avoided them for centuries until my wretched mother seduced my father into marriage. But Claud was too tactful to ask about her, not that I knew. I had heard nothing of the woman since her third marriage ended in front-page adultery.

Then he spoke of my grandfather, of the scholarly elegance of his letters, and how much he wished that he had met him, and how amusing my comment at the press conference had been.

"I didn't mean to say it, but I was caught out, stuck." And who came to the rescue? I did not need to ask myself. My relations with my secretary were and would remain utterly platonic, strictly those of business. But I was aware that the world might take me for a chip off the old rip's block. "That

79

Miss Arden is on leave from Global Airlines," I said carefully, "and she wanted a holiday job, so I decided to employ her. One is rather besieged with invitations, and I am finding her the greatest help."

"How very sensible of you," he said, drawing faint lines with his fork on the tablecloth to form a geometric pattern. "I don't see how you could possibly cope without a secretary."

At bargain rates, I did not divulge, but he was asking me about Drin. Claud Merriwell would know of its and our run-down condition, not that he hinted at that. *The nostrils of the affluent twitch afar off at the miasma of us paupers,* Grandfather said once.

But at the Duncattos' suggestion, I had fabricated a story which would explain suite-occupying wealth. My Irish grand-mother's sister had married a man in Dublin. They were childless, and she had outlived him to the age of ninety, and had left me a modest inheritance. "That has been a considera-ble help," I said — the trooper lying — not ceasing to astonish myself.

"I'm glad for you, Dougal," he said. I liked him now, a more human man than I had thought.

Then it was my turn to show tactful interest in homes and relaxations, but I avoided business, ever a closed book to me, and not one that I could open without revealing abysmal ignorance to the president of the largest steel corporation in Canada. Their two children were now grown-up and away, so they had moved from the Westmount house to an apartment, much easier for Laura, his wife, who was not very well. They also had a ski chalet in the Laurentian Hills, and a summer house by the sea.

"Do you ski, Dougal?"

"I used to go to the Tyrol for a fortnight every winter. But not lately." Too broke lately, I did not say.

"Sometime you must come with me to Aspen, Colorado. Four hours door to door in our small jet, which makes the occasional weekend possible. It's too high for Laura — she has troublesome emphysema — but the skiing is superb, and the après-ski is not too bad." He addressed himself gravely to his fork or to the four-lane highway he was tracing lightly with it, a bit of a dog, the president? "Weekend skiing or weekend golf, that's all I have the time for. Do you play golf, Dougal?"

"I used to, but I gave it up."

"You're young to give things up," he said. "How do you keep so fit, then?"

"I walk ten miles a day at home, more or less. Golf might be a good idea here, though, while I'm in the city."

"I can lend you clubs. Perhaps we could play on Sunday if you're free. Now, if you'll forgive me, Dougal, I must go. I have labor troubles on my head. Seven thousand blue-collar workers, and the strike deadline is with the midnight shift."

"But I had no idea. I would never have taken up your time."

"I have two mottos or watchwords in business, Dougal. One is: *If you can't delegate, you shouldn't be where you are.* And the other is: *People who can't leave their work behind are invariably second-rate.*

He was immensely sure of himself, and with good reason, and yet conceit might lurk. We went out and down the steps, and the bottle green Cadillac drew up. "That reminds me," he said. "If you're touring gardens in the country, you're going to need a car. Our son is in Europe this summer, and his BMW is sitting idle. May I send it round to the Ritz garage for you?"

I had decided to rent a small machine for the duration, and here was another windfall, lobbed into my lap. Forgive the mixed metaphor. "It's wonderfully kind of you, but . . ."

"Not kind at all, I want my Scottish cousin to enjoy Canada."

"But supposing I smash it, Claud."

"If you smash it, there's insurance. All you need is your British driving license."

I had that in my wallet. He waved away my halting thanks, and said: "Grenier will run me to the office, and be at the hotel for you in about ten minutes."

The heat was burning, ninety-eight degrees, the hottest

weather I had known since Aden's furnace. But we drove round Montreal at an air-conditioned seventy — by the new tall city, by old Montreal, and on and round and up to look over shimmering buildings to haze beyond the river, and caterwauling sirens were wild and weird in canyons of the city. We walked on the mountain of Mont Réal for half an hour to Beaver Lake and back.

"I thrive on heat," Diana said. "But I must say your cousin's little runabout begins to beckon."

She was a most entertaining companion/guide through the city of her youth, making me laugh in English, and Grenier laugh in that outlandish patois, often unintelligible to me. Her youth had been slightly checkered, one might gather.

There was no hint of the secretary until she spread out all ten fingers to indicate the appropriate pourboire for Monsieur Grenier. Back in the sitting room, she said: "I spoke to Mr. Farrow at lunchtime again. I said that you yourself were reluctant to take any honorarium at all, would not even discuss it with me, but might I venture to advise?

"Why, certainly, he said. *I wish you would, Miss Arden.* So I mentioned your worldwide renown, the very heavy expenses you were incurring, including the services of an executive secretary, myself, and the many other engagements you would have to forego if you were to give full meticulous attention to the Country Garden Club. Well, Mr. Farrow stopped me short at that, Mr. Farrow was quite agitated, and Mr. Farrow said: *Upon my soul, Miss Arden, the last thing we would wish is to be held niggardly. Do you think Sir Dougal would be kind enough to accept five thousand?* His suggestion, it wasn't me at all."

"Well done," I growled. It was the least I could growl, still troubled by the remnants of my conscience. Five minutes of verbal sorcery by telephone, twelve cents' worth at a dollar an hour, and she had put five thousand dollars in my pocket. It was so miraculous as to be quite frightening.

"You're scowling, Sir Dougal. Have I done wrong?"

"No, no, Diana. On the contrary, I am profoundly grateful.

82

But I do hope that in the future you will not get too far ahead of me in such matters."

"That I promise, I really do. It's this fault of being carried away by my enthusiasms. So if ever you find that I exceed my authority, do just give me a metaphorical spank."

"I'm infecting you with my florid linguistic ways," I said, and we had a jolly laugh together, amity restored.

It was nearly six, time for a bath and change. "By the way, Sir Dougal, I took the liberty of having your two other suits pressed. They were rather rumpled."

"Thank you, Diana. I forgot that."

"Do you want me to come along to the interview? Or would you rather go it alone?"

"Please come," I said. "Yes, for heaven's sake come." As this first formal day of work wore on, I realized increasingly how much I depended on my secretary's guidance and selfless, if at times impetuous, concern for my interest.

"In that case perhaps I could have a quick shower in the other bathroom. I feel sort of grimy after our torrid walk. May I, Sir Dougal?"

"By all means, Diana."

"And I'd better get out some ice for a television stiffener."

When I emerged for my stiffener she was typing, but turned to consider me with care. "You look just lovely. You look good enough to . . ." But Diana left her sentence uncompleted. "Say when," she said briskly, with the whisky bottle.

My interview on "Meet the Celebrities" was not so bad. The girl asked me about home, the boundless acres of heather hill, the river, the lively Drin that I loved so much and perhaps described quite well, and she asked me to quote Robert Burns in Scotch, and she asked me about gardening, and it was done.

Diana had watched on the monitoring set. "You were super," she said. "You were just yourself. Like a young Gregory Peck, only more stalwart sort of. Wonderful when your face lit up about the river, perhaps a teeny bit ponderous when it came to those rhododendron things."

If my secretary's praise verged upon the fulsome, she could also criticize in kindly fashion.

"Let's go and have some dinner."

"I know a nice small restaurant, Sir Dougal."

We had a banquette table, sitting across the corner. First bone-dry martinis; and then crabmeat with cantaloupe, sweetbreads, a bottle of Chablis, lime sherbet.

A man played an accordion, but quietly, insuring private talk. "I came here once with that guy I worked for."

"The one who went to prison?"

"Yes, him. Well, actually, Sir Dougal, he was the only man I ever have been secretary to until this very day. But I had been with him a year by then, and he wanted me to see at firsthand his business methods on the road, so I came along to Canada that time, Montreal, Toronto, Winnipeg, Calgary, Edmonton, Vancouver, selling as we went.

"There were only two lines or items, and the whole shipment fitted into one strong suitcase, that was the beauty of it. The white-gold brooches were the first thing, the most gorgeous flamboyant designs by Giuseppe Como. As you know, of course, white-gold is an alloy with platinum, and it has the loveliest soft luster, and stamped on the back with the authentic monogram of Como; they were fabulously expensive. The other things were pocket lighters, not just ordinary eighteen carat ones, but with new everlasting fuel and ignition systems, and he had an exclusive franchise. I hope I'm not boring you, Sir Dougal."

"Certainly not, Diana. How would you like some crème de menthe frappée?"

"Just adore it. Well, we sold as we went, from one gilded establishment to the next. He was a quite fantastic salesman, always casual and easy. And as we moved west and I learned his methods, he began to let me do a little selling too."

"I fancy, Diana, that you were an apt pupil."

"Aptish, perhaps, but you should have seen that man go selling tough jeweler cookies. Now, one stipulation he made was payment down, and one idiosyncrasy he had was to take

84

each check at once to the bank and cash it into the biggest denominations. And so, by the time we had sold the last of our stock in Vancouver, his special inside pocket contained a nice little wad of ninety-four one-thousand-dollar bills."

Diana glanced round the dimly lit room and lowered her voice, and the man was yodeling mellifluously to his accordion. "Up to our last day in Montreal before flying back I had never had the slightest hint of shenanigans. When I first went to work for him, he said: *The essence of our business is discretion. If I talk, if you talk, sure as hell some S.O.B. will steal the deal from us. So when you leave this office, you close the door on what you know. That clear, Baby?* He was a little racy in his ways and speech, not at all like you, Sir Dougal, and for that I'm grateful, I mean to you. So, of course, I never breathed a word, not that there was anything funny-peculiar to breathe about. At keeping my trap shut, I'm a natural, even if you may think otherwise." She gazed at me with a small reproachful pout.

"Indeed, I do not think otherwise, Diana."

"One day when I had worked for him about six months, he locked the office door, *to keep the underworld out,* he chuckled, opened the safe, and removed a box in which were jewels — emeralds, diamonds, rubies and one sapphire — all cut stones, and some huge. He taught me a little about them; values, the best colors, flaws and so on. Then he put them away again. He said nothing about secrecy; people do trade in precious stones, and it all seemed perfectly aboveboard.

"It was in this very room, Sir Dougal. Di, he said. He always called me that, and I wished he wouldn't, and I hope you won't, I like being Diana in the round. *Di,* he said. *Do you want to work up to full partnership with me on equal terms?*

"*Gosh, yes,* I said. Then he whispered: *Do you object in principle to a little smuggling?*

"*Lord no,* I said. *I draw the line at drugs, that's wicked. But decent smuggling is just a game that everybody plays.*

"*Good. Then tomorrow I'll show you how we turn an honest*

profit. And he tapped his lower right tummy where the ninety-four grand was nestling."

Diana finished her crême de menthe. "Do you mind if I stop a minute to make a quick telephone call, Sir Dougal?"

✻ 11 ✻

I, Dougal Trocher, indigent baronet, sat alone in this hospitable strange land, savoring *Cordon-bleu,* and I wondered and I wondered. And then suddenly I saw Tirene, not the happy Tirene of the fishing dream, but the enraged Tirene of Crummock railway station, it was so vivid a glimpse and I had lost her.

Here came Diana Arden, for the first time revealing forthright exasperation. "It really is a bit much. Jenny, the girl whose pad I flopped in on the sofa last night, promised faithfully that if she decided to go away, she would leave her key with the janitor. Well, she hasn't, and he flatly refuses to let me in, says it's more than his job is worth, and I suppose it is in this goddam larcenous city, and there sits my luggage. I could kill Jenny, the silly little thing, she's lost her moonlit pants to some beastly Turk in Buffalo.

"Ah well, not a stitch to my name, but I'll think of something. Now, where was I, Sir Dougal?"

"You were at a little smuggling game, Diana, do go on."

"Next morning we were whisked by Chrysler Imperial to a Montreal suburb called Outremont and to a house in its own capacious grounds, a butler at the door, *please be seated,* and so we were, surrounded by a marvelous nineteenth-century collection — Degas, Cézanne, Gauguin, van Gogh, you can name it. And then another man came, quite a different slab-faced type with a wrestler's torso and extra bulges that might just possibly have been burgeoning muscles underneath his arms. He said not a word, simply cocked one finger.

"The oak paneling of the next room swung open by silent magic, and we went into the windowless secret chamber where a small man stood beyond a refectory table. He had an ascetic Jewish face, and he smiled and bowed and motioned us to chairs. The door clicked shut, and there we were.

"On his side of the table was a strip of black velvet, and on that a dozen sparkling objects, and beside that a pair of forceps. On our side of the table was a strip of the same, balance scales, similar forceps, a pad of paper.

"Then he picked up one cut diamond from his velvet and put it onto ours with the forceps, and my boss picked it up, and weighed it in metric carats — that's two hundred milligrams, Sir Dougal. He had brought his own weights, it's the etiquette, apparently. He made a note, and studied the stone with his optician's glass, another note. About one diamond he shook his head and picked it up and gave it back, and the man nodded.

"At last my boss spoke. *Seventy-five*, he said.

"*They will surely fetch a hundred and twenty in London, and so my price is one hundred thousand.* He was very polite and quiet, and he had those suffering Semitic eyes. I guessed now by looks and voice that he was probably an Armenian.

"*They're good all right. Let's call it ninety.*

"And that was the end of it, Sir Dougal, no haggling, just two professionals at work. My boss took out his wad, counted four from it and put those back, and handed the bills one by one across the table. He held each up to the light, an overall quick look through his glass, put it down and took the next. Afterward, he counted them through like a bank teller, lightning fast. *Ninety*, he said. *Sincerely, I thank you.*

"Only then did my employer take the pillbox from his pocket. Now they were his, he popped those things into that box with as little ceremony as if they were the so many marbles I spoke of earlier today, and he snapped on a rubber band.

88

"*Cheers, then,* he said, *perhaps next month.*

"*Perhaps next month,* the small man said, bowing.

"The panel door swung open. Slab-face herded us to the butler, who shepherded us to the limousine. At the Queen Elizabeth, where we were staying, he said: *Go to the drugstore, Di, and buy a three-cake gift set of the most expensive soap you can find.*

"He was like that, rather peremptory except when wheeling and dealing. Anyway, I got the Lanvin, super bathsize. He was waiting in the room with a small vice already set up, and a hair-thin hacksaw. He undid the cellophane without breaking it, and in a very few minutes the chosen cake was sawed exactly in two, crosswise, like the two shells of a clam. Then he laid out the eleven smashing diamonds, and for each one he made its nest in one half of the soap with a special curved knife, a drop of water on each one to anchor it, put the halves together, shook them, listening, not a rattle. He mixed up some epoxy — *joins anything to anything,* he said — made a thin line of it round each piece a little inside the edge, wedded the two, put them back in the vice to set.

"After half an hour, he buffed the join and polished it, and there was a perfect cake of soap, perhaps an undetectable mite smaller because of the saw cut, and worth just one hundred and twenty thousand dollars. *That leaves two cakes to sweeten the wife,* he said. He had a spouse somewhere, but she never swam into my ken.

"That night we flew by different airlines. *Have a well-earned holiday, Di. See you Monday week, then, Gorgeous.* But I didn't see him on Monday week or ever again because they caught him next morning at London Airport.

"At first, I thought that some swine, perhaps even the Outremont people, had squealed. But not so. It transpired at the trial that known diamonds stolen in New York had been finding their way at intervals onto the London market, and when Interpol slipped the word to Scotland Yard, it was only a matter of the patient flatfoots keeping tabs on who kept flying when and where. I'm sorry to say it about such a brilliant

89

man, but he was too clever just one time too often. They say you can get away with a big one once, Sir Dougal, or even two big ones twice, but that's it."

"Tell me, Diana, did the police give you personally much trouble?"

"Not a sausage, because they knew nothing about me. You see, he abhorred stupid red tape and ridiculous taxes, and so he always paid my salary in fivers, and of Diana Arden, Secretary, there was no record in his office, period. You know, Sir Dougal, I don't think he did anything so very bad, not in my book. He sold his merchandise quite honestly, and with the proceeds he paid for the diamonds quite honestly, don't you agree, or don't you?" Her gaze earnestly solicited my worldly wise opinion.

"There was the matter of buying goods that he knew to be stolen, and there was the matter of evading customs duty on them. Both acts were surely criminal, Diana."

"Well, to start with, those diamonds were taken from plutocrats who could well afford it, serve them right. And to go on with, I'm sure he would gladly have paid the customs duty, but under the circs he couldn't very well. *D'accord*, Sir Dougal?"

"Not entirely *d'accord*, Diana." I paid my bill, consulting her about the tip, total cost sixty-four dollars. As we left the restaurant, I was thinking that I had never known anyone like my secretary. Her knowledge of life was clearly encyclopedic, and yet sometimes she revealed a naiveté that was almost childlike.

"Thank you so much for my lovely dinner. Now one hour's typing, and I shall be up to date."

"But, Diana, there's no need to type tonight. You can finish the letters in the morning."

"And get behindhand. No, Sir Dougal, sorry. My invariable motto is: *Never lay your head to rest until the job is done*."

"If you insist, then. But mark it down as overtime."

"*Overtime!* Do you realize that a half share of the bill for our delicious dinner represents four days' wages? It would be a pretty sleazy trick to charge you overtime."

The lights were against us at the next corner, and we waited. It was dark now at nine-fifteen, a cool touch of air came up from the river. "Sir Dougal!" she said, looking down at her shoes, black with silver buckles reflecting light.

"Yes, Diana?"

"The trouble is that I have nowhere tonight to lay my head, and if I go to some hotel without a single piece of luggage, those horrid desk clerks will think and wink, and . . ."

"You spoke of other friends, new left people and revolutionaries. Why not stay with one of them, Diana?"

"I can't, because they're all away this week at some hideout in the Gaspé, plotting world insurrection. So that's hopeless, and so what I wonder is could I possibly sleep tonight in the little bedroom where I wouldn't be a nuisance to you in any shape or form, and then tomorrow morning — I might have to ask for your influence and help — somehow or other I'll get into that flippertegibbet Jenny's flat where I belong." This poured out in a bashful torrent. "Please, Sir Dougal, could I?"

"But surely, Diana, in the eyes of the world that would not be quite proper."

One polished shoe stamped heel and toe, clip-clop. "In your eyes and mine it would," she said indignantly. "Who cares about the smutty-minded world? I don't. Do you, Sir Dougal?"

"Of course not, Diana."

"Then my only need is a toothbrush from that drugstore. Hang on a mo."

"Early to bed for me," I said, on arrival at the sitting room. "It's been a long day, and worse for you, Diana."

"To work for you is a privilege, Sir Dougal, and I love it." She deftly linked paper to carbon to paper and rolled it in. "Now, before I start typing, may I order some milk? Scotch whisky and milk is a wonderful *architekton* of sweet dreams."

I retired with whisky and milk and *Time* magazine, and read for a while in bed, as is my custom. I tried to understand about Equalization Payments, Lobbies, Lame Ducks, Packed Courts, HEW, but it was all incomprehensible to a simple Scotsman.

The typewriter chattered faintly next door, and I put out my bedside lamp, and that sound stopped as I slid toward sleep, seeing dreamlike images of what had gone before, of yesterday as we trundled out at Prestwick, the stewardess playing dumb crambo to another voice, first with the life jacket, then with the oxygen mask that would pop down, then pointing to the emergency exits.

"Sir Dougal!"

⌖ 12 ⌖

I CLIMBED BACK to wakefulness, a word still in mind. "Is there some emergency, Diana?"

"Yes, Sir Dougal, there is some desperate emergency."

I switched on my bedside lamp, and beyond its modest beam, I saw Diana Arden. She wore a brief sarong from slender waist to swelling thighs. She wore her tiger stripes of silk.

"I can't stand it one more second, that's the emergency, Sir Dougal."

"But, Diana!"

"No buts," she said, and lithely she came into my ample bed. She kissed my brow, and she kissed each cheek, and she said: "We could call this overtime, if you like."

That small mocking comment made the utterly unexpected somehow quite instantly inevitable as she kissed me on the lips, "Darling Sir Dougal." In thirty seconds the monastic ways of half a lifetime took their leave. I was a man, and in my pajamaed arms there thrived delectable, soft, supple woman.

"No hurry," she said. "We have the whole long night before us. Just lie there like some sultan while I toy with every single button."

I was lost, and as the errant moments sailed, I heard my true love in the car beside me:

Perhaps you might learn as well as teach in Canada.

I'm sure I shall. But how do you mean, Tirene?

93

Oh well, you know, live and learn, live it up a bit.

But two minutes later she had told me to verb off, stuffy old adjectival prig.

Is it you, Tirene, toying with every single button? No, Tirene, it is not. Please leave, Tirene, go away. I sighed profoundly for treasonous delight.

"Was that a happy sigh, Sir Dougal?"

"Happy is not quite the word for it, Diana."

"And this is the very last one. Oh, mercy me, my goodness gracious." She drew off my lower, slipped me from my upper, and I had my will with her tiger stripes.

"I bet there aren't two more naked people anywhere in all the world."

". . . Bliss," she said, as a quiet time came drifting. "Have you done much of this sort of thing, Sir Dougal?"

"No, Diana, I have not, and I do apologize for clumsiness."

"Not to worry, you were born to tumble."

"And so were you, Diana." Her head lay on my shoulder.

"You smell of man. And that's what you are, man through and through. The moment I saw you at the airport, my pulse did a carioca dance, and I wondered why, it so rarely does. But it was when you came to my rescue and shook that fat bastard like a jellyfish, that was the moment of decision. Then and there I vowed to myself that Sir Dougal and I would be happily horizontal in no time flat, well, it did take two days, and here we are, and am I grateful."

"But, Diana, you gave no hint of any such intent."

"I certainly did not. I know you think I'm simple, Sir Dougal, and so perhaps I am, but not as simple as all that. From the very first looks and words exchanged, I knew you were a man shy of woman, and I knew that if I revealed the slightest cuteness or come-hither, you would flee like the noble stag when hunted. So little sister was my only hope. But once or twice I nearly gave myself away."

"Did you, Diana? I never suspected."

"Last evening, for instance, when you had changed. It's possible for a girl to say to a man: *You look just lovely,* that

could be a friendly sort of joke. But if a girl says to a man —
and I barely stopped myself in time — if a girl says to a manly
man: *You look good enough to eat,* there is invariably a sensual
connotation, now I'm talking just like you, Sir Dougal. But
we're buddies as well, that's what's so lovely."

We were entwined, and we were comfortable, and we were
buddies.

"Have you forgiven me, Sir Dougal?"

"One does not owe forgiveness if one has reaped a harvest of
delight, and if one intends quite shortly a renewal of the same.
But I do have some questions to ask."

"Let's have a drink, and then I'll answer them."

"Isn't one A.M. rather late for a drink?"

"In a night of love — you're kidding. It's an encourage-
ment. What's yours?"

Diana was soon back with spanking whiskies, and we were
more than ever comfortable. "I know your questions can't be
anything but honest, so I promise to give honest answers."

"Diana, you have already told me why you concealed your
physical designs. How many of the other things, the stories
you have told me, have been the children of a fertile
imagination?"

"But, Sir Dougal, every single thing was true, oh well,
except for little jokes and leg-pulls. All that about my boss was
gospel. But to one fib I must confess. I made it up about
Jenny because I knew that if I didn't get in at once and storm
the citadel, so to speak, I would be sure to betray my feelings
during working hours, and you would be sure to throw me out.
Actually, Jenny was wailing on the telephone about that
beastly Turk in Buffalo."

"You sound a mite unsympathetic to the lovelorn Jenny."

"Yes, I am, and I'll tell you why, because all this soppy
romantic love most girls drool on about I simply cannot
recognize. The only love I know is making love, shameless
lovely love with a terrific man like you, and if you think I'm
just promiscuous, you're wrong, because I haven't slept with a
man for simply ages. Real men are few and far between, and

you are one, and by the time I've taught you all I know, you'll be the best lover any woman ever had."

"Thank you, Diana, but there is one thing I must tell you, and it is that I do love another woman in the total way that you simply cannot recognize. I love her altogether, mind and body, and am terrified of both."

"Poor you, Sir Dougal, but I tell you what: Couldn't you pretend I'm her, I mean put her in my place? That might make you braver for the body part if chance should ever offer. I don't think I can help about the mind."

"Both are lost to me," I said, and the air conditioning gently hummed. "What are you thinking about, Diana?"

"I am thinking carnal thoughts, Sir Dougal, and they make bad poetry:

> *"Love me again before we sleep,*
> *Love me slow and love me deep.*
> *Love me through,*
> *And I'll love you.*

". . . Yes, Poetry," she said later, from her now-established place in the hollow of my shoulder. "My God, what that loved-one of yours is missing. Darling Sir Dougal, now good night."

When I awoke, it was to bright morning through the chinks, and to no Diana, and I felt the loss.

"Coming," she called, and strolled in naked. "I was combing my hair and mussing up the bed, both for appearances, not that the latter will deceive." She clasped her hands behind her head, and boxed the compass. She was nature's child, no less perfect of body than Tirene, whose form was evident, if not unveiled, never to be unveiled, oh, damn Tirene. "Do you like me, Sir Dougal?"

"I like you very much. You arouse in me a most cordial tumescence." For once I had stated thought and feeling with precision. "What time is it, Diana?"

"Just eight o'clock, and the *Star* man doesn't come until eleven, so we have lots of time for what we have a mind to, and another thing I have a mind to is to ask you one or two frank questions. Shall I ask them before or after, Sir Dougal?"

"After, Diana. Come here at once."

"How could you learn so quickly? Now it's me to learn, to learn you every inch." And that she did with grave concern until I toppled her and made her victim, supple eel. Then she was laughing, brown eyes happy. "That's what I mean about love for its own sake, love for fun. Thank you a thousand times, Sir Dougal, three times actually so far."

"Thank you, Diana. Don't you think that now we're getting to know one another a little better, you could drop my dreary handle and just call me Dougal?"

"No, I can't. If I called you Dougal in private, then sure as hell the ever-latent sensual would surface taking notes in public while you judged some plutocratic stuffed shirt's garden, and my traitor tongue would give our private show away. *Sir Dougal*, it must always be.

"But if you imagine that now I'm your ardent mistress I'm going to be any less your ardent secretary, you're mistaken. Just one favor I would ask. May I promote myself to the confidential category of amanuensis?"

"Indeed, you may, Diana."

"In that case, Sir Dougal, spill the beans."

"How do you mean, Diana?"

"I mean that some can stretch the truth convincingly, and some cannot, and into the latter group you surely fall, although I must say you're improving."

"I don't quite understand, Diana."

"You travel first class, you're living in the lap, and I don't mean to boast, Sir Dougal, but my lap could also be called *de luxe*."

"Luxissima, Diana."

"But from various small things you said, half-said, or stopped yourself saying, I tumbled in short order to the fact that you're not a rich man at all."

She lay on her side, cheek in hand and propped on elbow.

She had me cornered, figuratively speaking, on the tilting ground. "Diana in the bonny buff," I said.

That merry laugh, and she was blushing. It was quite charming. It was innocence. "You're trying to put me off, Sir Dougal. Well, I won't be. You kept saying you were here on business, and then you made an odd remark about the Country Garden Club being big enough to be worthwhile, but it was when you boggled at taking a fee that I said to myself: Sir Dougal's funny old conscience is bothering him. Now why? Sir Dougal is the soul of honor, that stands out a linear mile. Sir Dougal is so terribly British that he thinks it wouldn't be quite cricket. You're smiling, Sir Dougal."

"I'm smiling because you read my very thought."

"Please tell me, then. We're as close together as a man and woman can reasonably be. Don't you trust me?"

I stood at the brink, as once Black Dougal had stood above the Fall of Drin. "About the other chap, your first employer, was that all true?"

"I told you," she said, blushing again, this time with annoyance. "Damn you, Sir Dougal. Every single word was true. But cross my heart, if you insist."

Diana Arden crossed her heart, and I told my tale of vacillation and despair, of the goading by my stout friend which had forced me to decision, of the help that Tarquie and Lois had given me, of the vague plan that now began to take a firmer shape. I told her all, omitting only mention of the wayward, adorable Tirene.

"What a superlative conception. Sir Dougal, you're a genius, Captain of our ship. What an honor it is for me to be Chief Officer."

"But, Diana, there are many risks involved. Don't forget what happened to your previous employer."

"He was too clever once too often. That was his comeuppance. But we're going to be clever — no, I don't much like that word, *too clever by half*, it reminds me of, finagling — we're going to be ice-cool intelligent just once. Now first, we must get these rich goons and their riches under one weekend roof together, and that means a super full-fig party."

"Surely goons is hardly the word, Diana. They're probably very decent people."

"The bloody rich are all goons to me, and please don't interrupt . . ." She thought aloud and brilliantly, my incredible Chief Officer. It was small wonder that the boys on the Far East route had said that our Diana should be running the whole damned airline. ". . . It's all your original thinking, Sir Dougal. My job is to tie up loose ends and details. But our worst mistake would be to plan too much too far ahead. What we must do first is shape things to our way.

"For instance, we might make a quick preliminary tour of all the gardens, perhaps with Mr. Farrow, and choose our venue, best of all mold him into thinking it up as his own idea, he sounds quite a malleable old codger.

"But it's after nine, time to ready ourselves to meet the day. Shall I order a huge breakfast? I'm absolutely famished, and I hope you are. I want you fighting fit."

⚹ 13 ⚹

"A CHAP WHO DOWNS orange juice, porridge and cream, a jolly spiffing kipper, two eggs and sausages and bacon, not to mention buttered toast, Chivers Olde English and a quart of coffee — that chap goes a long way to insuring equilibrium as between his appetites. Ah, sweet languor, I feel marvelous."

She had borrowed an iron for her dress, and for the ubiquitous tiger stripes, worn this morning at her neck. "Diana, you positively glow with health."

"I positively purr," she said. But that thing rang again. "Sir Dougal Trocher's office. Oh, thank you, please send it up. A Special Delivery, Sir Dougal."

"You open it," I said when she had tipped the bellboy an hour's worth of her wages.

It was a letter from Jonathan Farrow, venturing to enclose a check for my honorarium, also a list of the country gardens, and his wife and he so much looked forward to meeting me at Camelot on Saturday evening, and might he send a car? And in the meanwhile was there any way in which he could be of service, however small? With every kind regard, sincerely.

"Who is Jonathan Farrow? He writes like one of those men of distinction one hears about."

"He is, Sir Dougal. I copied him from the hotel *Canadian Who's Who.* Here's the entry." It was crisp-secretary time.

There were three typewritten sheets about Jonathan Farrow, industrialist and financier, born 1905, son of, educated,

100

married, joined Bocabec Pulp and Paper, Executive Vice President, President, Chairman, Honorary Chairman of the Board; Directorships: Chemicals, Railways, Bank, Gas, Breweries, Oil, Trust Company, Steel . . .

"Mr. Farrow has retired now to his thirty-seven directorships, I counted them, Sir Dougal, all huge outfits. Mr. Farrow is a charter member of the adjectival enemy.

"And look at Mr. Farrow's War. Director General of Munitions, sending our brave boys to certain death from a safe office desk in Ottawa."

"One might think, Diana, that Mr. Farrow was using his best endeavors to send the enemy's brave boys to certain death."

"Ah, poo! And look at Mr. Farrow's recreations: gardening, conservation, country pursuits. What are country pursuits, Sir Dougal?"

> *"I chase thee to mossy dell in Nature's Garden,*
> *That is a country pursuit, Diana Arden."*

"Gosh, it's a riot being your secretary but as I always say, business is business is no time for the libido. Now, what I suggest is that you in person telephone Mr. Farrow, express thanks in your inimitable way, for the bread I mean, and then suggest that a quick tour of representative gardens on Saturday would be of the greatest help in assessing your task, which you so much look forward to discussing with him that evening."

"All right, Diana. What's his number?"

"I will place the call, Sir Dougal."

"I should do it myself. It's damned bad manners to keep anybody hanging on the line."

"I quite agree in principle, but not in practice. As I said before, you must be grand. You must be on a pedestal apart, ever courteous, and, with the exception of Cousin Claud, never never be on first-name terms. That would spell the ruin of our cause. You must be the august Sir Dougal, his olde worlde self. That shouldn't be too hard, and that way we can work wonders for the sake of Drin . . ."

"Good morning, Mr. Farrow, it's Sir Dougal's secretary speaking. It's cooler, you say? That's nice. Then I look forward to going out." The pause was momentary, and the blush was flooding. "Sir Dougal would like a word with you himself, if it's convenient. Here he is."

"Goddam stupid bitch," she muttered, passing me.

Mr. Farrow thought the preliminary tour an excellent idea, and might he drive me? And since we would in some measure be discussing business in the evening, would I care to bring my secretary to dinner? Mr. Farrow was a cultivated-sounding man, with an accent that hovered somewhere in the mid-Atlantic. Until Saturday morning, then.

"I'm not very pleased with you, Diana."

"I know," she said, crestfallen. "It was just one of those hasty boo-boos I commit. But actually, Sir Dougal, lots of secretaries on the road share suites with their employers without any funny business."

"Surely not secretaries like you, Diana."

"Not secretaries like me with employers like you, that I do admit. So there will be some cozy chit-chat, but they will approve the austerity of our public relations — I am always Miss Arden to you, Sir Dougal, practice it — and they will admire you for carrying on a bold family tradition. Am I forgiven?"

"Yes, Miss Arden, what the hell."

"There are these letters to sign. Now, about the check, I don't think that at this stage of our operation it would be wise to take a leaf from my late unlamented's book and convert it into five at a thousand smackers each. Such denominations are not so easily negotiable for bus fare, and across a counter they cause searching looks because they are used by a very different kind of person from the upright likes of Sir Dougal Trocher. Which does not mean that we mightn't need the big boys later when we step beyond the pale into the big stuff. So I suggest you put it in the bank. Do you have a Montreal account, Sir Dougal, or just traveler's checks?"

"I have four hundred dollars in traveler's checks, but I also

102

have a credit of a thousand at the Laurentian Bank. There was a letter from them asking for instructions."

"That's easy, then. Dear Sir: With reference to your letter of 30th June concerning the thousand dollars which you hold for me, I shall be obliged if you will open a current account in my name. I also authorize my secretary, Miss Diana Arden, to deposit the enclosed check for five thousand dollars. Herewith two specimen signatures. With my thanks. Yours faithfully.

"Now endorse the back of the check: *Please deposit to my current account.* That stops me absconding with the lolly."

"Diana, you're a secretary beyond compare. I notice you spending your own money for tips and so on. Are you keeping a careful note?"

"I certainly am, Sir Dougal. Here is the petty cash account, written up to date. And here is the wages account."

"Only three hours overtime, but surely . . ."

"Don't argue the toss, Sir Dougal. I simply will not overcharge you for my overtime."

"Very well. But there is something else of great importance that we must agree upon. I refer to our terms of partnership."

"Let's talk about it this evening at our leisure. That *Star* man will be coming in a minute. I don't think you need me, do you? Your self-confidence is increasing by such mighty leaps and bounds. This would be a convenient chance for me to go to the bank, and fetch my belongings, and do any other little jobs you want."

"You might get me some picture postcards, say a dozen. And if you happen to see a good one of a Saint Bernard dog, please buy it."

"Oh, I adore Saint Bernards, so wise and pensive and majestic. Do you have one?"

"Yes, Diana. His name is Bernardo, and I miss him."

"You know, Sir Dougal, they say that a man and his dog oft come to bear resemblance."

Where's your alter ego? Tirene inquired at a dogless meeting in the month of May. "Do they say that, Diana?"

"They say that, Sir Dougal. I should be back by twelve-fifteen, and I'd better buy some Smirnoff, a favorite tipple with the press, serving as it does to cover the news."

"Diana, you think of everything. Did you think, by the way, that it might be tactful to leave your bags downstairs until he has gone?"

"I thought of that very thing. Toodle-oo, Sir Dougal."

Interview over, the Montreal *Star* was grateful for two bloody marys while we had frosty sherry. With me, Diana was at her most secretarial. With him, she was quite girlish, a very different Miss Arden from my stewardess. I could not but observe her impact on men. Slightly bemused by vodka and the *femme fatale,* he took his leave. We had our lunch upstairs. "Shall I drive you along to the Botanical Garden? It would be a chance to learn the BMW."

"You aren't a gardener, are you, Diana?"

"No, Sir Dougal, not yet I'm not. And I confess to some reluctance about seeing exotic botanicals all afternoon. But I tell you one thing I must do, and that is acquire a spurious smattering of horticulture and learn those Latin names."

"There are very many, Diana, and difficult for a beginner."

"Not for me, Sir Dougal. I read them once, and they're imprinted. That's the kind of memory I'm cursed with, or I suppose in my secretarial capacity, blessed with. Could you lend me a gardening book?"

I had left the books in a suitcase, and produced them now.

"Huge tomes," she said, without enthusiasm. "Hopeless chest-flatteners to read in bed. Isn't there anything? Oh yes, here's a slimmer one. But how madly exciting, how marvelous! You never told me. That was mean."

"I have told you much, Diana. I have not yet had time to tell you quite my little all."

"*Upon My Garden*, by Dougal Trocher. What a lovely title."

"It is from the Song of Solomon. 'Awake, O north wind; and come, thou south; blow upon my garden . . . Let my beloved come into his garden, and eat his pleasant fruits.' "

Diana hugged the dilapidated book. " 'Let my beloved come into his garden.' That stirs my ever-latent sensual. But as some other great author wrote: *To everything there is a season.* Now, let's go."

She rode the BMW like a thoroughbred polo pony, in and out and stop and start and weave to full gallop past common steeds. "Super car," she said. "I love you. Now I must hurry back to read the book. Sir Dougal, as a special favor may I have the hospitality of your couch to read your classic?"

"You may, Diana. But I should warn you that of my classic a mere seven hundred copies were sold."

"Copies sold do not a classic make. Shall I give you some boodle for the taxi home?"

"I have enough, thank you. But I must cash a traveler's check and hand over the proceeds for your accounting."

"Okay. From now on I shall pay for everything, and that will be in keeping with the lofty image. And so home sweet home to do my homework, and then a little snooze to make up for overtime, and then I shall wait upon my Captain's pleasure."

I spent an enjoyable afternoon, finding much of interest at the Botanical Garden. Sleep was catching up, so I asked the taxi driver to stop a few blocks east of the hotel, and I walked the rest. It was cool and cloudy, in pleasant contrast to yesterday, and a brief shower splashed my head.

There were two letters at the desk. One was from Ida Peebles, saying that no sooner was I out of the house than the library floor sagged six inches in the middle, and she was feared it was the dry rot. Like most of us, Ida enjoyed imparting doom and gloom. *Have a grand time, Dougal, and mind what I was warning you about.* She had warned me about North American women, not those of Danish/Australian/French extraction.

Lois wrote that Bernardo and Garry were having a lovely time, but had been rather naughty, roughing up a pregnant sow, no harm done except to Tarquie, who was apoplectic.

And Harry Zee had called from the United States, much interested in my welfare, and where could he reach me by telephone? I wondered whether Lois might have dropped some hint to Mr. Gilpin that had intrigued him about this expedition. More likely it was to be a quid pro quo, a free weekend for free gardening advice. It would not be my first experience of that shabby trick by the affluent. But never could I bring myself to send a bill. That, however, was the old Dougal Trocher.

We hope that your working holiday is a smashing success. But she ended rather sadly: *Not a word from Tirene since she left. She might be in another planet. I don't think she cares about us one little bit. Best love, Lois.*

I would have said: *Tirene does care. But Tirene is unhappy, Lois.* I could not say that, lost in unhappy thought at the cashier's desk in another continent, another planet. "You just sign it again," the girl explained to this nincompoop, and so I signed it and put a hundred dollars in my pocket.

The air conditioning gently hummed, no other sound, Diana would be sleeping. I opened the bedroom door to glimpse her loveliness in slumber, but she was awake, and the poor girl wept. Her siesta gown was a transparent frivolity of scarlet, and *Upon My Garden* lay upon her lacy bosom, and her cheeks were wet. Alas, they were laughter's tears. I had forgotten about that review from the *Illustrated London News.*

> Mr. Trocher is a gifted landscape gardener with a notable aesthetic sense, and his concern for simplicity of line is admirable. We might wish, however, that this love of simplicity extended to his literary modus expressi as he would doubtless call it. In common language, his style reminds us of that old garden favorite, the convolvulus or morning-glory, so well named for the twisting, intertwining convolution of its habit.

"Do you find my book so laughable?" I said, offended.

She wiped her eyes and sat up straight. "I certainly do not, Sir Dougal. I loved its every word, especially because it reads just like you sound; and I might say I learned more about gardening in two hours than I had learned in all my life, and now I can pass any exam you care to set me in Latin names, just try me out. So I had a lovely snooze, and when I woke up, the clipping was half-out of the last blank page inside the cover, and I just thought that crummy reviewer had quite a point about the convolvulus or morning-glory of the family *Convolvulaceae*, there, you see? But I was laughing with you, Sir Dougal, not at you, it was just so funny. I hope I haven't hurt your feelings."

"No, Diana," I said mollified.

"Then divest yourself of those offending garments — there I go, it's a disease — and let us seal the bonds of friendship."

Later, we had a policy discussion. It has been said that the human mind works less efficiently when the thinker is recumbent. But Diana and I did not find this. We agreed, differed, mooted that early evening, as on other mornings, afternoons and nights until our final plans were made. The cool discussion, and careful thought, and Eros waiting in the wings. All plotting is enjoyable, yet I fancy that no plot in history came more enjoyably to life than ours.

One subject we discussed and argued at that session was our partnership agreement. "But, Diana, if my task is only to keep the victims occupied in sensible gardening clothes away from bedrooms, and your task is to clobber the loot, as you describe it, then all the risk is yours, and none is mine, not one iota."

"Sir Dougal, for a brilliant man, you are sometimes inordinately dense. Without your great prestige and fame as magnets, those goons would not be there at all. I am simply the willing tool. My cut's ten per cent, and that is final."

"Ten per cent is ridiculous, Diana. Equal shares, I say."

"If you are obdurate, out of your bed and out of your office I do go. Then what happens to fourteen thousand precious acres?"

She was browbeating me again.

"I love it when you growl, deep as your friend Bernardo."

How often had Bernardo growled, and at the mention of whose name?

"Don't look so sad, Sir Dougal. You have vast possessions

and demands upon you. What demands do I have upon me as a single girl? Well, I must say I have more demands upon me than some less lucky single girls just at this moment, but that is not the point. The point is: Unto each his needs or hers, no more, no less, true socialism. Well, that's settled."

⚬ 14 ⚬

AT THE BEGINNING of my story I wrote that one's childhood memories are isolated pebbles on a dusty path. Perhaps adult memories are not much different, the pebbles more frequent, more clearly seen, but most of the path back there is dusty. So it is with my recollections of that time in Canada. The press conference remains with me complete, but interviews and appearances run hazily together.

The lecture to the Institute of Horticulture, "Some Thoughts Concerning Form and Color in the Garden," was erudite, factual, dry, fitted to an audience of knowledgeable people. Tactfully, they pressed a check upon me for five hundred dollars, and with grateful protestations I accepted it, honestly earned income.

The big success was the Highland Society Banquet. I made a jolly ten minute speech and then, abundantly fortified by Glenlivet, found myself singing "Roaming in the Gloaming," "There was a wee cooper he came frae Fife," "Sandy MacNab Was the Bridegroom," my kaleyard repertoire in what Lois called my heathery baritone. Diana inspected me — lace, velvet doublet, kilt, badger sporran, waist belt, skean d'hu tucked into diced hose below my knee, buckled shoes. "Oh, mercy me, my goodness gracious." Despite an earthy vocabulary from which I endeavor to spare the more gentle reader, she expressed ultimate admiration in those Victorian terms.

And there was the game with Cousin Claud, whose business success might in one small measure be explained by his fierce competitiveness on the golf course. It happened that in my Cambridge days I had been a fair golfer with a handicap of two. Now, in Canada, I had every reason to be grateful to Claud Merriwell for the loan of a superb car, so when I realized on that day at Bruno how much he cared, I decided to indulge him wildly, and we arrived at the eighteenth tee all square. Diana was invited, invariably the case by any male who had set eyes on her. She walked round with us, charming Cousin Claud to whom she had taken a strong dislike. *You could cream that foppish goon with one hand tied behind your back,* she hissed, aside. *Sir Dougal, do please beat the bugger.* But I flubbed a bunker shot and missed a last short putt to give Claud victory and pleasure.

Then there were the twenty-three gardens to be meticulously evaluated in two working weeks, north, south, east and west of Montreal, much travel in the BMW. However nefarious my ultimate intent, I was determined to give good value for the honorarium. *Take a note, Miss Arden, please.* Ulmus glabra pendula, *I think the finest specimen of the Camperdown that we have seen.* — Hydrangea arborescens, *a somewhat blousy shrub alone, as we see it here. How much more effective when massed together. For artistic design, five marks out of ten, have you noted that, Miss Arden?* — *Five out of ten, Sir Dougal, that is duly noted.*

I marked the gardens strictly, which was as well, because the best were of high quality. But, with one exception, my recollections of them are a hotchpotch.

Let us go back to that first Saturday. We had spent the day with Jonathan Farrow in his chauffeur-driven Continental, making ten brief stops for preliminary inspection, had been dropped at the hotel to change, and were now traveling the Eastern Townships' Autoroute, eighty miles an hour, a comfortable idle, myself at the wheel. Speed was of the essence to Diana. For her, as for dear Tirene, speed ever beckoned from here to yonder. But I had pointed out that we must never be

110

caught by the police nor be in any way conspicuous, and she had yielded.

"What do you make of him, Diana?"

"Well, I could sum it up by saying that Mr. Farrow is not too altogether ghastly for an old goon from way back."

"Diana, that word bothers me. The terminology seems inappropriate."

She drew in breath, and I turned to glimpse displeasure's frown. But she said nothing until I had negotiated a toll booth soberly. Her method, before my edict about never drawing attention, had been to run the narrow lane at forty miles an hour, flipping a quarter into the basket with nonchalant dexterity and unfailing aim.

"Sir Dougal, may I utter a few respectful thoughts as we tool along at this dreary dawdle?"

"Pray do, Diana."

"In the plane you said: *When I'm nervous of people, I become long-winded and pontificate.* Are you nervous of me?"

"Indeed not, Diana. Among many delightful discoveries in our relationship, that has been the most delightful."

"You do use rather long words, though, and I am finding the habit insidiously infectious. But what I'm getting at is that when we first were chumming it up like nohow, you confessed that you loved another woman altogether, mind and body, and were terrified of both, and I opined that practice with me might make the latter aspect less intimidating. Bluntly speaking, has it?"

"Indubitably so, Diana, thank you."

"Well, it seems just possible to me now that I could help with your mental block. I don't mean to be impertinent, Sir Dougal, but when you are terrified of your loved-one, do you pontificate, and does that annoy her?"

"It infuriates her, Diana."

"Then what I suggest is that in our times alone — never in public, but alone — you practice jazzing up your speech. You sure have learned at record speed to whoop it up in the hurly-burly. Couldn't you try whooping up the other?"

"I could, let me see, I could have a crack at it, Diana."

"Good on ya, Mite. Now may I please drive for the residual modicum of this splendicious thoroughfare?"

"Sure can, Baby. She's all yours."

It may seem surprising that we should be such passionate, indeed purple lovers, and yet remain casual chums. But such was the case, my thoughts and my longings ever with Tirene.

Jonathan Farrow had given us a map with directions to Camelot, which lay ten or fifteen miles from the autoroute. It was rolling country of woods and fields, at a superficial glance not unlike that part of Crummock where the lowlands and the highlands meet, but the greens were less green, the growth more violent, the wilderness at hand, untidy. People in Canada often said: *It's so like Scotland.* And I would politely mutter agreement. But Canada is the wilderness, the big hard wilderness to be despoiled and feared, and one could love it too.

I was thinking that as we turned in between wrought-iron gates, but then, about a place with the grandiose name of Camelot, my thinking was revised. To one side belted cattle chewing the cud beneath stately tree in park, to the other a hardwood plantation spaced and manicured, ribbons of lawn along the drive. It was not wild Canada, nor was it my decrepit Scotland, but it was not far off lush England.

We drove for a quarter of a mile or so, crossed a river bridge, the lawns widened, and there was Camelot.

"Golly, Sir Dougal, this could be it."

"I'm with you, Diana."

She parked the car, and we walked on tarmac toward the gray stone house, about the size of Drin. Below was a formal rose garden, flanked by Etruscan urns, centered upon a fountain beneath Venus errant. Beyond that first terrace was a swimming pool of azure blue, beyond that the park, beyond that a dip to wilderness, a rise to high hills in the south.

The front door opened, and I turned to see the portly Mr. Farrow, a man for whom I had taken a liking, and must curb it. "Your roses are magnificent, Mr. Farrow. And the view!"

"The mountains of Vermont," he said. "With acknowledgments to Uncle." He bowed slightly to the United States. "My wife is in the upper garden. Shall we go there first, or would you like a drink?"

Upper garden elected, we went across lawns, greener than our own had ever been, without a single broad-leaved weed, unlike our own, and with a sprinkler system. To the right was a lake. It curved toward us in narrow sickle shape, at this end a small boathouse. To our left the lawns were bounded by an immense herbaceous border. Ahead, in succession, we came to rock gardens, a lily pond, statuary, shrub borders, each entity leading, hinting to the next. Below the house the general effect had been contrived, too perfect. But this upper garden, or succession of gardens, had a casual air that was most appealing. "Very fine," I said. "I do congratulate you, Mr. Farrow."

"My wife is the real gardener in the family. I am tree man. Having spent my working life gulping Canadian forests, I now try in a small way to make amends." He chuckled, amiable plunderer.

The path swung back to the shore of the lake. "Such black pellucid water, Mr. Farrow. Is it deep?"

"Twenty feet, Miss Arden, more or less."

"It's all so beautiful. We just wander on to new surprises." Diana's newest surprise was the inlet brook, a wooden bridge across, fat trout therein. "I don't see how any other garden imaginable could possibly compete. Am I speaking out of turn, Sir Dougal?"

"It would be improper to prejudge the competition, Miss Arden," I said in mild rebuke. "We have, after all, seen only a representative selection."

"I misled you by including our garden on the list because I thought that you would like to see it. But we used to win with somewhat embarrassing regularity, so when I became president of the club, I persuaded my wife that we should be disbarred. As a matter of fact this has been a source of some disappointment to dear Mildred.

"Of course, the prime purpose of our annual competition is to foster pride in the gardeners we employ. Here at Camelot we are so well blessed with the incomparable Luigi and his family team that it would be hardly fair to compete."

"So then the incomparable Luigi never has the fun of winning." Diana made her girlish moue. She was doing it to this old boffer too.

Farrow patted her bare brown arm. "Ah, but my dear young lady, the gardening world pays homage to Luigi."

"The gardening world makes pilgrimages to Camelot — what a lovely idea, Mr. Farrow, like some Mecca. And yet someone else must get the prize — it does seem just a little mean."

We had crossed the bridge, slightly arched in Japanese style. "That path continues around the lake. See the cedars that come in hedge-form to the shore, we never limbed them, and they conceal the working plantation beyond. This other path leads upstream through the wild garden."

"Jonathan! Come here this instant."

"Coming, Mildred! Oh Lord," he muttered. "Something awry." Mr. Farrow hastened on.

The wild garden was quite charming on both banks of the stream — a variety of ferns, some pitcher plants, a showy lady's slipper, *Cypripedium reginae,* green moss in hollows.

"I told that fool, Luigi. I gave him perfectly explicit orders a week ago to spray the paper birch for sawfly."

"But, Mildred dear, you know Luigi's theory about Malathion and similar insecticides — that to use them is to have to use them in increasingly heavy application. Leave the birches alone, Luigi says, and they recover every year."

"I will have you know, Jonathan, that this is my garden, not the garden of that ignorant opinionated wop."

"Oh, tutt-tutt, Mildred."

"Tutt-tutt yerself." Mrs. Farrow was a tall woman with barrel hips, her pink anger manifest, a potent and unlovely female. "How do," she said at introductions, with a nod. That

114

was a change from the Canadian custom of shaking hands morning, noon, and night like Frenchmen.

"It is such a pleasure to see your garden in its multifarious variety, Mrs. Farrow."

"Glad you like it."

I have found it advisable, when dealing with a certain type of amateur horticulturist, to establish early an upmanship of knowledge. "Interesting," I said about the paper birches, which were not badly molested by the sawfly. "This specimen is *Betula papyrifera cordifolia,* the cordate variety. See the heart-shaped leaf, Mrs. Farrow, distinctly different."

"H'mm." One of those who never admits to ignorance.

We walked down to the bridge. "You said that path continues around the lake, Mr. Farrow. Could I go that way? I would so love to look back across the water at this beauty."

"By all means, Miss Arden. And you, Sir Dougal?"

"Mrs. Farrow, would you like to show me the garden again? There is so much to admire."

"Let's split up, then, for the homeward jaunt. After you, Miss Arden."

"My husband is an inveterate bottom-patter," Mrs. Farrow remarked over her shoulder. "But I expect she's used to it, an airline hostess when not in or at your service, so I gather?"

"Miss Arden is on leave from Global Airlines, and wanted temporary employment," I explained stiffly. "She is the most competent secretary of my experience."

"Sounds versatile," said the awful Mrs. Farrow. "Now look at this *Prunus cistena,* infested with aphids. I told that damned idiot to spray it, but would he? No! This organic gardening is a lot of twaddle. Do you agree?"

"Not entirely, Mrs. Farrow. If the garden is sufficiently isolated, wholly organic methods can be most successful." I pondered my words, aware that I must be in the gorgon's good books. "But in the case of this *Prunus cistena,* I am in entire agreement — Malathion or the like. I note that you do make extensive use of honest farm manure and compost."

"That improves the humus content. But it is Vigoro, inorganic, that provides the balanced oomph. Anyone who says otherwise is talking balls."

The more my antipathy for this female grew, the more fulsomely I praised her water lilies, rock gardens, shrubs, annuals, herbaceous borders. "Surely there can be no finer garden in eastern Canada, Mrs. Farrow."

"By miles the best, Trocher, and every stitch of it I made myself. My husband thinks the sun rises and sets on Luigi and his pizza crew. Well, he's a good enough performer, but self-satisfied and lazy nowadays, progressively more idle since Jonathan's ridiculous false modesty stopped me winning the garden competition."

"Couldn't you, perhaps, prevail upon your husband to let you enter this year again? For myself, I would hardly like to award the accolade to a lesser garden."

"I see your point," she said, with incongruous hint of bridle. "But they're a jealous lot of bitches. The moment I entered, they would all drop out."

I knew that Diana's circumnavigation of the lake was with at least one purpose — to work similarly on Jonathan Farrow. "I do sympathize that your masterpiece must be a treasure unseen. And Luigi in his lesser way — a head gardener does need praise to put his best foot foremost."

"I like you, Trocher," said Mildred Farrow. To be called Trocher plain by this insufferable Englishwoman was almost worse than the incessant Sir Dougals, keep your distance, that my secretary insisted on. But it was useful to be liked. We entered the mansion of Camelot.

⋈ 15 ⋈

DIANA AND I TOOK our drinks down to privacy at the swimming pool while the Farrows changed for dinner.

". . . You did a good job, Sir Dougal, I'm proud of you. And I think I also sowed the seed without the teeniest suggestion. He allowed as how his dear Mildred did feel deprived of the accord that was her due, and that made her less than tolerant of Luigi who, in fact, had designed and made it all, a gardening genius. But he, J. Farrow, did find himself in no man's land, as it were, exposed to a crossfire between these two wonderful people. So I said: *Ah, praise, Mr. Farrow, how we mortals feed upon it, fail often to accord it.* So he said: *By Jove, Miss Arden, I will speak to Mildred. Why not ask them all here? Yes, why not? And peace will reign upon my garden.* So I said that was the title of your classic, Sir Dougal, and it was then that he lightly quiffed my bottom once or twice.

"A single item more to report: Beyond the head of the lake is one of his tree plantations — things called cedars, and quite a decent logging road winds over and down the other side to a highway. Now listen, Sir Dougal, the lake is twenty mysterious Cousteau-feet deep, and from that boathouse near the outlet it's only a hundred yards and a covered approach to the house, do you see what I mean?"

"Yes I do, Diana. What an inspiration!"

"Is anyone in sight?"

"No, Diana."

"Come here then briefly to help me forget what I endured at the hand of amiable billygoat."

Returning to the house, I said: "I fear that Mildred will not yield much in the way of gems."

"I wouldn't be too sure, Sir Dougal. You couldn't know about such sordid things, but all randy old men expiate their concupiscence."

Mrs. Farrow swept in on her husband's arm, and both were beaming. She wore a mauve silk pantsuit, and she sparkled with precious stones, powdered, rouged and lipsticked, a miraculous transformation.

"More martinis, Jonathan," she commanded, and to me she said: "It came to me out of the pale blue yonder in the tub. The results of this inane competition are normally announced at the winner's house amid much unmerited kudos and backslapping. Now, if we entered, the result would be a foregone conclusion, those envious bitches would opt out, and Jonathan's pet baby would be a flop. So what I have decided, Trocher, is that you will announce the results at Camelot."

The woman paused to down martini. "It will be a bang-up party, what in the old Indian days we used to call a *bara tamasha*, great celebration. The most civilized couples will stay with us. The rest can find their own way to dinner and dance and buffet lunch at the swimming pool, and then the culmination: a tour of the Camelot gardens on Sunday afternoon, the twenty-third, conducted by you in person, Trocher." A pause for martini. "Anything to add, Jonathan?"

"You and I are in full agreement, Mildred. But we haven't yet asked Sir Dougal for his opinion in the matter."

"You approve, Trocher?"

"I approve, Mrs. Farrow, Madame Farrow, Signora Farrow, Ms. Farrow, but not Farrow."

I took that risk because I could not endure more Trochering from this egregious monster, king's-ransomed as she was. However, having tumbled more martini down the hatch, she shook with elephantine mirth. "Sir Dougal Trocher, you're a Scotty sex-pot, and I like you."

"Mrs. Farrow, might I wash my hands?"

"Go to the loo, y'mean. Upstairs, first door on right. Help yourself, gel."

"You spoke of old Indian days, Mrs. Farrow."

"Yes. Daddy was governor of Bengal. That's how I met my Jonathan. He arrived on some forestry do, fell for me hook, line and sinker, fell for my hips at first sight, he said."

"Come come, Mildred."

"Come come, yerself."

"Dinner is served, Madam," said the butler.

Darkness had fallen as we drove back from Camelot.

"Her jewel case was open on the dressing table. I just peeked, Sir Dougal. They were fabulous. Know what I think?"

"That seems less than certain, Diana, but I'll buy it."

"Well, the first thing is that dear Mildred has fallen for her Scotty sex-pot. And the second thing is a very painful thought for me, but if you were prepared to sell your manhood to her mighty hips, you could soon acquire her jewelry by honest purchase."

"Diana, that is a preposterous suggestion."

"It is no suggestion, Sir Dougal, let me tell you. It is merely the secretary of the ways and means committee doing her duty. But in my other capacity I speak a very different language. One move in that direction and I would have to chop you."

"Would that be a karate chop, Diana?"

"That would, Sir Dougal."

"May I ask a question?"

"You may, Sir Dougal."

"How could you, so slim, so willowy, so feminine a girl ever have learned this chopping business?"

"I told you once. I said: *I've been up and down and in and out and around and around the goddam mulberry bush.*"

"One more question: Can this chop be lethal?"

"Yes, Sir Dougal. This chop can be very very lethal. And perhaps the time has come to drop a very very tiny hint. I noticed at one of the gardens today that your gaze wandered and again wandered to the daughter of the house, a comely enough bikinied dish. My hint is that so long as I am your current mistress, I will not share your precious favors. What you did not do before, and what you may do afterwards, was and will be none of my business. Got the message?"

"Got the message loud and clear. Now slow down, dammit, you're doing ninety."

"Sorry, Sir Dougal, I was thinking ahead to bliss beyond this boring autoroute. But let's talk business. That will keep my speed down.

"Tomorrow is golf with your cousin Claud. I can't say he appealed when he came to lunch, so smooth and natty and conceited."

"I agree. But there is this car, so let's be nice to him."

"Then Monday is the Highland Banquet. And all the next fortnight you will be judging gardens, with me at your elbow, but not quite all the time perhaps. There are so many little details that must fall to me. For instance, the most bothersome thing is disposing of the loot."

"That bothers me constantly. Would you by any chance remember the house where your first boss bought the diamonds?"

"Of course I do, Sir Dougal. Address and telephone number are indelibly imprinted. They may have moved or be in prison or have been shot dead, but I think I should try that one, and alone, because they are sure to have seen your photograph. When, is the question?"

"Will they remember you, Diana?"

"Well, it's like that blasted memory of mine. I never seem to forget anything. And no one ever seems to forget me."

"Diana, you are as gloriously unforgettable in character as you are in person."

"You say the nicest things, Sir Dougal darling."

"No, Diana. Stick to driving and to business."

"Sorry again. Now about that little Jewish man, I would bet he's absolutely honest. That's one task for me. The second task starts with me, and goes on with us both. Tell me, Sir Dougal, aren't there such things as Scottish Nationalists?"

"Very much so, Diana, there are such things."

"Are you one, Sir Dougal?"

"I think we all resent being given second best by Whitehall when most of Britain's poor old best comes out of Scotland. In a nonmilitant, theoretical sense, I suppose I am."

"Could you bone up on the militancy? I mean more than banner wagging. I mean armed revolt, seizure of power, death to the Sassenach, is what I mean."

"Please explain, Diana."

"You remember I spoke about my anarchist friends? Well, they aren't really friends, I'm scared stiff of them, and if you ever see those people, you'll know why. But they call me their friend and honorary sister because once I did save one of them from certain death.

"They call themselves the Dagoes, a somewhat derogatory term in common use, perhaps clever because they are anything but common, a small fraternity of fanatics dedicated to Destroy All Governments of Every Sort, you can see the same burning obsession in all of them. Republicanism, Conservatism, Liberalism, Socialism, Maoism, Russian Communism, Fascism, any boring ism you care to name is their enemy to be destroyed, nothing remaining but the nothingness of Nihilism. Do you understand so far, Sir Dougal?"

"Not altogether, Diana. Please go on."

"The point is that at our only meeting, they swore to serve me if I should ever need assistance in a rightful cause. Now, Sir Dougal, if the Dagoes knew that you intended to rob these goons only in order to restore your great estates to feudal splendor, they would take a very dim view of it. But supposing they knew that you intended to rob them in order to raise the funds to light Scotland-for-Ever's searing flame, to butcher the oppressor . . ."

"Diana, you are talking wildly."

"No, Sir Dougal, I am talking in sober deadly earnest. Now, just listen: Those Farrows haven't the slightest reason to suspect us. In fact, they're both terribly pleased with themselves for thinking of having the prize-giving there, and when the great day comes, you will have a cast-iron alibi, expounding the beauties of Camelot. And I'm thinking of a way for me to get a cast-iron alibi through Global. But we need more than that. We need to have a false trail laid that takes all suspicion in the wrong direction — I mean across the border to those great United States. Now listen . . . !"

". . . As a plot it's a masterpiece, Diana. But can we trust these Dagoes?"

"The answer is that if they trust us, we can trust them to the death. And the us in this case means you, Sir Dougal, because I already enjoy their trust, and a very queer trust it is to enjoy. But they won't know you from Adam because they never read newspapers or see TV — despised lackey tools of government.

"Now, if you can convince them of your quality, which is evident, and if you can convince them of your fanatical intent to tear asunder the strangling bonds of English persecution, then we've got it made. They may not be so hard to convince because, like all fanatics, they believe what their fanaticsm makes them want to believe. Strike the right rough, tough, brutal note, and they'll believe you."

"Rough, tough and brutal, Diana, I don't think I'm much good at that."

"Don't annoy me. You're a consummate actor when you want to be. And there always for all to see is your shining, manifest integrity."

"My shining, manifest integrity is leading me in rather odd directions. Had you thought of that, Diana?"

"I had thought of that, Sir Dougal."

We were in the city now, slowly up Mountain Street to stop outside the garage. "You go ahead," she said.

For the sake of decorum, we came in separately at night. It was my sixth night in Canada, my fifth night with Diana.

I got myself a drink, and one for her when she arrived, and she sat on the arm of my chair, her cheek against mine.

"Diana, these risks you want to take — it's even a risk to go to that house in Outremont. Why are you taking them for someone you've only known six days?"

"Dear Sir Dougal, because I'm fond of you. I don't mean in love or any silliness; that passes me right by. But I think your whole original idea was so wonderfully mad, and now doesn't seem quite so hopelessly altogether crazy as it did. It's dangerous and it's fun and it even looks like being possible, and please don't say thanks to me, because it's both of us together, point and counterpoint."

Point and counterpoint, I had thought that about Tarquie and Lois, and they had made Tirene.

"That's your sigh again." She kissed me. "I've been feeling last time all day long, and now it's next time. That just could be a reason too. Come to bed, Sir Dougal darling."

✖ 16 ✖

Hi, Tirene, dear ole Gorgeous,

'I'm writing this in my slap-up suite at the Ritz, which is a swell joint in both meanings, and the varlets look after me just like it was feudal home. Well today I played golf with my third cousin Claud Merriwell, Captain of Industry. I allowed him to cream me on the last hole less out of my familiar will to lose than out of my jolly decent wish to please. Claud lusts to win at work and play, typical plutobourgeois, but I'm very grateful to him for the loan of a humdinger of a *char*, a BMW Bavaria hot job (just your cup of tea), hence defeat.

Talking of hot and job the weather is the former and I have the latter. I'm judging a garden competition getting a smashing wad of lolly for it and will be busier than a bird dog for the next two weeks so busy ackshly with "Meet the Celebrities" on TV, interviews, Highland Society Banquet (that's tomorrow), lectures on my own green thumb line, and this and that and so on around and around the goddam mulberry bush that I have had to engage a secretary who is as plainly competent as her years are uncertain.

But all is not nose to grindstone and I'm following your instructions to the letter: *Live and learn, live it up a bit.* In fact this male chauvinist reactionary dodo and stuffy old adjectival prig is getting himself into a buncha capers that would make your tangled locks stand right up from the comb.

Letter from your mum saying Garry and Bernardo naughty, roughed up a pregnant sow but no harm done except to the Lord Lieutenant's apoplexy. That's a rib tickler, eh? Also worried at no word from you. You're a meany Tirene, bad baby, ring them right

124

away reversing charges as per usual. Hope you're enjoying your job and have novels to read about the honest self-respecting fornication you enjoy, not that Californian sod's perversion. Heard from Ida too, says library floor sagged six inches — good old dry rot. Drin kin buckle for all I care.

Canadians are real decent folks, more matey than us stuffed shirts, less cunning hypocrites that's my sage opinion.

Hoping this finds you as it leaves me, happily in the whisky bottle.

SWAK

Dougal

I read this maniacal effusion through, addressed an airmail envelope to her at Duncatto with *Please Forward*, found a fifteen-cent stamp and hastened along the corridor to drop it down the mail chute before sanity returned.

It was seven o'clock, high time for the whisky bottle. I sat with my first drink and made a few notes for that after-dinner speech. But where was Diana? She had telephoned the number stored in her memory bank, and when a man's voice answered, she said in French: *Is that 101 rue de la Baleine?* The line went dead at once. *I don't like it, Diana. — I do*, she said. *If the telephone's unlisted, and the address is right, what else would he do but hang up? Not to worry.*

That was at four o'clock, and still no Diana at half past seven. I was bothered, the more so because she was drawn to risk as the moth is drawn to the magic lantern. To call the police was more than slightly out of the question. Should I telephone? Should I go to the rescue?

At ten to eight the key sounded in the outer door, and it was Diana. But she was not in the sunniest of moods. "Goddam bloody everything," she said, and threw a vast Sunday newspaper to spill all over the floor. "Gimme a drink," she commanded, somewhat in the manner of Mrs. Farrow ordering up martini. But she soon quietened to tell her tale:

"The first thing was that the taxi driver wouldn't wait, but I didn't pay him off until that same butler answered the door bell. He looked a bit nonplused, but I said: *Do you remember me?* And he nodded. So I paid the taxi bastard, and was allowed into the art collection, and some ages later the huge bodyguard beast arrived. The atmosphere was less than cordial, his right hand across inside his jacket, and he barked in Teutonic fashion and the rude familiar: *Was willst du?*

"Perhaps they thought I was a female cop planted on my late unlamented, or perhaps they thought that this was blackmail. Anyway, things looked kinda ugly. So I was quiet and demure, said I didn't want anything except to make an inquiry on the same subject as had occasioned my previous visit.

"He screamed: *Hilde, Komm mal her,* and a rat-faced hag appeared instantly from the wings and frisked me in a loathsomely efficient way. She remained to glower with a hate as manifest as your integrity, Sir Dougal. Sorry I was cross when I arrived, but it's been a hellish evening.

"In the end I was led to the secret room beyond the panel, and the Armenian was bowing me into a chair, and without any preliminaries I stated my possible business.

"But he said just as bluntly: *Nothing is bought here.* So I said: *Can you tell me, please, where things are bought?* He looked at me for a long, long time, boring through me with those sad, omniscient eyes, and then he said: *I cannot tell you that. But I can give you a telephone number, and when someone answers, say one word: Loris. L-O-R-I-S. Here is the number.*

"With that he stood, and made his bow, which I reciprocated, and asked whether I could call a taxi, and he said: *A car awaits you.*

"It was a new Imperial, they must favor Chrysler products, and there were two men in front, and I thought, Oh my God, I'm being wafted off to torture or taken for a ride, but I appeared cool as the proverbial, saying: *Au Reine Elizabeth, s'il vous plaît,* because it had already occurred to me that the QE is as good a place as any in the city to get lost in numerous directions on the surface or by catacomb. Well, we went straight there, which was a relief. But I was studying the man in the passenger's seat, a nondescript type in a bluish suit, the only faintly noticeable thing about him a cheap Panama hat with a maroon ribbon, and they're common enough.

"I said *mille remerciments* as we drew up at the hotel, got out, strolled in, whipped round to that shop next the door, and I saw the car drive off along Dorchester with no passenger.

"I therefore betook myself to the Ladies, and when I came out, I spotted him in his dinky hat, so stupid to wear anything distinctive. Sometimes I think, Sir Dougal, that you and I could teach the rest of the underworld a thing or two.

"Well, I bought the Sunday *New York Times*, and the burden of that didn't exactly help on my subterranean saunter to take the Metro west from University, and there he was, my faithful tail, next car along. So on and on and ever west by bus and taxi, stop for a cup of coffee, never seem to hurry. It was a nightmare, but in the end I lost him by biding my time at a light on Greene Avenue, and hopping aboard, saying: *Five bucks to run that yellow,* which he did as it turned to red, and I dropped the five on the seat beside him, and we were corkscrewing round Westmount, super taxi man, he loved it. I had finally shaken the bastard off, and I gave the driver another ten, and here I am, exhausted, with nothing more for all that than a telephone number, and one word: *Loris.*"
Diana slouched, dejected. "Gimme another."

I brought her the needful. "Diana, you're as brave as a lioness, and as clever as a barrel of monkeys. Now why not go and have a nice bath, and you'll feel better."

"Barrels of monkeys, God, what next? Go and have a nice bath, pet poodle."

I was at my heavy-handed worst, and the reason: Madness. What could have possessed me to write the letter to Tirene? Facetious, boastful, the acme of vulgarity. And yet in a sort of way, the germ of the idea had come from Diana.

But I confess that when she returned in a trousered negligee of flimsy stuff, in happy mood again, I forgot that lunacy, and took this marvel in my arms and carried her forthwith to bed.

"I wanted to wait until tonight, but you soon changed my

mind for me, or danger changed my mind for me, or both, I really was quite scared this afternoon. *Oh, that's good. That's everything and good and good.*"

We had our late supper and a glass of wine. Diana often asked, not inquisitively but with casual interest, about home and Grandfather, particularly Grandfather. *I think you're rather like him,* she said once. *How, Diana? — Oh well, in your ways and so on.* But she never asked me about my peculiarly celibate life, nor any other intimate thing. As to her own past, she had mentioned it vaguely on the plane, but shied from the subject now. *I'm very happy at the moment. What else is there?*

The love, the idle talk, back always to the planning. Those weeks were, and have remained, a life within my life. It was life simplified to one single golden purpose: Save Drin at the expense of those to whom the cost would be so many marbles. All scruples vanished excepting one, that the Captain was letting his Chief Officer bear the risks. But Diana made short shrift of that and me. *Stop talking noble balls, Sir Dougal, idiot. Can't you see it's meat and drink to me?*

Some of her stratagems and schemes were as improbable as those conjured up by Winston Churchill in time of war, the many wild ideas and, like his, the few gems of the imagination to be coldly considered, rationalized, refined, Dougal Trocher, devil's advocate.

There is a thing called inspiration, a flash, it cannot be denied. But without uncessant careful thought it vanishes, just that, a flash. That is why so many self-styled poets never do write poetry.

But I digress. We were amiably entwined, and I was sleepy. "It's all right, then, if I take the whole day off? You can manage to find your own way to those first two gardens?"

"Yes, Diana. We settled all that before."

"I know, but it sort of bothers me. In the morning I'll see Jenny, that's no problem, except more bleeding heart about her beastly Turk in Buffalo. In the afternoon I'll make the Dagoes contact and fix up for Tuesday. Also, they must often have to swim bubbleless to the rendezvous, so they can probably help over the lake part too. It's the middle of the day that bugs me, lunch with Global, oh damnation!"

I sensed dismay, a tremor of it, but I did not ask why lunch with her airline should be *oh damnation*.

"You're such a comforting old rock of ages," Diana said, her breath soft on my shoulder. "Would you like me to roll away for slumber? Or shall we sleep together just like this? What is your fancy, Sir Dougal dear?"

"My fancy is let's sleep like this." And so we slept. It was the clamor of the telephone next door, or it was the abrupt loss of her that woke me up at ten past seven.

"Sir Dougal Trocher's office. Oh yes, Mr. Gilpin, Sir Dougal spoke of you. No, it's not a bit too early. Sir Dougal's schedule is so busy, I've been at my desk for half an hour. Yes, he may be. But he would insist, Mr. Gilpin, absolutely as it's you. If you wouldn't mind waiting just a second, I'll go and knock him up."

Diana hammered on the open bedroom door. "Sir Dougal! Please please wake up! It's Mr. Gilpin on the line."

I growled displeasure as our paths crossed back to bed and on to telephone. "Hullo."

"Ah, Sir Dougal, this is Harry Gilpin, and what a pleasure to talk with you. But first let me apologize for calling at such an outlandish hour. The fact is that as the evening of my years climbs on, so do I find myself rising ever earlier with the morning lark, and I forget that better men still rest in the arms of gentle Morpheus. So my apologies and how d'you do."

If Farrow and Merriwell were smooth by telephone, this one was polished marble. "How d'you do, Mr. Gilpin. But please don't apologize. I was just waking when my secretary knocked."

"How courteously you indulge my importunity. As I think you know, Lois Duncatto telephoned some two weeks back to tell me of your working holiday in Canada, and to suggest that I might look out for you, should you happen down our way. And I am calling now simply to say that Gloria and I do so

129

much hope that, work over, you will come here for a few days of rest and relaxation before returning home."

"That's extremely kind of you, Mr. Gilpin."

"Not in the least, Sir Dougal. Lois spoke of you in such glowing terms, and even Tarquie came on the line with a tersely gruff encomium: *Dougal's a good type. Hope you'll do what you can for him.*

"What a couple they are. Indeed, what a family! I never met their boy, Ian, but I saw Tirene again last year, a fascinating girl, and so amusing. How is dear Tirene?"

"Fine, I think." I spoke abruptly.

There was a pause. Lois had said that about all things except his little Gloria, Harry Z. Gilpin was uncannily astute. "It would be delightful to see you at our island hide-out off the coast of Maine. We live simply, but in reasonable comfort — Gloria, our small son Harry, and myself. Pray do honor us, but when?"

"It's most kind of you. May I just look at my engagements?"

May I just consult my secretary who has put on my pajamas? Diana materialized with the calendar. D-Day was Sunday the 23rd. Return Day was Monday the 24th. Sales Day was Tuesday the 25th. Her pencil rested on Wednesday the 26th. "If you're sure it's convenient, Mr. Gilpin, I suggest Wednesday the twenty-sixth as a possibility, but it's a little difficult to be certain yet."

It was only faintly possible to be possible, far less certain.

"The twenty-sixth, how splendid! And if there should be any change, please telephone me here. All dates are alike to us this summer as we rusticate. We can confirm precise times later so that I can send a plane to Montreal. And if there are still remnants from your heavy work load, do please bring your secretary."

Thanks from me, and more urbanity from him, and au revoir.

"Diana, why in God's name did you answer that telephone, and then *knock me up,* of all expressions?"

"I'm terribly sorry. I just didn't stop to think."

"When you stop to think, you're more than a match for anyone I've ever met. In future, do please always stop."

"I'll try, Sir Dougal. But did it matter so really much?"

It might matter if Harry Z. Gilpin dropped a bland word across the Atlantic, how lucky to catch so busy a man with an early morning call, his office open, and so on. Probably it did not matter. What might matter very much was that Mr. Gilpin seemed remarkably keen to have me.

"I can see you haven't forgiven me yet. And I know it was thoughtless of me, I deserve a spank. Go on, castigate."

I laughed and gave her a token belt on the bottom and that started us again. ". . . Am I forgiven now?"

"Yes, Diana, you're forgiven. You could get away with murder."

"Don't say that," she said sharply. "I might have to."

The thought was sobering. It was ominous, bringing home to me as nothing had before — that this was no game of tiddlywinks. I felt that tingle in my neck and spine. We got up to face the day.

✱ 17 ✱

WE DROVE INTO THE swell of the Laurentians. They were small compared with our Scottish hills, and everywhere wooded except for the slash and interweaving curve of ski slopes, improbable patterns in high summer.

I took the Sainte Emilie exit from the pleasing autoroute and soon came to a single street of shattering tawdriness, gasoline stations festooned with bunting, luminescent signs of shocking pink, belching motorbikes and music, the Sweet Slumberette Motel, Coke, Pepsi, Seven-Up and Sprite, fat women in white satin top-to-toe all bulging, fat men in hats and swimming trunks with belly roll. It was unhappy. They were unhappy, and I said so, but Diana did not speak. The new shopping center was less awful. I parked the car near Chartrand Pharmacie, and waited.

"You won't expect them to be like other people, will you?"

It was the second time that she had said it. "Not to worry, Diana," the laconic phrase she used herself.

"It's just that every single thing depends on this." She sighed, not the cheerful, insouciant Diana. "Here he comes."

The man was dark. He could have been a Mexican, South American, Moroccan, Spaniard. "Come with me." The voice quiet, the face and body curiously still. He walked away.

"See what I mean?" she said. We followed him to a Jeep Wagoneer. The evening was unpleasantly humid and oppressive, overcast. Thunder rumbled in two quarters.

"You in front," he said to me.

We crossed bedlam street, passed two villas fronted with imitation brick, beside each an outsized car, one royal purple and one shamrock green, on the rear windowshelves tasteful posies of artificial flowers, a woolly bow-wow and a cute teddy bear dangling from each inside mirror. Could these be the people whose fathers carved so exquisitely in pine?

Good riddance to honky-tonk Sainte Emilie, we were on country roads. For the next fifteen or twenty minutes we ran a forest maze by hill and valley, turning so often, no glimmer of sun to point the west, that I had no idea whether he was driving deliberately to confuse direction, or was taking the shortest way from Sainte Emilie to somewhere.

But now we left the road for a narrow trail, climbing over a shoulder and down to a stream. He pulled the lever back for four-wheel drive, and we surged through water, climbed again.

"It's a grand serviceable machine ye have," I said in Scotch, which was to be my language of this evening, as it had been of last evening at the Highland Banquet, if briefly and in song, and my hangover lingered, but residually.

No comment from the driver. Our way was barred by a stout metal gate, mature maple groves on either side of it, effective roadblock to anything except a heavy tank. The gate swung up and open by unseen agency, clicked loudly shut behind us. The trail wound on until we breasted a rise, and there was a farmhouse with contiguous shed and barn, all of weathered cedar, gray. The clearing was flanked on three sides by low cliffs, a setting of some quiet charm, gnarled apple trees, a well. A man and a woman stood at the door, no other people or cars in sight. An American robin, orange-breasted endearing bird, tugged at a worm and flew away. A squirrel chattered somewhere, rustic scene.

"Out," our driver said, terse and explicit. I removed the thin plastic raincoat which I had worn to conceal the kilt (of sober Hunting Trocher), and which had contributed to my discomfort since we left the air-conditioned BMW, but he was so intimidating that I had not quite liked to take it off. One

133

thunderstorm was nearer now. Another grumbled in the distance.

The woman was blond, a cheek-boned Slav. She searched Diana and motioned her in. The man was very black, but sharp-featured. He took some time with me, and, not much liking it, I growled. He pushed me impolitely through the door.

They sat in a curved row on kitchen chairs at the end of the room, which was otherwise bare of furniture. Diana was given a chair at the side, no seat for me.

Hands on hips, I considered them, a polyglot collection, my own age in average, eight men and three women, Nordic, Iberian, Japanese, Semitic, Negroid, Slavic and indeterminate. I stared at them in turn, and they all stared at me, the same curiously still gaze. *You won't expect them to be like other people, will you?*

But they were like other people, like individuals one saw occasionally, consumed with thought. These were eleven consumed with thought, and I understood why Diana feared them.

"Fer a thousand years and mair . . ."

I spoke in the plain language of Lowland Crummock, not quite broad speech, for that would be unintelligible to any foreigner, including the bloodstained Englishman. I told my tale of Scotland's bondage, and since I must convince these most peculiar people, I must convince my peculiar self.

To that end, I had rehearsed the speech, or rant, in the bathroom in the Ritz-Carlton Hotel in Montreal in Quebec until I made myself believe it, almost. Then I moved to the sitting room and delivered my tirade to my Chief Officer. *What a terrible story*, she said. *Is it really true, Sir Dougal?*

I did not reply until I had simmered down. *Old truth blended with new balderdash*, I said. *You took me in completely*, said Diana Arden, not the simplest soul alive.

Rough, tough, brutal and black-bristled, I let them have it to the peroration:

"Fer Scotland! Ay, it's fer Bonnie Scotland I'm tae plunder

134

the blood-suckin' rich! Heed tae the worrds o' the immortal bard:

> "Scots wha hae wi' Wallace bled,
> Scots, wham Bruce has aften led,
> Welcome to your gory bed
>   Or to Victorie!
>
> Lay the proud usurpers low!
> Tyrants fall in every foe!
> Liberty's in every blow!
>   Let us do, or die!"

One can work oneself to fearful passion, and I had. I glowered at them, arms akimbo. "Queries?"

There was only one question, from the Japanese. "When you have extirpated the alien ruling swine," he said in excellent English, "what form of government will you establish?"

Diana had warned me to expect that trap. "Nae government at a'!" I bellowed. "The currse o' mankind is government."

Every head moved in acquiescence. "You show sincerity," said the biggest man among them. "But to believe does not suffice." His accent was strongly German. "Now we test your quality. First is marksmanship. You may choose the weapon, pistol or small rifle, choose."

I could not hit a barn door with a pistol, but a rifle was another matter. "A point two-two wud do me fine."

"Raus!" said the German.

I did not much like him. "Raus, *bitte!*" I said, and Diana's head swung to me, anxious.

All trooped outside, and all were silent except the German, master of this ceremony. He held the rifle, a semi-automatic. "Ten — ten — fifteen," he said. "Ten shells are in the magazine. Ten targets will appear. You have fifteen seconds. Is it understood?"

"Ay, understood. But I'll need a sighter."

"No sighting shot. The rifle is zeroed. You may view the

targets." He pressed a button on the farmhouse wall, and ten human heads appeared round the foot of the cliff. They were life-size and life-like, as varied in physiognomy as my hosts. He pressed another button, and the gruesome faces disappeared. A shortish man stood near me, Tommy gun slung from shoulder, the muzzle delicately pointed somewhere off my stomach. The German cocked one into the chamber, and handed the rifle to me. "Say when you are ready."

I came up to the aim to get the feel of it, a bead and a V, the best sights for this. "Ready," I said.

Ten differently aimed shots in fifteen seconds is fast shooting, even with a semi-automatic; but the human head at thirty yards is a large target. I toppled all ten of them, cleared the rifle, and handed it back. "Yon's easy," I said.

"The next test you may find less easy." He changed magazines. "The target will cross from right to left, and you will not have a preliminary view."

In the killing days of boyhood, rabbits were still a pest at Drin, and I learned to shoot them running with a point two-two, no great skill, but a skill few people learn.

This target was a running figure, a manikin in quarter scale, presumably on rails. "Easy," I said again, when the pattern of bullet holes had been inspected.

"Now we test you for steadiness of nerve." It was the Slav woman. "Against the wall, and keep still, I advise you."

I did as I was advised, resting my head against a cedar shingle. Few women can throw, but in this woman's hand was a throwing knife. I raised my eyes so that I would not see the thing come spinning. I raised them to a multiple fork of lightning above the cliff, and I counted up to eight before the thunder rippled, crashed and boomed, and louder than thunder a first knife *thwicked* into the wall beside my right ear.

An American goldfinch, jet black and vivid yellow, arrived to perch on top of an apple tree. *Goldfinch, you are beautiful,* I tried to make myself think as other knives came in succession, left ear, overhead, astride the jugular, a quivering

136

handle touched my skin. "That is all," she said. "You may step out."

I turned to consider the outline of my head in throwing knives. I shuddered, but a quick cough might have covered that.

"Now we test you as a fighting man," said the Japanese. "You may choose wrestling, boxing or jujitsu. Choose."

"Boxing," I said.

It was the German who removed his shirt, a man of about my own build, but with a bulge of diaphragm. I took off my khaki shirt and gave it to Diana. "You're doing fine," she murmured. "Bash 'im."

I hope you don't have to bash 'em at the press conference, said the captain, but that was a long time ago. It seemed almost as long a time as the thirteen years since I had last been in a ring. I broke his jaw and concussed him into hospital, and never boxed again until this evening on a rough lawn in French Canada, barefisted.

I held out my hands to shake, but he came in punching, and I sidestepped. That first rush was enough to give me his measure — a fair boxer with a knock-out in his right. If he connected, I would be in trouble. But I would not let him connect. With my much greater speed, I would work to his body, and wear him down and finish him off with an uppercut to the flat of the jaw, least damaging to knuckles. But a hangover, much travel to the realms of Venus, I must be quick about it.

We circled as the rain began, a few large cool drops, and then at once a downpour. The onlookers took to the verandah, human enough for that. It was storm twilight, with vivid lightning close, with calico-tearing, CRASH.

He rushed me again, child's play to avoid this lumbering slugger, but my rubber sole slipped on wet grass, and the punch exploded above my left ear. I would have been down, but was close enough to clinch, and I hung on. "Break!" they shouted.

My head was clearing, and I broke, and now I went after him, flat-footed for stability, feinting a lead to the chin. His hands went up, and my left went under to the solar plexus — one, two — his stomach muscles took the first punch, but not the right jab that followed it. Down out. He croaked for breath, writhing on the grass.

"You hit him low." Remarkable protest, *that's not cricket.*

"I didn't. I hit him here." I put my hand on my diaphragm. My blood was up, and my head was aching, and I had forgotten to talk Scotch, but they did not seem to notice.

"The blow was not low." This man spoke for the first time. His *blow* and his *low* sounded very English. "Come inside." The lightning and thunder were simultaneous.

I was handed a towel, and dried my upper half, and Diana gave me back the shirt. "All okay." I just heard it.

"Now what is it that you want of us?" It was the Englishman.

"Do ye hae a blackboard?"

There was no blackboard, but a large sheet of paper was pinned up. With a marker pen I drew a map of Camelot — the house, with an arrow pointing south to indicate the direction of the American border, the lawns above, the lake curving round, the garden or gardens winding up between hill and water. I made a dotted line down the lake to the boathouse.

Nobody spoke until I had explained our fledgling plan. Then the Englishman, who might be the leader, if anarchists had such, said: "The diving equipment presents no problem. We have it. But I see two main difficulties. The first is in precise timing."

"It'll be nearer the day afore we can be sure of times."

"The other difficulty is to lay a false trail across the border. Fifteen miles, half an hour, but that is too long. Every customs post would have been alerted. There is a better way, if it is possible."

Diana and I had thought of that better way, but let him

think of it. "Brother Joseph, are there helicopters, four to six place, in the eastern townships?"

"Two Miller six-four G single turbocopters operate out of a pad near Magog. *Forest Surveys Inc.* Away all week, back Friday late." Brother Joseph rattled that off.

"Can you fly that type?"

"Flew 'em in Cambodia."

"Would it be easy to get one?"

"Piece of cake on a Sunday. Nobody lives at the hangar. Lock it up and leave it, not much theft problem, because not many chopper pilots." He was the one who had held the Tommy gun, Canadian or American, spare of body as in words. He looked neither more nor less dangerous than his fellow Dagoes.

"Understand," said the Englishman to me, "that if we decide to do this thing, it will not be primarily in the cause of Scotland's freedom. All government is tyranny and so we approve your cause. But far greater challenges engage us than the liberation of a few million people from what is now tepid, bureaucratic slavery. The reason that we would help is that we Dagoes owe a profound indebtedness to Sister Diana. We have tested you this evening solely in her interest, to ascertain your caliber in marksmanship, in coolness under fire, in fighting quality.

"Brothers and sisters, do we find this man worthy to be the colleague of our honorary sister?"

"We do, Brother Henry."

"Do we decide, then, to render assistance?"

"We do, Brother Henry."

"You may go," he said, nodding to me. Then all the Dagoes stood and clenched both fists at shoulder level to their honorary sister. "Brother Pedro will drive you back."

The German stood by the door, his face pale and his breathing heavy. "Are ye a' richt?" I inquired chivalrously.

He stared, no glimmer of a smile. Not one of them ever smiled.

The rain was stopping, and thunder had moved on. Once more the steel gate rose at some invisible behest to let us through, and we drove back to Sainte Emilie, no word from Brother Pedro, no word between us until we had left the dreadful street behind — it looked less dreadful, though, somehow a relief to see prosaic dreadfulness.

"That was a horrid punch, but jeepers creepers you socked him back good. Does your head hurt still?"

"It aches and sings a bit. Diana, did you know that I would have knives thrown at me in your interest?"

"No, Sir Dougal, I did not. He said that they would have to test your nerve and so on in my interest, but I think in this case my interest is also slightly yours, or isn't it?"

"Yes, Diana, sorry."

"Don't mention it, Sir Dougal. And hearty congrats for not even blinking."

"I didn't see them. My eyes were raised to the fulgural heavens, and to a goldfinch. May I satisfy my curiosity?"

"Well, it depends. Well, what about?"

"What did you do to incur their profound indebtedness?"

"I smuggled one called Brother Dimitri — he wasn't there this evening, on sentry duty, I expect — I smuggled him out of Hong Kong and into Sydney, New South Wales, by Global."

"How did you manage that, Diana?"

"I preboarded him by wheelchair, and one of the toilets was marked out of order, very simple really. Then, later I let him out, and half an hour before Sydney he suffered a fearful coronary, rushed from the very planeside to the hospital, which the ambulance somehow never reached."

"Why did you smuggle him, Diana?"

"Because he was on the run from Red China, and that old reactionary, Mao Tse-tung's thugs were on his very heels, and I'm a sucker for the underdog. That is all slightly true. Any further questions?"

"Only one: Are you an anarchist, Diana?"

"I'm as much of an anarchist as you're a Scottish Nationalist.

Stupid governments annoy me, and at the moment you annoy me."

Since yesterday Diana's moods had been capricious — edgy, bad-tempered, penitent by turn. Something troubled her. Was it the daring, ingenious alibi with Global Airlines? *Fixed,* was all she said about that. Was it apprehension about our meeting with the Dagoes?

"Dougal," she said, as we were negotiating the stark spaceage interchange after the autoroute. "I'm sorry I've been bitchy, and I promise not to be again." Nor was she bitchy again, and not until much later did she call me Dougal, plain, again. It was absurd, and touching somehow.

⌘ **18** ⌘

DIANA AND I ARRIVED on that Saturday afternoon to find Camelot in a welter of preparation for Mrs. Farrow's *bara tamasha* or great occasion, and bossing the welter was Mrs. Farrow. As is so often the case in the homes of successful men, Jonathan Farrow was understrapper to his Mildred.

"Mrs. Farrow, I would like to stroll through the garden once more, if I may, and give Miss Arden some notes for tomorrow."

"Help yourself. Don't be too long-winded about it. Swimming party starts at five. Jonathan, how many more times am I to tell you not to trail damned cow dung into my house?"

"It is my damned cow's dung, dear," he pleaded. There was a strange devotion.

This was our fourth visit to Camelot, much encouraged by the Farrows. I did not give Diana notes, but said: "Let's just run through tomorrow afternoon again."

"Okay, Sir Dougal. Three forty-five I park Jenny's VW and come to the edge of the lake, hiding behind the cedars. Four o'clock I slip into the water. Four on the dot you start the pilgrimage from the house. Four-thirty you are leading them over the inlet bridge en route to the beauties of the wild garden. Four-thirty plus or minus a couple of minutes I emerge in the boathouse, whip off aqualung, open waistbag, whip on overalls, gloves, sneakers, beat it under cover to the house.

"By then all Mildred's minions are in position at the lily

garden. That's her own operation order, thank God the woman is so highly organized. At four-fifty I am once more submerged, and at that same hour you are crossing the bridge again, followed by your adoring flock. And if I may make a suggestion, Sir Dougal, it is that tomorrow, at the climax of your dedicated labors, you can unbend a little, show them the quick Sir Dougal who makes me giggle. Okay?"

"I'll try, Diana."

"Then, at five, proles are plying plutocrats with refreshments, and at five-five P.M. you make your brief prize-giving speech. At five-ten precisely the helicopter arrives. It is out of sight from the lily pond, but you all hear its loud inimitable blatter, and perhaps you refer to it casually, even ask Mildred if she expects the press — that will excite her madly.

"Prizes awarded by the horticultural aristocrat, winners and losers gravitate to see the visitor from the skies, its whirly-birly spinning. But they are brought somewhat abruptly to a halt, because, facing them, are two masked men with Tommy guns."

"Unloaded, of course, Diana."

"Unloaded, my foot, Sir Dougal."

"But Diana!"

"Don't look so shocked, and do please grow up. The Dagoes are on the most wanted list of every police force in the world. They never stir abroad without being literally armed to the teeth in self-defense. And Brother Henry even made a big concession. He promised me that if there was trouble, they would fire one warning burst, if at all possible, that is."

I stood on the rustic bridge, staring down at plump Jonathan Farrow's plump rainbow trout. Faced now with the deadly realities of crime, of my own crime, I groaned.

"Cheer up, Sir Dougal. The Dagoes aren't trigger-happy. The Dagoes are ice-cool. And besides, these goons value their precious skins too highly to try conclusions with two Tommy guns. And don't you see that it all adds oomph?"

"A plethora thereof, Diana."

"At about that time, little innocent the Naiad — anagram

143

for me — is clambering from the deeps to vanish into Mr. Farrow's giant cedar hedge of which he is so rightly proud. And at about that time two other men come running from the house, and all aboard, and up she soars before the eyes of the dumbfounded audience, and off she beetles in a beeline for the fair mountains of Vermont in those great United States.

"Now let's go back and have a swim. That's one thing you don't shine at. In a swimming pool you remind me of Sir Dougal's faithful friend, Bernardo."

Diana was in high spirits, danger beckoning. "Old gloomy," she said. "It's going to be okay. You'll see."

"But so many things have to be right, Diana. Take the weather."

"There's a high pressure system the whole way to the Rockies. Certain fine for forty-eight hours. And London is good too. What's in between doesn't matter with jets."

"But flight delays, you have almost no margin for that."

"Quite true, but everything's going to be all right, I can feel it in my bones. There is just one gloomy aspect, a fearful deprivation."

"Your lack of sleep, Diana, I suppose."

"No problem, I can snooze anywhere. The deprivation is that we can't make love for two whole days."

"I was thinking about that. And I was wondering how I could have endured the bleak, inhospitable years without a happy woman in my bed. Already in, let me see, in nineteen days, it has become a jolly habit, makes a chap feel fighting fit."

"This chap too, Sir Dougal, very many thanks. Now shall we join the hoi polloi?"

Mrs. Farrow's program was on the dressing table:

SEVEN TWENTY-FIVE O'CLOCK: COCKTAILS IN THE DRAWING ROOM.
SEVEN FORTY-FIVE O'CLOCK: DINNER.
NINE FORTY-FIVE O'CLOCK: DANCING.

Diana's room and mine were widely separated. I had

grumbled mildly to Jonathan Farrow that I had notes for my prize-giving speech to dictate and so on. But the reason for my complaint was to strengthen the validity of Diana's alibi. He looked upset. *I said that to my wife, but the most she would allow was the use of my study. The fact is, Sir Dougal, that dear Mildred is, ahem, a bit of a bluestocking in such matters, quite unjustifiably, I know full well.*

Having heard about the Highland Banquet, Mrs. Farrow had implored me to wear the kilt, and I yielded, anything to indulge the woman safely. Thus, at seven twenty-five, I was a male Scotch peacock among the dinner jackets and the smokings. Three weeks ago I would have been shifty, ill at ease. But kindly Canada had banished many inhibitions. Indeed, I had to watch myself to preserve the formality that Diana and self-knowledge both demanded. What a hypocrite.

Daiquiri in hand, I made the rounds of ladies present, some stately *grandes dames* with blue hair, some comely in early middle age, some in their appealing thirties. They were charming, and their jewels more than came up to expectation. I have to say that on the whole I found North American women more lively, less conventional than their men.

Diana was much the youngest, looking quite ravishing in a short evening dress, the honey blonde, the beautiful. If only Tirene, who was much more beautiful . . . Oh damn Tirene.

Martinis down the hatch, Mrs. Farrow said: "Trocher, you look good enough to eat," that well-worn phrase, and took my arm.

Seven round tables, six people at each, the shrimp ramequins (and such a sauce!) were being removed when the butler appeared.

"What is it, Murton?"

"Madam, the personnel manager of Global Airlines is on the phone for Miss Diana Arden."

"Tell 'im she's at my dinner party. Tell 'im to take a running jump."

"Madam, the gentleman says that the matter is most urgently important, involving emergency duty."

Mrs. Farrow swung to me, and her emerald earrings pendulumed. "She's your floozy. What about it?"

"Miss Arden mentioned some stipulatory clause when I engaged her. Perhaps she should speak to him if it's so urgently important."

"All right, Murton," and the message was imparted.

"That ogre!" said Diana, loud and clear, and to her host sitting opposite: "Please excuse me, Mr. Farrow." She went out, frowning.

Petit poussin, infant carrots, peas, new potatoes. "Grew 'em all maself, including the chickens."

"And this delicious jelly, Mrs. Farrow?"

"High-bush cranberry, *Viburnum trilobum* to you, Trocher," adding gamesmanship to her other charms.

But here came Diana. "Sir Dougal, it's the most awful thing. Oh, Sir Dougal, I don't know how to tell you!"

"Calm, Miss Arden, please."

"You remember what I said about what us girls call the blue moon rule because it's so rarely invoked, which is that in return for one extra week's annual furlough we declare ourselves available at all times for duty in emergency. Oh, Sir Dougal, why was I such a darned little idiot as to tell the hotel where you would be?"

"Control yourself, Miss Arden. What is it that you want?"

"This other girl, damn her, no, I mean poor thing, she's been rushed to the hospital with an appendix, and I said to that stinker: *I simply can't, I absolutely won't.* Of course, what I should have said was I'm in bed with a high temperature, but I'm no good at telling lies. Oh, Sir Dougal, I am so sorry." Diana's cheeks were wet with tears.

"Stop yer blubbin'," snarled Mrs. Farrow. "Out with it!"

"That stinker said in his ice-cold tones: *Either, or, Miss Arden.* Either I report for duty on Global Flight Eight-six-two departing Montreal at twenty-three twenty hours tonight or else I'm fired with a month's pay docked into the bloody bargain. And another one of their stupid rules is that I have to stopover twenty-four hours in London, so I can't be back until

Monday afternoon. Oh, Sir Dougal, I'm most terribly sorry to let you down." She laughed and sobbed.

"Miss Arden," I said in tones as ice-cold as those of the hated personnel manager. "Stop these histrionics at once. It is a grave inconvenience, but you did warn me of the possibility. Now, calm down, pack your bags and, let me see, yes, you had better take the car and leave it for me at the hotel. You have three hours, ample time if you start immediately. Where are the notes I began to dictate this afternoon?"

"In Mr. Farrow's study, Sir Dougal."

"I shall do what I can. Make haste, then."

"Hysterical frippet," said Mrs. Farrow, with a contemptuous toss of earrings. "No quality in this hippy generation."

Madame Labouisse on my other side said: "The poor child is most upset, but naturally. You are unfair to her, Madame."

"Ah, poppycock, Madam yourself."

It was easy to understand why Mrs. Farrow was not one of the most popular women in that small ultimate circle of society, French and English.

But what a dinner! It is often said that North Americans subsist on three inch steaks. Not that lot, take my word for it.

It was a long evening of duty dances and much champagne, and I was in bed by half past twelve. Diana would be one hour on her way to London, due there at 10:15 A.M., change out of uniform, take Intercontinental Airways Flight 363 back 11:30 A.M., arrive in Montreal at 1:35 P.M., picking up her friend Jenny's Volkswagen at the airport. It was a tight program, a cold gamble against delays in flight.

But supposing they stamp your passport, Diana. Where is your alibi, then? — That is taken care of. With Global, I am Diana Arden, Chief Stewardess. Economy on Intercontinental I am Donna Andrews, Australian Schoolmarm, horn-rimmed with a bun. — Does that mean you have a false passport, Diana? — For a brilliant man, Sir Dougal, you do ask the dottiest questions sometimes.

There was much that I did not know about Diana Arden.

For instance, I did not know that I would see her at the hotel on Monday after a fourth Atlantic crossing. I did not know that I would see her again at all. It was an uncomfortable thought, and I dismissed it.

⧓ 19 ⧓

I WOULD GO TO Jonathan Farrow, and I would say to him: *Mr. Farrow, suspicious characters are lurking in the woods. With my own eyes I have seen them, and I am convinced that devilry is afoot. The underworld has learned of this distinguished gathering, of the garden tour, of a deserted house with many treasures.*

It was ten minutes to four on Sunday afternoon, a fine time to have second thoughts, to be skewered by a sword of guilt. "Do you realize," I muttered in my luxurious bedroom at Camelot. "Do you realize that never in your life have you stolen anything, not one penny? And now it is your diabolical intent to steal from honorable people who have employed you, housed you, fed you, trusted you?"

How could I have even contemplated such an abominable crime? How could I have planned it cheerfully, coldly, cunningly, zestfully? But I had.

Mildred Farrow's orders were on the dressing table.

FOUR O'CLOCK: TOUR OF THE GARDENS OF CAMELOT, CONDUCTED BY
 SIR DOUGAL TROCHER OF DRIN. DRESS: SENSIBLE GARDENING
 CLOTHES.

FIVE O'CLOCK: TEA AND REFRESHMENTS AT LILY POND.

FIVE MINUTES PAST FIVE O'CLOCK: COUNTRY GARDEN COMPETITION.
 ANNOUNCEMENT OF RESULTS AND PRIZE-GIVING BY SIR DOUGAL
 TROCHER OF DRIN.

SEVEN O'CLOCK: BARBECUE AT SWIMMING POOL. DRESS: UNDRESS.

NINE O'CLOCK: DISPERSE.

I looked at hills to the south, but turned away from them, and in the eye of my mind I saw the gaunt hills of home, the waterfall, the Den, the beech trees and the House of Drin, vignettes of places dear to me, the cause of this wickedness, and wicked I would damned well be.

Tirene said in May: *Old fuddy-duddies like you and Daddy are just root-strangled by the ages. To be rootless — that's the only truth and freedom.*

But I fought for the roots of seven hundred years.

"You go to hell, Tirene, Darling love," I said aloud, and went downstairs. "Are we all here, Mrs. Farrow?"

"All present, Maestro, every man Jack and his little Jill."

"Shall we begin, then? What a delightful afternoon it is, the cool breeze blowing. And may I say how privileged I feel to accompany so many gifted gardeners on this tour of Camelot?

"Now let us stroll first along the great flower border, predominantly perennial, but artfully augmented by such old annual friends as *Nicotiana alata*, whose fragrance fills a summer's eve . . ."

4:10 P.M. All being well, she would be nearly halfway down the lake, emitting no bubbles from the frogman breathing unit.

"Mrs. Morris asks how best one may attract birds to the garden. In my brief stay in Canada, I have been fascinated by the wealth of birdlife. Now, to attempt an answer: First, we need plentiful water to slake the thirst and bathe the feathers. Second, we need widely varied cover to give shelter, to encourage the happy families that tend to follow nidification, avian or otherwise. Third, we need an abundance of foods, to name only a few: rich ruddy worms to please the ruddy robin; then the several wild cherries, the apple, malus, rowan, and perhaps prime favorite of all, *Amelanchier canadensis*, its pale blossom so appealing to the human eye in spring, its sweet red fruit a feast to birds in summer. Then there are the many flowers that appeal to your nectar-sipping sprite, the hummingbird. Last, I have a negative suggestion. The poet wrote:

"Oh lovely Pussy! Oh Pussy, my love
What a beautiful Pussy you are.

150

"To which I might add my own humble contribution:

> *"But beautiful as Pussy Cat may be*
> *We birds are happier without Pussee."*

"Sir Dougal, you should be on the stage."

"Thank you so much, Mrs. Morris."

4:25 P.M. The bridge ahead of us, to the right cedars rimming the end of the lake. She had said that she would break a small branch and stand it upright at the water's edge, and it was there. My pulse raced up.

"I should like now to pay tribute to Mrs. Farrow and to Signor Luigi for the sheer witchery of their landscaping, for the economy of line, for the simple curves that lead us on to ever new delight."

Fearful for my stout Chief Officer, I was overdoing it, but Mrs. Farrow and Signor Luigi, dapper in the background, beamed.

4:45 P.M. Diana would be, Diana should be stealing back under cover to the boathouse, neat toolkit zipped into one pocket of the overalls, trophies zipped into the other.

". . . And so we bid farewell to *Lobelia Cardinalis*, the Cardinal-Flower, worthy prince of Nature's church, to the many graceful ferns astride the burn, I beg your pardon, astride the brook, to the Indian Pipes, those pallid parasites of ghostly beauty, no wonder that they hang their heads . . ."

5 P.M. Beside the lily pond, the English butler dispensing drinks, Signora Luigi at the Georgian teapot, four sloe-eyed Luigi maidens proffering sandwiches and cakes.

5:05 P.M. "Maestro, time to pick the little winners."

There were mutterings from some present.

"Ladies and Gentlemen, Mrs. Farrow elevates me to the dignity of maestro, but it is with profound humility that I come now to the culmination of my task. Heaven forbid that I should take issue with our gracious hostess, but if the winners were little winners, my decision would have been an easy one. Yet every garden that I have visited has had quality. Any one of them would, in less rare company, be a worthy winner . . .

"After most careful thought, I have decided to award the Grand Challenge Cup to Monsieur et Madame Pierre Labouisse, whose seigniory on the banks of the noble Saint Lawrence is a sanctuary to which pilgrims wend their way in awe and wonder. *C'est pour moi vraiment un grand plaisir* . . .

"And the second prize I am much honored to award to Mr. and Mrs. Jan Morris of Hudson Heights, both dedicated lovers of our earth and all the fruits thereof. Beauty rests in their cloistered garden."

Loud clapping. Jonathan Farrow then thanked me briefly and gracefully, and Mildred Farrow put her word in: "Thanks, Maestro, you did the little winners proud."

But as the dreadful woman spoke, a sound grew quickly. Diana had called it a loud, inimitable blatter, and it was, the chop-chop-chopping of a chopper. Not thirty seconds could have passed from the first sound to the momentary glimpse as it sank beyond a coppery cluster of *Acer platanoides* Crimson King.

The noise moderated to a throaty coughing. "Are you expecting other visitors, Mrs. Farrow?"

"Not that I know of, Maestro, old chap."

"Or the Press, perhaps?"

"Oh, I say, Maestro, that's a thought. They may want to photograph a real garden. Come on, let's have a dekko."

Mildred Farrow strode from the lily pond, between the rock gardens, and round a border of tall double pink and white rugosas in abundant bloom, her maestro reluctantly at heel.

At the end of the emerald sweep of lawn was a chunky, white helicopter, FOREST SURVEYS INC., the rotor spinning. This side of it stood two men, with feet apart, with masks, with Tommy guns cradled in familiarity. The stubby barrels weaved to and fro across us.

I heard others approach from behind, and gasp, and beat retreat, but Mildred Farrow stood her ground, and so did I, sheltered in some degree by an immensity of hip and torso.

152

"Unbelievable," I said. It was unbelievable and it was true.

Arms akimbo, Mrs. Farrow stood her ground, just as I, arms akimbo, had stood my ground before these people in circumstances of less immediate menace. I thought that I recognized the lean jaw of Brother Henry. And I thought that I recognized the bulky shape of the German I had clobbered.

"What are the bloody fucking bastards up to?" It was a frank inquiry, and she shook her fist at them, and the muzzles now stared squarely, roundly at us.

"Better retreat," I said. "They look rather businesslike."

"Retreat? Don't know the word." But we moved back out of sight, and no bursts followed us. "Robbery, Trocher! They're covering for other buggers in the house." Jaw set, eyes flashing, Mildred Farrow also looked rather businesslike. "Whole armory in the gunroom. Have to get there. How, though? Got it, flanking action behind the herbaceous border. Don't stand there dithering," she snarled at her husband, whose face was blotched purple pale. "Do something!"

"But Mildred, we are unarmed, and there is open ground beyond the border. You mustn't risk your life."

"What's bloody life, if you don't risk it?" *Will the real Mildred Farrow please stand up?* And this was a real Mildred Farrow. "None of you softies got 'ny guts?"

No one in the stricken assemblage moved. "Come on, Trocher, you have guts. Follow!"

Perforce, I followed her. I followed my hostess because if I did not, I would be put to shame. I followed my hostess because it was one thing to steal her jewelry, another thing to be accessory to her murder. The one sin might be called venial, the other mortal.

Bending low, I followed her mighty backside in her straining trousers behind her great herbaceous border. But that came to an end as all borders must. The helicopter still coughed throatily. We crouched, under cover from the masked men, in full view of the garden people.

There were some yards of open ground to cross, then cover

153

behind a pergola of climbers, then a short open distance to the house, and I was thinking that even a Dago might be human enough to pay back a knock-out punch with interest.

"You're a stout chap, Trochei," she said calmly, happily. "We'll rush it in one from here. The gunroom's just inside. Then we're going to pump the buggers full of lead."

She ran fast for a woman of her astonishing dimensions. She was behind the pergola, and I nearly so, when a burst of bullets crackled overhead, and on she ran, and on I ran, and then the pergola was splintering apart about our ears, and I took the only possible course of action. I tackled Mildred Farrow by the pants, felled her, lay on top of her mountainous frame while the devil's chatter was all about us, and I wrestled her into a slight depression. But shooting ceased. The helicopter blattered into view above the tangled ruins of the pergola of climbers. Unharmed, we stood to watch the machine fly south.

"You saved my bacon, Trocher, thanks. It's the breed that counts. Look at those gutless wonders!" The other Mildred Farrow was standing up.

"I disagree with you, Mrs. Farrow."

"Call me Mildred. You deserve it."

"Thank you, Mildred. But what you tried to do was suicidal."

"You did it with me, Dougal boy. And my God I liked the weight of you in that tumble."

"Glad to hear it, Mildred. Now, shouldn't we go and see what happened?"

"Well, I suppose so." She did not seem particularly interested. "My God, we showed 'em what stuff we're made of."

But here was Jonathan Farrow. "Ah, Dougal, how can I thank you? How can I express my gratitude and admiration for your bravery in shielding my dear Mildred's body with your own? We all saw it, a wonderful act of courage."

"It was nothing," I said, strangely light-headed. "I was saving my own skin as much as your dear Mildred's bacon."

154

It seemed that the incomparable Luigi had crawled forward in time to see two women, not men, dash out of the house, bags in hand. We all repaired to bedrooms to count our losses. My cuff links were there, and so was Grandfather's gold cigarette case, which I had nearly sold last month to pay Drin wages. Diana and I discussed the matter, and she had settled it: *No, Sir Dougal, I will not be weighed down by chicken feed. These are conservative golden goons, not diamond-studded gangster types. Forget the men.*

But the women's reports were unanimously of disaster. *All my best things,* all said. Most of them were philosophical about it, perhaps knowing that what the insurance policy would not adequately cover, Daddy surely would.

There were some tears, however, about jewelry of sentimental value. "Oh George, the darling pin you gave me for breaking my leg at Val-d'Isère on our honeymoon, remember?"

"Don't cry, Nancy dear. We'll find another just the same."

"But it couldn't ever be the same for me."

"Stop yer blubbin'," said Mildred. "What have you got to moan about? You didn't move an inch to save your bloody pin." She was at her most awful cock-a-hoop, and at a new low ebb of popularity, for every woman of active age there present knew that Mildred had shown herself to be the better woman.

"The necklace was made from Grannie's tiara."

Being so rooted in the ages, I was bothered by that, for my own grandmother's tiara had long since been sold, not stolen.

But on the whole the mood was cheerful, an unwonted dangerous excitement, a being-in-the-self-same boat, a certain feeling of *fin de siècle*. Oh to hell with it, let's have another drink. I had good cause to admire Canadian calmness and aplomb.

And I should add that it is often easier to admire when one is oneself the object of admiration. If to all my fellow guests Mildred was the gallant loathsome enemy, to all of them I was the hero of the hour.

It is perhaps given to few robbers to be the hero of their robbed. I was also pleased with myself for two reasons. First, it had troubled me that all my risks were being taken by Diana, but as events transpired, I had taken a fearful risk. How fearful will be known to those who have heard and felt their immediate inches of this lovely world being torn apart by Tommy-gun tattoo. The second reason was a simple one — I had saved dear Mildred from certain death.

Choosing a moment when my hostess had left my side — I was her hero too, unfortunately — I slipped off and up the garden quite alone, being most anxious about Diana. *I'll take the branch away when I get back,* she said, and it was gone.

Returning in the cool, in the soft play of sun and evening shadow, I was surprised to hear the characteristic chunking of a helicopter. Surely not? Come back to get me? Terrified, I ducked into cover. But the sound was lighter, the machine a small bubble-nosed type, CFCZ-TV.

So, the police in hordes, the media like busy bees. Well before dark the Forest Surveys' helicopter was found abandoned near the village of Bellamy, Vermont, a clean first getaway by the desperadoes, a massive manhunt already launched in the United States. No vestige of suspicion rested here, but it was after nine before all particulars of stolen jewelry had been taken, and we were free to go, and I could accept a lift into Montreal.

Jonathan Farrow bade me an affecting farewell. In trepidation I faced dear Mildred, who was a few seas under with martinis and Viennese champagne.

"I couldn't care lessh about the bloody rocks. Lots more where those came from, eh, Jonathan?"

"Of course, Mildred dear."

"But I tell you what, Dougal boy, after the taste of our clinch together, I'd give all the jewels ever possesshed for a proper roll in the hay with you."

"Tutt-tutt, Mildred dear."

"Tutt-tutt yerself, old randy."

I was engulfed in her mighty hug, from which I broke with

156

my mighty strength. It did occur to me that if I had been less of an honorable decent sort of chap, and more of a dishonorable indecent sort of gigolo, I could have saved Drin without peril, without crime except against self-respect.

I was safe from Mildred, but other dangers had not yet begun.

⚝ 20 ⚝

Something brought me from a long way down. From peace to mad muddle to be awake on Monday morning, and it was a long ring again. "Hullo."

"Sir Dougal Trocher?"

If I heard my damned stupid name just once more, I would open a window and scream into the abyss of Sherbrooke Street. "What is it?"

"Sorry to disturb you, sir. London is calling."

"Put it through, then." But I pulled myself together to be the amiable crook I was. "Sorry, operator, still half asleep. I didn't mean to be rude."

She chuckled, kindly woman. ". . . Go ahead, please."

"Sir Dougal, I'm terribly sorry to call so early, but I've been beside myself with worry. Are you wounded?"

"What on earth do you mean, Miss Arden, am I wounded?"

"It's a late flash in all the papers here, about that huge robbery, and how you shielded that Mrs. Farrow with your own body from that awful machine-gun fire, but no details. Oh, I've been so anxious."

"I am unwounded, Miss Arden, thank you."

"What a blessing! The other thing, then, Sir Dougal, is that my flight is due at fourteen fifty-five, which means I can report at the office by half-past four, and I just want to say again how terribly sorry I am for letting you down, but thank God you're safe. Good-bye, Sir Dougal."

I had realized that the robbery, in view of its scope and daring, would make a big, brief splash. But, simple coot, I had not realized that my own action would be newsworthy, the human interest to lend the spice. Last evening they had photographed me with Mildred Farrow, who was as keen on that idea as she then was to dominate and domineer proceedings. So, having described the masked robbers to the police as best I could, I sneaked off to pack my bag and hide from reporters.

Not to much avail, it seemed, for with my morning tea there came the *Gazette*: GALLANT SCOT SHIELDS STOUT-HEARTED HOSTESS, the story of the robbery, and not a bad picture of Mildred Farrow and myself. *Stout-hearted* was true, and in the context of the photograph, quite an amusing euphemism for Mildred's shape. The total value of the theft was estimated at almost a million dollars.

I had not finished breakfast when a call came from Jonathan Farrow's secretary in Montreal, saying that he was anxious to complete the records of this year's Country Garden competition, and did I have any given or Christian names other than Dougal? Dougal Colin Lisclibborn Trocher. I spelled out Lisclibborn, my Irish grandmother's name.

During all these three mad beautiful weeks Diana had been with me, but now no Diana, now nothing mad and nothing beautiful, and if she came this afternoon, what would she bring, and where the hell did we go from here?

To make matters worse, the telephone began to ring, requests for interviews, congratulatory calls from Claud Merriwell and others. And then it was the reception desk to say that the media were in the lobby, and might they come up?

I had not played shy before. Indeed, some publicity had been our policy. So to be too much the shrinking violet now might seem suspicious. I telephoned and asked whether a room could be made available for a brief press conference at twelve o'clock? Easily arranged, and then I called my friend the head porter for help.

He smuggled me out by devious ways to the alley behind.

Thence I went to the garage and got the car and took it to be serviced. That at least was something to do. Now nothing to occupy myself with until twelve o'clock, but walking the streets was something — which I did on another hot humid morning. So many troubled faces one saw. Surely people in London, in Edinburgh, looked less unhappy? My own face must have mirrored the trouble that I felt, but my spirits rose a little as I walked, and I managed to face the press at twelve noon, play the modest hero, disliking myself. To state that I felt remorse, however, would be to misstate.

After that, a lonely lunch upstairs. It was just a month ago that we had sat beside the river. *Plain theft,* Tarquie said. *How about that one, Dougal? — It's clean. I like it. A weekend party sort of thing. I was turning over in my mind.*

So there the thing had started, and here the thing had happened in just such a way. *Plain theft,* how simple that sounded, but if I have made our crime seem simple, I have oversimplified. Like all good plans, it involved an intricate complexity of trivia, all linked, all slaves to chance.

To illustrate this complexity, I mention one small aspect — Diana's use of cars. She had left the BMW at the hotel garage on Saturday night. Then she had picked up a suitcase and had gone by taxi to Jenny's apartment. Jenny was visiting the Turk in Buffalo and had left her keys with Diana, who asked whether she might borrow the Volkswagen over the weekend. That was all Jenny knew.

For two reasons, Diana took the VW on Saturday night. First, time would be of the essence on Sunday, so she would drive direct from the airport to Camelot. Second, she must not be seen in Montreal, so she could not go back to Jenny's janitored apartment. She would go to a motel for two hours that evening, Donna Andrews, Australian schoolmarm. But there were still two risks: First she had to park the car for another night at the airport, and she had no two-night parking ticket alibi. Second, she had to leave the jewelry in the car. It would certainly not fail-safe, but it would have to do.

Punctually at half-past four there was a knock. "Ah, Miss Arden, safely back!"

"It's not me being safe, Sir Dougal, but you. I read all about it in the *Star*, coming in. How brave you were and what a merciful deliverance." This for the benefit of the man, whom she tipped. She looked as if she had just emerged from twelve hours of refreshing sleep, not from four Atlantic crossings.

But when he had gone, and I had applied the safety chain, she looked at me and began to laugh. Diana laughed and I laughed too. "Darling Sir Dougal, Mildred's hero boy. Please tell me. No, don't tell me. Come here first."

It was wonderful to have her back, to be in bed again, sensual fun, that was the thing between us always. "It might have been a month, not just two days." Her brown eyes were so happy and so honest and so innocent, extraordinary girl.

But in my arms in friendly lassitude, she said: "You thought I wasn't coming back. You thought I would skedaddle with the loot. You did think that, didn't you?"

"Don't be ridiculous, Diana."

"Oh yes, you did. I felt your heart go thump just now. It gave a lie-detector jump. Well, let me tell you that any woman who wouldn't come flying back to what I have gratefully received, that woman would be just plain crazy. Now give me half an hour to make repairs, and then I'll show you."

I had a bath and dressed, wondering how Diana had guessed that I cherished some inkling doubts or faint suspicions. But with so cryptic a partner who would reveal almost nothing about herself, it was inevitable that one should have some reservation, some mental insurance, as it were. The truth was that I had not thought it, but had given thought to it.

"Are we locked up solid?"

She opened her crocodile purse or handbag, smart and expensive, like everything about her, and she spread the swag on a green baize table where we usually kept the drinks.

"Rich goonery," she said. "They bore me." Diana was that *rara avis,* a woman who disliked precious stones.

Diamonds, rubies, emeralds and sapphires — bracelets, brooches, pendants, earrings, and one small tiara, I remembered it on Madame Labouisse, prize winner, charming woman. Two pearl necklaces, and the larger one was Mildred Farrow's — had been Mildred's. "Pearls aren't much nowadays." There were two fabulous diamond solitaire rings. "This one is eight or nine carats, and a perfect stone. Worth eighty thousand, even a hundred. But all the big ones will be recorded, so they have to be spirited elsewhere, I believe Hong Kong is the very best marketplace. Some might even have to be divided and recut. That means halving the value or quartering it."

I was seeing a few of them again. I was seeing this ring on this woman's wedding finger, that ruby and diamond pendant on that delicious décolleté of Mrs. Morris, and so on, interesting. "What are they worth, Diana?"

"On their rightful owners, nearly a million, I suppose. Out of their settings, recut, hot, I don't know, Sir Dougal, perhaps a quarter."

But I was far away at Drin, workmen tearing the library apart, and then all restored, the Den replanted, the . . . "What did you say, Diana?"

"I said that the time has come for Loris."

"I'm not sure . . ." But the telephone rang beside me.

"This is the front desk, sir. Mr. Farrow's chauffeur is here with a parcel for you. May I send him up?"

Diana whisked everything back into the handbag. "I'd better vanish."

I opened up for Prentice, the Farrows' chauffeur, a cheerful type, with a refreshing absence of *Sir Dougals.* "Mr. Farrow's compliments," he said. "You did a good job, tacklin' 'er, saw it myself. None the worse, I hope?"

"I'm fine, thank you, Prentice."

"Mrs. Farrow's a bit under the weather, poor thing screwed

'er backside up, nothing serious. She's a killer, that one," he said with some admiration, and went away.

Dear Dougal,

I owe you an apology for the rather lame ruse about Country Garden records, but we did want your initials for the binocular case. I trust that you will find them of service when "spying the hill" at Drin.

I would very much have liked to bring this small gift in person, but Mildred is laid up and I cannot leave her side.

In falling yesterday she suffered a sprain in the lumbar regions, and by this morning the pain was intense. However, our doctor assures me that it is nothing serious, and she is resting under sedation.

Not many a husband can be grateful for his wife's sprained back, but for dear Mildred's I owe you a debt of gratitude that can never be repaid. Yours was a splendid act of gallantry.

Thank you also for making our garden competition so notable a success, marred as it was in aftermath by outrageous armed robbery.

Mildred joins me in wishing you a safe journey home, and be assured that our house is always yours. Please give my compliments to Miss Arden when she returns from London . . .

Diana read the letter while I opened the parcel. They were Leitz Trinovid, ten by forty, superb small binoculars, far better than my own of twice the weight and size.

"He's a decent old codger," Diana said. "Just the right kind of present, the best in the world, but not too grand. And now I seem to think I have a soft spot for Mildred too. What I wouldn't give to have seen the two of you." I described that action, which was not entirely funny in retrospect. "Were the Dagoes shooting to kill?"

"Yes, they were, Diana, after one warning burst."

"And if you hadn't tackled Mildred, would they have got you both?"

"Yes, they would, Diana."

"Sobering," she said. "And a sobering thought is Loris."

"Wouldn't it be better if we put them in a safe-deposit box, and waited, say, a year?"

"We've discussed that so often," she said, but patiently. "If we waited a year, things would be no different. If we waited a year, you wouldn't have the money you need so desperately. We daren't smuggle them into the United States or England, and even if we did, we have no contacts there. I thought we might find a contact through the Dagoes, but that one encounter was terrifying enough. And yesterday, after repaying their profound indebtedness to their honorary sister, they tried to kill her lover-boss. No more Dagoes, thank you very much. Now, why don't you go and get the car, and I'll be thinking while you're away."

"You won't do anything until I'm here?"

"I dunno." She was quite testy. "Just fetch it."

But when I had brought the car to the hotel garage, and was in again, she said: "I called Loris. A man asked for a number to phone me back, but I said that I had no number, so he said: *Call again in ten minutes.* Which I did, and I'm almost sure that the man who spoke was the Armenian." Diana produced a Texaco map.

"He told me to take the road by Lachute, that's on the north side of the Ottawa River, and turn off here, drive four miles and two-tenths, come to an open gate, turn left, half a mile to the lake. *Arrive at ten A.M. and wait. Come alone and unarmed, and you will be perfectly safe.* Somehow or other I absolutely trust that little man."

"I don't, Diana. And you are not going alone."

"Oh God, am I to explain everything a thousand times? You were known before, but you might have got away with it. Now, since the robbery, everyone who reads a paper or watches TV must know you. Okay, so you're linked to the jewels, so you're open to blackmail for the rest of your life. Me, they don't even know my name. Now, have some sense."

"I'll hide if you like, Diana, and you can deal with him. But I'm coming. All woods and lakes, isn't it?"

"Yes," she said. "We used to go fishing up that way."

"Very well. I will lurk in the back, and somewhere between the gate and the lake, you slow down, and I hop out."

164

"Do you have a gun, Sir Dougal?"

"No, I don't. I have my skean d'hu."

"What's that?"

"It's the knife I wear on my right leg with the kilt."

"Oh yes, I remember. Could I see it?"

I fetched the skean d'hu, and she admired the cairngorm in the handle, and drew the small knife from its sheath. "Golly, it's sharp," Diana said. "Not for show at all."

"Not altogether," I said. "Shall we go out for dinner?"

"That would be lovely, Sir Dougal."

"To the place we went the first night?"

"No. It reminds me of my late unlamented first employer."

We dined well, and walked back quite early. It was a fine night, the moon not yet up.

Diana took my arm in the troubled city and we were quiet until she said: "I'm glad you're coming."

She had been entirely confident about the robbery, and it had gone without a hitch. But now she was not confident. We both faced the morrow with foreboding.

⚡ 21 ⚡

It had been Diana's idea to hire the car, a Chevrolet. *The BMW is too rich and rare, and there could be a lead back to you through Cousin Claud. Not very fair to his corporate image, either.* She was in good spirits again this morning. *But what about your driving license? You have to show that, don't you? — Donna Andrews has an Australian license,* she said indulgently to the nitwit. *I'll pick you up at the corner of Crescent, two blocks along.*

That was an hour and forty miles ago, and nobody had followed us. "We turn right here," Diana said. "Four and two-tenths to go. Now I think you'd better pop over."

I lay on the floor between the seats, seeing sky, treetops, power lines. "Any houses?"

"No," she said. "Forest primeval. Still no one following that I can see." We rolled along smoothly. "Now a fence on the left, one of those wire-mesh fences about five feet high, snowmobile proof, I guess, and TRESPASSERS WILL BE PROSECUTED signs in French and English. Here's a gate, and it's open, in we go. Are you ready?"

"Yes. What's the surface like?"

"It's a dirt road, but smooth as tarmac. Now we're going round this bend, you're telling me we are. A good place ahead, a small bridge and a stream, thick cover. How do I know where to pick you up?"

"Either at the bridge, or at the lake, or if in between I'll put

166

a six-inch stone in the middle of the road. And if no sign of me, don't wait. I'll find my own way back."

"It's quite a little walk, Sir Dougal." Her voice was calm, ironical, the car slowing, a small jerk as it changed itself to low. I held the door handle. "Now."

I was out, stumbled, got my balance, into thick alders by the stream. I crouched there. The car had moved on. The sound of running water robbed my ears a little. I must risk it. I moved noisily through undergrowth, away from the stream. Now I could listen.

The ground rose ahead of me in the lake direction, sun behind my left shoulder. There might be a quarter of a mile to go, a slope to climb, perhaps to a vantage point. It was a young spruce forest, unlimbed and dense. I could not move quietly; I could move and listen, move and listen. A white-throated sparrow sang its sweet high song, Sam Peabody, Sam Peabody, the Canada bird. I had learned most of the common species. *In my brief stay in Canada I have been fascinated by the wealth of bird life,* thus to the Country Garden people, pontificating, true.

But here was a path, crossing my direction, running north and south. There were deer tracks, and droppings too. The deer made use of it, as they would always use an easy route, but this was a human path, trees limbed on either side to head-height, the floor clear of twigs. It was a patrolling path, along which men could move silently on rubber soles, and men did, two different shoe patterns in soft ground.

I looked for trip wires, none, but they would be useless with deer about. I crossed and stopped to listen again. The forest was thinner, young spruce and cedar mixed, and between them, among them, a nightmare tangle of dead old brush.

I heard two sounds, first the muted snarl of a big outboard motor. It grew steadily, and then it cut off, and water lapped. The lake could not be far away.

The other sound came from behind on the left, a swish of tires. I could see the ribbon of the road. It was a long, black, glistening car, two men in front and one behind.

167

"Yeah, come in, Joe." The voice was alarmingly close to me, beyond the clump of cedars in which I lurked.

"You looked 'er over yet? Jeeze, Kurt sure is right. Best bitta tail I ever seen. Now she's parley-vooin' with Loris. The tits on 'er, you should get a load o' those, Dug."

"Comin', Joe." I had a glimpse of the man running, a green shirt, a walkie-talkie in the hand near me, left hand.

The man Dug had run left, and I ran ahead. The woods changed again at the crest of the hillock, this time to a stand of old white pine, and I made no sound on dead brown needles.

Now I was on a downward slope, crouched again in cedar. The road widened to a turnaround, three cars on the far side, in shade, our rented green Chevrolet, the black rich Leviathan, a third nondescript. The new binoculars hung from my neck inside my windbreaker. I put them up. Diana and a small man were walking to the floating jetty. He gave her a courtly hand into the boat, Diana in the bow, small man in a city suit amidships, boatman in the stern. The motor started, and the boat surged up, planing to the island. I looked at that, a white house set in trees, a long, low, modern-looking house, the shore steep and rocky. Soon the sound fell as the boat slowed to a jetty.

Below me, the chauffeur sat in the car, reading a newspaper. I saw no one else until a man in a green shirt and trousers, a peaked green cap, crossed the road. He had a holster at his right hip, the walkie-talkie in his left hand. He looked like the lanky man whom I had glimpsed, and he went into the shade of a large deciduous tree, a red maple.

He led me to see two other men, who stood in deep shade, one dressed and armed similarly to the first, the other a bigger man in a suit, and he was talking, whispering, one might think, from the closeness of their three heads together.

It was twenty minutes to eleven. So long as I stayed where I was, so long as the sun did not reflect from my binoculars, so long as they did not have dogs, I would be safe and be quite useless. Two armed men, and the third probably armed too, a

168

bodyguard for Loris. And they were plotting. If they were not planning some future thing, why the earnest discussion?

A bluejay called harshly and yet melodiously on the hill. *Bluejay on the hill, water in the mill* was the old saying, a farmer had told me. But the day was fine, a shadow of cloud low beyond the lake, a mile, two miles across.

It was after eleven, and still they talked, and what good was I here, what good was I anywhere with only a small knife, its sheaf tucked into the occasional pocket in front of my trousers, its handle held by my belt? Why in God's name had I not bought myself a gun? That would have been easy enough in Montreal. But guns were against my principles, bloody fool. *Jeeze, Kurt sure is right. Best bitta tail I ever seen. The tits on 'er, you should get a load o' those, Dug.*

The three men were still together, the driver still in the car. I moved downhill toward them, but slowly now, another path. This one ran east and west, parallel to the road. I had crossed three north-south paths, and this was the second east and west, about a hundred yards between each. So a criss-cross network perhaps.

I spied again round a rock. One of the three men had disappeared, the lanky one, Dug. The others still talked beneath the tree, out of sight of the driver. I rolled into a patch of wild raspberries.

He cleared his throat and spat. "Jesus, I don't fuckin' know," he muttered, not far away below me; then louder: "Yeah, come in, Joe."

"Where ya at, Dug?"

"Two North Able."

"Wait there. I'm comin'."

Two North Able, that sounded like a reference in the manner or code of any roadmap. *Two* could be the second path from the lake, parallel to the shore; *North Able* could be the first path on the north side of the road, and parallel to it. That way, or the other way round, it must mean an intersection, something of the sort.

Dug's voice had been faint, and the other metallic voice through the walkie-talkie fainter still. I crawled downhill. It was steep, prickly juniper, broken rock, painful crawling, but just below was a bramble thicket, and from that thicket a quivering nose, a pair of eyes, two large ears faced me squarely. The doe snorted and ran, the white flag of the white-tailed deer, her dappled fawn after her.

It was my chance, and I took it, into the brambles, face stinging, scratched. "Fuckin' deer," Dug said, near at hand.

My heart steadied down. I heard the other one puffing as he climbed. "Okay, Dug, we got it all worked out. Here's what happens: Loris comes ashore first, same's usual, says to Kurt: *Tell them to patrol Charlie North and Charlie South*, same's usual, gets us out of the way, protectin' the flanks, give 'er safe passage out. What the little bastard calls his code of honor.

"Well, that's where same's usual stops. Soon as the car goes and the boat starts back to pick 'er up, I move behind the tree. You cross over and wait near, out of sight.

"She comes ashore and to the auto. Jeeze, that little arse in them tight pants, you seen it, Dug?"

"Sure I seen it. Got a hard-on, lookin'." I sweated. That was my sex talking, I was one of them.

"So I stick 'er up nice and quiet until Rudi's back at the island. Then I call you, and you lift the purse and we take 'er a distance back in the woods, and we got two hours until Kurt gets back in the Mustang. Then she's his for the screwin', fair enough. And we split three ways even. Hell, you're actin' shit-scared, Dug. Don't you want to screw the bitch?"

"Sure I do. But how do we know Kurt's playin' square with us? Who gave Garry his last year?"

"Kurt did. Anyone cheats Loris, gets his."

"Ain't we cheatin' Loris?"

"Sure. But we're in it together with Kurt this time. How's Loris to know?"

"He'll know. Sure I'm shit-scared of that little kike, and so are you, and so is Kurt. What if Kurt runs out on us?"

"Kurt won't. Kurt's crazed horny for 'er. And by the time

170

he's used 'er good, it'll be dark and we can row out 'n dump 'er."

"Dump 'er? Jesus!"

"Are you crazy? Kurt says she knows the house address and the phone number. Let 'er go, and she calls 'im right away. You want yours from Loris?"

There was a pause, and then the one called Joe spoke again: "Kurt says she ain't a reglar. Even Loris don't know who she is. We park the Chevy in Lachute tonight, and that's it, no trace. What I come to say from Kurt, and it goes for me too: You're in this, Dug, or else. Are you in?"

"Sure I'm in. Who says I ain't in?"

"You better be. Kurt! Callin' you, Kurt. Over."

"Ja?"

"That's okay, Kurt."

"Goot. Dug, patrol One North Able to Four North Able to Four North Charlie to One North Charlie. Joe, the same thing south. Check in each ten minutes. Could be someone with her, so keep a sharp watch, and listen for me. Out."

They both moved away. If I had guessed the code rightly, they would be patrolling rectangles north and south of the road.

It was after twelve, and a hot breeze was beginning to riffle the lake. Nobody moved at the island. I tried to think, and there were three alternatives that I could think of. The first was to wait for the mysterious Loris to step from the boat, walk straight over to him and tell him what his staff planned to do. But it was a virtual certainty that if Kurt did not shoot me out of hand at first sight, he would shoot me the moment I opened my mouth. And even if he did not, Diana would have broken her word to come alone — then what about the Loris code of honor? They were all afraid of little Mr. Loris.

So that was ruled out. The second thing I could do was to ambush Dug, jump him as he patrolled. But they had to check in every ten minutes. Imitate that slurry voice? Impossible.

The third alternative was the best slim hope: Move back, cross the road out of sight of the cars, work forward on the other side to that maple tree. But when Loris and Kurt had driven off, there would be one unarmed girl and one man with a four-inch knife and two men with pistols. Joe had said: *I move behind the tree. You cross over and wait near, out of sight.* One man at a time. Take Joe first. That was my best hope, slim indeed.

I moved a few feet to spy again. Kurt sat under the tree. Of the others no sign, no movement at the island.

But where was Dug? If my guess was correct, he would be patrolling about three hundred yards east, two hundred yards north, three hundred yards west, two hundred yards south, a thousand yards, say fifteen minutes until he passed me, and I could follow. It was eleven minutes since they had parted.

There was sudden loud movement, and I turned to see another deer, this one a stag with antlers in velvet. But in Canada they called them bucks and does, and horns, not antlers. It stopped, looking back, uneasy, perhaps disturbed by Dug. Then it caught my scent, and was gone.

And for a brief time, far less time than it takes to read, I was in the high corrie on Ben Drin. We had stalked him all day, a Royal, with a noble broad spread of antlers turned to us, watching downwind, an easy shot at two hundred yards.

He's so bonny, Dougal. In those days she still spoke with a touch of Scotland.

Yes, he's bonny.

So bonny, Dougal, please don't shoot.

But the bead was true and steady below and behind the left shoulder. *Please don't!* she said urgently as my finger squeezed, and I shot the stag through the heart. She had come stalking with me many times, and loved it, but something had happened to her at that moment on that day. *So cruel,* she said, and turned and ran. I watched her running, my leggy friend of twelve. That was the day I lost my friend, because something also happened to me. *Good-bye, Tirene,* running downhill and out of sight. Men of twenty-five simply must not fall in love with girls of twelve. It is indecent. It is Lolita. It is perversion. And at willful seventeen, almost grown-up, the old man of thirty is a bore.

But I was back now here in Canada. I heard him coming. He passed below me, moving east. I gave him a minute and followed on the path, carefully, ghostly as the Indian of myth flits through his forest on such a path as this.

I heard him check in with Kurt, giving position *Three North Able*. He was on a regular anticlockwise circuit, and the paths were as I had thought, about a hundred yards between each intersection. I left that one and moved down to the road, alders again, the cars and the lake not in sight. But where was Joe on the other side?

Diana had been three hours and a half with Loris on the island, surely not much longer. I must risk the crossing. All I met was a rabbit, tamer than any rabbit I knew. It hopped a few feet and pricked long ears. They called them rabbits, but it was a snowshoe hare, of the genus *Lepus*. Hares were rabbits, grouse were partridges, kestrels were sparrow hawks, warblers were redstarts, a mixed-up bunch of nostalgic kids, those old settlers must have been. It was wet ground here. I dirtied my bloody face with alder muck.

I moved west now, and to move fast and quietly I risked the path, stopping often. I gambled that Joe would be patrolling anticlockwise. I had read somewhere that exercising prisoners almost invariably walked their wire or enclosure anticlockwise, perhaps stronger right legs, the spin of the earth or something.

"Come in, Joe. Where are you?" It was the voice of Kurt.

"At Four South Baker."

"Go to Three South Baker. Loris moving on the island."

I crawled forward. It was cedar again, soft foliage on my brambled face, sweat stinging my eyes.

The boat was coming. It made a healthy muffled roar on the short crossing, a minute or two, a quarter of a mile. Now get the statistics right. Joe was at Three South Baker. When he was told to patrol Three South Charlie, he would disobey orders and come to the tree, which was about One South Able,

173

two hundred yards or a little more, I would have that time to play with.

The motor had stopped. I heard footsteps on the wooden jetty, and I heard a new voice, quite a different kind of voice, "Tell them now to patrol North and South Charlie for fifteen minutes. Then they may leave."

Kurt gave those orders, and was acknowledged twice. Two car doors opened. Two car doors closed with expensive clunks. The car drove away and so did the boat.

I ran to the maple. There was one low branch. I jumped for it, swung a leg over, and stood in a crotch about ten feet up. I would be hidden by leaves from anyone outside the spread of the tree, but entirely visible to anyone below.

I drew my skean d'hu, which had gralloched a good many deer in its time, my time, my father's time, but not any men yet, so far as I knew. A red squirrel chattered above my head, chattered, chattered, stopped.

Joe came running. He panted below me, leaning against the trunk. The Chevrolet was a few feet away on the road. Now the boat again. Diana sat in the bow, her fair hair flying.

Now? No, wait until the boat started back, until his hand moved to draw the gun. He was a stocky broad-shouldered man. She said something to Rudi in the boat and then walked this way. It was true what these members of my sex had said about her. And I was one of them. I happened to be one who knew.

She was nearly at the car when his right hand moved. I jumped then. The knife went beautifully like into butter into the inner side of his arm between elbow and shoulder, the ulnar nerve, a little trick the wicked army taught me, and I had never used it but had not forgotten.

The gun fell to the ground, and so did he at the impact of two hundred pounds in a free fall of five feet or so. Joe was down and out, and I gave him good extra measure with the butt of his pistol.

Diana smiled at me. God, she was cool. "Into those cedars, quick! Another one."

174

She obeyed, dived for cedars beside the path. I stood behind the trunk, peeking round it, waiting for Dug, the reluctant one. The odds were even money now, although perhaps not, because I was a bloody awful pistol shot, and it was Dug's job, he should be good.

"Joe!" he called. No answer from Joe.

He came cautiously into view, passing the cedars where Diana hid, his pistol in hand.

She was so quick that it had happened before I knew what was happening, before he could begin to turn. She chopped him from behind, heel-handed right, heel-handed left, two strokes at the neck. It was the collapse of neck and Dug. *Yes, Sir Dougal. This chop can be very very lethal.*

⚸ 22 ⚸

"I TOLD YOU I might have to get away with murder," said Diana Arden.

The squirrel chirped and chattered again above my head, peering down at me, rat-faced. "Oh, shut up," I said, but it did not. I leaned against the tree, drained out.

"Has he gone into the house yet?"

I put up Jonathan Farrow's glasses, the boat at the jetty, nobody moving. "Must have."

"Quick, then. Get these out of sight." We dragged Dug's body into hospitable cedars. Joe breathed heavily, unconscious. I did not know, but rather hoped that I had cracked his skull. However, the arm was bleeding badly, so I ripped his shirtsleeve and made a rough bandage, ever quixotic. Then we rolled him in too. I washed the mud from my face in a puddle.

"You scratched yourself. What about the guns?"

"Keep them. Throw away later." I sat behind the wheel.

"Just a mo," Diana said, going back to the tree. "It would hardly do to forget you, would it?" she remarked to her crocodile bag, and we were off.

The gate was still open. I turned onto the first paved road, no one in sight, no one following. Diana took the ubiquitous tiger stripes from an outside pocket of her purse and wiped the guns off carefully. Then we were on the main highway, some traffic, but light, a side road again, a pond, no houses. "This should do nicely," she said, and lobbed them in. "I'd better wash your knife too," which she did in the pond and got in again. "Keep on this road. I'll sort of feel our way back to the city. Now tell me what happened."

I omitted the interim intentions of Kurt and Joe and Dug. But I told her that she would have been dumped in the lake.

"Guessing the key to those paths was great, top marks for genius. And waiting to jump him until he began to draw his gun, top marks for nerve. I think it's a good thing that Sir Dougal is a man of peace."

"I think it's a good thing that he never quite provoked Miss Arden into chopping. Do your hands hurt?"

"Not a bit, Sir Dougal, thank you for inquiring. One would have sufficed but, quite frankly, I felt like two."

"Now tell me about Loris."

"He didn't ask me any questions. I put the things in a pile on the table, and he took them one by one. It was so slow; it was until the end of time. *Beautiful*, he said once, that was the diamond solitaire, the oblong one. *Exquisite*, he said once, that was the small tiara.

"But he put Mildred Farrow's earrings apart from the rest, took off his eyeglass thing, a loupe they call it, and said: *I am so sorry, but these are paste.* You remember the emeralds?"

"Yes," I remembered them penduluming as Mildred rounded on me at the dinner table. *She's your floozy, what about it?*

"So I said: *Can I throw them in the lake?*

"*By all means,* he said. *It is very deep off that rock.*

"But when I came back, he smiled: *You trust me, young lady, and trust begets trust.* And he said: *I do not know you, and it is better that I should not. But you remind me of someone long ago.* Then he went back to the job.

"There were marvelous things in the room, a *sang de boeuf* vase, jade, ivory arm rests, other Chinese stuff, French furniture — and the paintings! It sounds out of place in a house on an island in a backwoods lake, but somehow it wasn't at all, it was lovely.

"And when at last he had finished, he moved a small

painting, Jan Brueghel, he said it was, unlocked a safe and took out banknotes. *Please count with me,* so I did, and he said: *They are all good bills and unmarked, I promise you.*"

"How much, Diana?"

"You tally them up when you get to the hotel. Now we'd better switch. I'll drop you off and take the car back.

". . . So when he had paid me, he said: *I have a fair bottle of Madeira, and then a light luncheon of cold salmon, avocado mousse, a peach, would that tempt you?*

"By that time I was quite hungry, so I tucked into the lunch."

"By this time, Diana, I also am quite hungry."

"Poor you, starving. Well, I admired his things, just as good as the ones in Outremont, and he said: *It is my small hobby. For some time now I have had my eye on a Corot of the Italian period. And in due course, when I have reaped profit from this transaction, I shall acquire it.*

"He was kindly, ineffably polite, the strangest man, sort of eery. *Excuse me while I have a word with Rudi, my jeweler.* He came back soon. *Rudi will take me first, and will come back at once for you. You will be entirely safe. You have never seen me. You have never been here. Is it understood?* That was with the hooded, hypnotic look.

"So I said it was understood, and I thanked him, and we shook hands, elaborate bows and all that. I didn't suspect a single thing until I saw that thug standing under the tree. Now, put the dollar bills in your inside pocket. See you later."

I walked to the hotel and, locked in, I counted the wad of dollar bills, an inch and a half thick, thousand-dollar bills. They were pink, with a picture of a covered bridge on the back. The color did not particularly appeal.

I counted two hundred and sixty-three the first time, two hundred and sixty-two the second. I am a hopeless counter. Try again. Try a fourth time. Yes, two — six — three.

Only some were new, so the consistency or crackle of paper varied. I held each one against bright light, and looked for the small green dots called planchettes, scattered haphazardly in varying number through Canadian bills. The printing was sharp on every one.

So far as an ignoramus could tell, they were the genuine article. Divide by about two point four — one hundred and nine thousand five hundred and eighty pounds.

I put them back in my pocket and let her in.

"Well, we did it," she said. I had so much to thank Diana Arden for that I could not emit a word of thanks, and we had done it, she had done it. Why had she done it?

It was after five, and Claud and his wife were coming to dinner. "Let's get tea and some sandwiches."

Diana ordered them, and I had a quick bath. My scratches bled a little but she stopped that with a styptic pencil. "I think I can make you up for Cousin Claud, but they'll show as soon as they start healing over. Oh, there's the telephone . . .

"Jenny's home from Buffalo, dying to pour her beastly Turk out to me. I'd better go for half an hour."

"We owe a lot to Jenny, so be nice, Diana."

"I'll do my very best, Sir Dougal. Now sit and I will cosmeticize you." She used a fine brush and powder from her compact, painted me most skillfully. "There! The rugged bronzed features are unblemished." Diana kissed me on the lips, but her own quivered a little after that. "Just think what it might have been today. Well, I'm off." She was gone before I remembered about asking her to get a present for Laura Merriwell.

I ate my egg sandwiches and drank my tea, thinking about the day, and that telephone rang.

"Sir Dougal Trocher?"

"Speaking."

"This is Inspector Fleming of the RCMP. Might I have a word with you, sir?"

I had been preparing myself for it, not to hesitate, nor let my voice betray. "Of course, Inspector. I'm just out of the bath, so give me a minute or two, and come right up."

A slight but noticeable bulge. I transferred the wallet to my hip pocket, and now the wad of notes did not show. Best to

179

hide them, best to carry them? Panicky, stop it. What else? Keep Diana away. I got an outside line and dialed Jenny's apartment. "Is Miss Arden there?"

". . . Yes, Sir Dougal?"

"Oh, Miss Arden, I quite forgot to mention it, but could you pick up a small present for Mrs. Merriwell, in Danish silver, perhaps, say fifty dollars?"

"Why certainly, Sir Dougal." Calling her Miss Arden on an outside line. She would guess that there was something.

If they suspected us, my line would be bugged, or would it? How do bugs work? How do you know you're being bugged? Well, you don't. I had done a few things in Canada, and still was clueless, the *outsized lamb* that Tarquie had mentioned.

I left the outer door ajar, the inner one open. A knock. "Come in." He was a moderately long-haired plainclothes inspector, a with-it policeman, carrying a briefcase, too good a cop to let his eye seem to wander. That was one thing I had learned, watching people, and people-watching. He produced his green card in a cellophane case, but I waved that away. "Do have a seat, Inspector."

He opened his briefcase and came to the point, if it was the point. "I showed these photographs and others to Mrs. Farrow, and to Luigi the gardener too. I think only the three of you caught more than a momentary glimpse."

They were full-length photographs of two men, a little fuzzy, clear enough. The men were not looking at the camera, but straight ahead, amid blurred people on city sidewalks, spy pictures blown up was what they were. One was of Brother Henry, the other of my boxing adversary whose brotherly name I did not know. "Do these remind you of anyone?"

"You mean the men at the helicopter?"

"Yes."

"The lean jaw of the smaller one, it could be him. And the big fellow's shape looks right." I shrugged. "But they were masked over eyes and nose, I really don't know, Inspector. I might guess that they were the same men."

"Luigi said just that. Mrs. Farrow seemed surer." The inspector smiled faintly.

"Do you know who they are?"

"We know who they are, but not by name, or not by any names that stick. They are members of a small brotherhood of anarchists who rather incongruously call themselves the Dagoes." He put the photographs away, frowning. "This job wasn't quite their usual form. When they need money, they take a bank, much more efficient, a hostage, any appealing hostage, a child, a pretty girl. No one argues with that, or if they do . . ." He left it unfinished, closed his briefcase. "But the shooting was true Dago style. I gather you had a near shave. Or did the redoubtable Mrs. Farrow exaggerate?"

"No. The bullets crackled, blew the place apart. I expect you know the feeling."

Inspector Fleming smiled. "Once or twice."

"How is the redoubtable Mrs. Farrow? I hear she sprained her back, or we sprained it together."

"The lady's back improves, but the tongue is a bit vituperative. Why the bloody hell hadn't we done our job and shot all those gangsters long ago? I tried to explain that the robbery was a provincial police matter, and none of our business until they crossed the U.S. border. *Poppycock!* was all I got for my pains." He laughed again, an urbane policeman who slightly kept me guessing. "Mrs. Farrow has but one hero, Sir Dougal Trocher." He looked at me: "And well she might," he said, adding without the least pause: "Your secretary got back from London?"

"Yesterday, Inspector. They called her for emergency flight duty on Saturday evening. But you heard that?"

"Yes," he said. "I heard that." He was watching me.

"Perhaps just as well. Like Mildred Farrow, Diana Arden is a mettlesome girl. She might have joined us, and three would have stretched the luck too far."

"Thank you, then," said the amiable inspector. "I must go. Mr. Farrow told me that you and Miss Arden leave for Maine tomorrow, so I wanted to catch you."

"What about these Dagoes? Any arrests?"

"Vanished," he said. "They have hide-outs all over the place. One in the Laurentians, we think. Some day at some cost, we shall get them."

"Won't you have a drink?"

He declined that politely, and took his leave. But I wondered. To this day I wonder whether my risk of life, grappling Mildred Farrow into safety did not cause a most astute policeman to dismiss certain thoughts about certain small matters of coincidence.

My Cousin Claud varied a good deal, sometimes quite human, sometimes transparently self-satisfied. One felt that two or three men lived at odds in Claud. And yet, to have achieved what he had by the age of forty-five, there must be some constant upon which his people could lean. I never saw him at work, so I never saw it. The one constant that I observed was in his clothes, invariably the band-box, whether wearing charcoal gray Bermuda shorts and yellow stockings on the golf course, or a gold-buttoned waistcoat with the watch chain.

But he was subdued on that last evening, and worried about his wife, who smoked and coughed and smoked, out of breath after walking to the dining room. She was much pleased with my silver bracelet, Diana's choice at seventy dollars.

"You must come and stay in Scotland next summer, Laura."

"I would love that," and she coughed, and lit another.

"She should be down at the sea now," Claud told me after dinner. "Not allowed to travel. Tried to stop smoking a dozen times. Can't do it."

It was a stilted affair, saved by Diana, who told Australian stories, and Laura laughed and coughed again.

Claud was to drive the BMW home. He seemed embarrassed by my thanks, and was apologetic that he had to fly to New York tomorrow, but Grenier would be here to take us to the airport. "Who are you staying with in Maine?"

"A chap called Harry Gilpin, friend of friends of mine at home."

"Good Lord, you mean Gilpin, the copper man?"

"I believe so. Do you know him, Claud?"

"I know of him. Harry Z. Gilpin tops the top league."

So it was good-bye at last. "I've never been so tired," Diana said. "But I can't stop thinking a hundred jumbled things, poor Laura, so painful to see her, isn't it? And that queer, gentle, deadly Loris, and you jumping from the tree, and what might have been. I feel one gigantic wobble."

"I don't think I'll ever get to sleep tonight."

"Let's both take a pill. I have some for after flying."

It was another first for me, a sleeping pill. "Darling Dougal, now good night. Try to forget about it."

But the pill took a long time to quiet my horrors of that day, not the horror of events, but the horrors planned by those *untermenschen*, submen, monsters. I slept alone.

We dropped off height above the woods of Maine. "About five minutes," said the captain by intercom. "Do up your belts, please."

The Jet Galaxy was most comfortable, six seats, a small sofa, a writing desk, two abstract paintings, Bukharás on the floor, yet a certain austerity. Aft of this cabin was a sleeping compartment with two berths. One might call it the top of the top league in executive jets.

"I tried to fix Kurt," Diana said. "I wrote on a plain bit of paper: *Ask Kurt what he planned with Joe and Dug,* and I addressed the envelope to M. Loris, 101 rue de la Baleine, Outremont, and I mailed it from the hotel. But probably it won't reach him."

We swung over the coast and a sparkling sea, came in to land and taxied to a hangar where four people waited. There was a blue helicopter, the same shape as the one at Camelot.

A spare man came to meet us, a gray-haired oldish man. He wore a patched tweed jacket and gray trousers. His face was acquiline, with a touch of Aztec about the cheekbones. "I'm Harry Gilpin," he said. "How delightful to see you."

⚘ **23** ⚘

ONE MIGHT HAVE EXPECTED that for guests of Harry Z. Gilpin, customs and immigration would be something of a formality, but not so. The one officer carefully compared faces with photographs, and checked our visas before putting on his stamp. The other dipped into every suitcase.

"You don't see many like these," he said about Grandfather's ancient cowhide. "Not too good for economy transatlantic. Okay by Mr. Gilpin's jet, I guess." He was casual, too casual? "A jazzy kilt and a dark job — I thought you folks just had the one plaid to your name."

"That's the dress tartan, and this is the Hunting Trocher."

"Too darned cold for hunting in the fall in Maine," he said, and went on searching. "My mother was a MacGregor from some place Aberfeldy. You heard of it?"

Nervousness about what was in my unsearched pocket made me lapse into the alien corn: "I know it well, a braw wee toon on the River Tay. You should go there sometime."

"Maybe I will. Mum'll be tickled pink you called it a braw wee toon. Have yourselves a good vacation." It was a clipped, lackadaisical drawl, a new American voice to me.

So then I had my first helicopter ride, a short hop to Harry Gilpin's island. A first marvelous mistress, a first robbery, a first disgustingness (extraordinary to be thirty-four, and never to have encountered that, sheltered poop), a first knifing (good

184

clean fun), a first cool dangerous cop, a first sleeping pill, and now a first helicopter, afraid of it.

We came over Camber Island. It was a mile by a half or so, mostly wooded above cliffs, one inlet with a sandy beach, a wharf, two boats. There was a long, low house, facing south, a pond below that, other buildings.

It was another new place to me, a countrified place, not loaded with people. *The world isn't only people, Tirene. — But it is. That's the terrible truth you funny old rustics are hiding from.* Darling Tirene, where are you now? You couldn't care less where I am. But you might be surprised to know that I hover above an island with two hundred and sixty-three thousand dollars in the pocket. I smiled to my gloomy self about that, and met the gaze of Harry Gilpin. The calm gray eyes were infinitely shrewd and rather small.

We landed near the biggest of the houses. It was not a top of the top league, new world country mansion like Camelot, but a clapboard house of modest size, painted white with the faintest touch of pink.

Waiting for us were a woman and a child. She wore a pale yellow pantsuit, embracing the hips, and our expiring rotor wind delineated that of which Lois had said: *It is a lovely bosom, don't you think so, darling. — Used to be pretty decent. Don't know about lately.* And to me in private he had remarked: *Gilpin's wife is a proper humdinger of a little peach.*

He was a sturdy small boy in swimming trunks, barefooted, summer brown, high-cheekboned, Harry Gilpin's son. And how-d'you-dos yet once again. I had met more new people in North America than I would meet in a year at home, and perhaps these would be nearly the last new people. All my life it had been a strain to me. That poem of Emerson's, *Brahma,* couldn't remember it. I had the *cafard* or the *weltschmerz.*

"You remind me of a younger Tarquie," she said, shaking hands. On her wedding finger was a square-cut ruby, diameter about that of a quarter, five new pence, probably worth more than I had just carried through the customs. Bloody money, riches, ostentation.

"Hullo," I said to the boy. Meeting children was always easy.

"You're Scotch," he said to me.

"Scottish, dear," his mother said.

"It says Scotch on the bottle, Mummy."

"Yes, I'm Scotch," I said. Even pedants like me say I'm Scotch, not Scottish.

So that was all right. I felt a bit better. Harry Gilpin led me aside. "The guest cottage has an office, which would be convenient, so I have tentatively put you and Miss Arden there, but if you would rather . . ." He glanced at me, tactful, solicitous host.

I very much wanted to be with my friend, my anchor, more than ever my friend and anchor. "That would be fine, Mr. Gilpin. I do have quite a few letters to write and answer."

"I don't wonder, after your intrepid act, duly reported in the *New York Times*. Come now, young Harry and I will show you. The jeep will bring your things along. Back in a trice, Gloria darling."

Gilpin walked with Diana, and I with young Harry.

"You know Maine, Miss Arden?"

"My very first time, Mr. Gilpin. It's such lovely clean air after the city, and so quiet, just the lull of the sea, poetical me, sorry."

He chuckled. How lightly and easily Diana won people. How lightly and easily Diana had killed a man yesterday. "Sorry, Harry, I didn't hear?"

"I was saying your face is all scratches. Did you get them from the bad men?"

"No, Harry. I fell into a prickly bramble bush, you know — blackberries. I was watching a very special bird called a Baltimore Oriole and it kept moving, and I kept moving and bumped into the brambles, pretty stupid."

A pause in the conversation ahead. Mr. Gilpin's ears had been cocked to that. As Diana foresaw, my scratches could not be camouflaged today. *He escaped with minor abrasions.* So he had. But he could not escape his recollections.

186

"Here we are," said Harry Gilpin. "In this case, cottage is only slightly a misnomer, but *summer cottage* can be anything up to Scottish Baronial, as no doubt you know."

There were a bedroom and a bathroom at each end, a living room, modern furniture and paintings, a kitchenette, an office with an I.B.M. typewriter, Dictaphone, photostat machine.

"Note the letter on the living room table. Drinks and luncheon await you at the house when you're ready."

"Come soon," young Harry said to me. He had a certain gravitas at the age of five or six.

The letter was from Lois.

Dearest Dougal,

I hope the garden competition has been a huge success, and your lectures too, and that you're having a lovely holiday with Harry and the twin-set.

The weather has been ghastly, cold and wet just when we need sunshine for the crops, and you know what that does to Tarquie. Worse for him than weather though is that we've had not one word from Tirene. When he telephoned those publisher people yesterday, he got a very snooty reception from some editor who said that Miss Duncatto's employment had been terminated, and they had no address for her. We were never accorded one either, part of the mystery or mystique, but she used to telephone every week. So we're a dim old bothered couple at the moment. *This bloody world*, he said last night. *What has it done to our happy child?*

I dropped in to see Ida yesterday. She was rather subdued, not at all her battle-axe self, wearying on getting you back, and she had had a dream of Dougal in mortal danger in some forest.

What a tale of woe. Garry and Bernardo must have eaten something very dead, because they were frightfully sick and we were terrified it might be poison, but all right again, lying beside me now. When I said, "I'm writing to Dougal," Bernardo sat up and howled the most doleful dirge, quite touching really.

Last thing is that HZG telephoned again (he uses transatlantic like a half-hour gossip on the local) to say they did so much hope you could manage it, and he would help you in any small way within his power. I don't know how, but I have a feeling. That man is positively psychic, very inquisitive and totally discreet, unlike his garrulous cutie. Better burn this.

Best Love,
Lois

P.S. A fine day at last, just going out with dogs.

The letter was postmarked last Saturday the 22nd, before Camelot. So she had lost her job, unhappy, defenseless — Tirene vanished. Tirene could not kill people with bare hands, but the one who could came from her bedroom, and put one of those hands on my shoulder. "I hope it isn't bad news, Dougal."

"Just troublesome, not bad." And then and there I almost told her, could not tell her, and we went to lunch.

Gloria Gilpin, for whom Lois evidently had it in, was not so bad, Harry Gilpin's treasure by Jacques Fath and Cartier, very feminine with the big strong men.

"It's such a thrill to meet you, and more than ever after reading about that heroic deed." There we went again, the adjectival hero. "Was that how you got those terrible scratches, but I think they suit you?" She gazed at me with limpid orbs.

"No, Mrs. Gilpin, I did that later."

"Could you please tell me what happened with the bad men?"

Gilpin replenished my Campari. "Well, you see, Harry, we were all up in the garden when suddenly these robbers swooped down in this helicopter, and there stood two men with Tommy guns, and I was pretty frightened, but this Mrs. Farrow, she was the lady who owned the garden, and a pretty huge terrible lady but the bravest of the brave, she said: *Come on, Trocher, follow me!* Well, perhaps I was more frightened of Mrs. Farrow than of the Tommy guns so I had to follow her to reach the house and get guns so we could shoot those robbers, but the men saw us and bullets cracked all round our heads, and the next thing I got Mrs. Farrow on the ground in a huge huddle. That was what happened, Harry, and then the helicopter flew away, thank goodness."

188

"Gosh! But how can a pretty huge terrible lady be the bravest of the brave?"

"Sometimes they come like that, Harry."

"So modest," said Gloria Gilpin. "Just like Tarquie. I think all Scottish lairds must be Sir Galahads, but he's a Lord and you're Sir Dougal. May I call you Dougal?"

"Please do," I said.

"And Sir Galahad shall call you Lady Gloria," said Harry Gilpin. Which remark made Diana giggle like a schoolgirl.

"Ah, poo, sarcastic beast." They doted.

We had cold lobster for lunch, and raspberries and cream. "Simple fare," he said. "We do live simply here for these few weeks away from the frenetic bustle." It was difficult to imagine this calm man ever living in frenetic bustle. Copper king, one-time ambassador to Chile, art collector and connoisseur of world authority, philanthropist and so on — Lois said that at seventy Harry Gilpin was more than ever master of his business empire, now diversified to include everything from the original copper to plastics, rocketry, computers, lasers. *You name the up and coming pie,* she said, *and Harry has a finger in it.*

Money, money, I thought again, that loathsome necessity. Yet stolen money for the sake of Drin was less loathsome than money for the sake of money, phony excuses for myself.

Diana and Super-goon, as she might describe him, were having lively conversation; Dutch art, the resurgence of Japan, troubled youth, for whom he evinced more sympathy than she did. In Canada, except privately with me, she had been ever the secretary, intelligently acquiescent. But now she argued on equal terms, and to Gilpin's evident pleasure.

Gloria spoke of Scotland's wonders, and young Harry asked me about home, what it was like, and did we swim? "Not much," I said. "The water is too cold."

"Ours isn't cold. Will you have a swim with me?"

"I would love to, Harry." He was a thoughtful, small boy, and seemed unspoiled.

"Later," she said. "After we've all had a little snooze. Even

189

you perhaps, Dougal. I'm sure you never snooze at home, but you must be so terribly tired after everything."

"I am, Gloria. Yes, I am." I did not remember being tired like this, a load of weariness, despondency.

"So now our siesta," Gilpin said. "Then the swim. And perhaps a stroll along the island before drinktime?"

"I would like that, if you're sure you're not too busy."

"I'm not busy in the least. Two hours on the telephone each early morning, a glance at business papers, and the rest of my day in idleness. Until later, then."

Back at the cottage Diana said: "What a lovely wicked old man. Super-goon, I just adore him."

"I guessed you right for once, Diana. *Super-goon,* I guessed."

"You guess me right quite often, Dougal. Lord, I'm sleepy."

I went to bed to escape to sleep, but I could not. No escape from what one did, from what was done to one, from what was done by two, from what was done by three. But it was never done. It was the intended horror. "For Christ's sake stop it," I said aloud.

But now I did escape. Now sleep was coming. *The only love I know is making love, shameless lovely love . . .* Shameful loathsome copulation thrashing.

"Dear God," I said. "No, Diana. Go away!"

"You screamed. What is it, Dougal? You must tell me."

"No."

"Is it the stealing?"

"No."

"Is it me, then, killing him?"

"Of course not."

"Then I know. It's what you heard them say they'd do."

"Yes, Diana. Please go away."

"And leave you with it always, leave it with you horrible. Dougal, you must forget, and I must make you."

It was a slow goodness, a slow kindness, passion growing, passion grown, and passion gone. She smiled. She always

190

smiled in loving, but this time differently. "Now forgotten?"

"Yes," I said, and it was almost true. "Diana, thank you."

"Someone else might thank me, if she ever knew. But she won't know."

ж **24** ж

HARRY GILPIN CALLED HIS swimming pool The Pond, and in appearance, in partial fact, it was a natural pond. The springs that fed it were natural; the sandstone ledge that sloped smoothly from ground level to seven feet at the deeper end was nature's fluke laid bare by bulldozer. But the walls were concrete, sandstone colored; the by-pass pipe for flood was buried; the filter worked in the woods, unseen.

"Do you own the whole island?"

"With the exception of the Camber family's house and a bit of land. They are fishing folk, and young Tom Camber manages the place, a proper sea dog, you must meet him."

The approach to the sheltered pond was pleasing too. A grass lane swung down from the house, on the lower side a dropwall to shrubs, curving round. "Did you do all this yourself?"

"Well, yes," he said, "the planning aspect. I took it gradually, with doubts and delays and second thoughts, really only working down from what the good Lord had provided. It's a small hobby of mine." Mr. Loris had said to Diana yesterday: *It is my small hobby.*

I had thought that Gilpin might welcome a little landscaping advice, but he needed none from me. "It's good," I said. "It's simple."

"Thank you, Dougal."

Those words, *simple, simplicity,* I know that they are

contradictions in long-winded, prosy me; just as perhaps a certain austerity in his landscaping, in the furnishings of his airplane, were paradoxical in a man who clearly loved to see his pretty wife dressed for the plage and wearing outsized rubies at lunchtime on a rustic island.

Diana and I threw a ball about with Harry, while his parents watched. She swam like an Australian, and young Harry very well for his age, and I floundered in pellucid water. Later, I went walking with Harry Gilpin while Diana typed a dozen thank-you letters.

"A remarkable girl," Gilpin said. "So vital, so entertaining, so intelligent. She tells me that her normal job is as a stewardess with Global Airlines, a waste of talent, I would have thought. Have you known her long?"

"Three weeks and a bit, since the day I flew over."

We were following a path along the island. The woods were much like those yesterday. *Yesterday.* It was unbelievable.

". . . Sorry, sir, I didn't hear."

"I said, I hope your visit has been a success."

"Thanks to Diana, yes, it has."

"A pearl without price." But he switched the subject as smoothly and quickly as that policeman: "Are you far from Duncatto? In a somewhat turbulent winter there, I don't think I ever visited Drin."

"We're five miles apart on the map, a world apart otherwise."

"Oh?"

"Duncatto is thirty thousand self-sufficient acres, admirably run by Tarquie. Drin is fourteen thousand down-at-heel, mismanaged by me."

"Surely you depreciate yourself, having only just inherited. And Tarquie told me once that your grandfather, a man whom he held in high esteem, was not the best of businessmen."

"To put it mildly, nor am I."

"We cannot be everything," Gilpin said. "Indeed, I sometimes wish that I did not have this flair for making money. Money! No doubt you will raise an eyebrow when I say that

193

making money is not the object; making things work is the fun for me. Wouldn't it be better for young Harry that he should know want? It bothers me. But what can I do?"

"He's a grand wee boy," I said. "Don't worry."

"*A grand wee boy*, that is music to hear. But an old father must worry. Indeed, any parent must worry in this troubled age. Lois says that she and Tarquie are so anxious at present about Tirene, not only because they have had no news of her for a month, but that lately at home she is so fractious and unhappy. I suppose you have known dear Tirene all her life?"

"Yes. We were great friends when she was young. But . . ."

"But?"

"Too many buts," I said, and he asked no more.

There was a rustic seat at the end of the island. An osprey was hovering offshore. I watched through my binoculars, hoping to see it dive for a fish. That could be another first for me, but the osprey stopped hovering and flew away, and I said: "The last time I saw Tirene, she called me a male chauvinist and a reactionary dodo before lunch, and a stuffy old seven-letter prig when I saw her off that evening at the railway station."

Harry Gilpin laughed. "I wouldn't say that you merited those descriptions. Or is it possible that North America and your secretary have served to round off the corners of the square?"

"It is possible," I said, and we sat companionably, and I wondered. Dare I broach the subject? *I'm sure he knows there's something*, Diana had said. *Let him bring it up.*

"Lois mentioned that you might have some small problem about transferring funds. May I be of assistance, Dougal?"

For reasons best known to himself this potent man was offering help. Either he should know nothing, or he must know it all, so tell him. "I do happen to have quite a large sum on me." I showed him the wad of bills, held by an elastic band.

"All thousands?"

"Yes, sir, all thousands."

"May I venture to ask how much?"

"Two hundred and sixty-three thousand dollars."

"H'mm," he said. "Not too bad for a reactionary dodo. All genuine bills?"

"We think so."

"Never in my misspent life have I seen such a roll. May I ask how you rolled it?"

So I told Harry Gilpin my shameful story. ". . . That's all, except that an RCMP inspector came to the hotel to show me photographs of the two Dagoes, whom I failed to identify. Then, with a quick, casual change of subject he asked me about Diana's return from London, so quick and so casual that it did just make me wonder. But there isn't, there can't be a particle of evidence. And Diana says that nobody at the airline except the personnel manager himself knows the truth about her emergency summons, and he is completely safe."

"That leaves only the Loris connection. Now, the bodyguard would have returned to the lake to find one dead man and one wounded man, and to do some very rapid thinking. My guess is that in order to avoid incriminating himself with Loris, of whom you say they were all terrified, he would consign two bodies, not one, to the depths of the lake. In that way, their disappearance would seem to be a vamoose with Diana's dollars."

"Exactly what we thought."

"As to the mysterious Mr. Loris, Diana's anonymous letter may not reach him, but I fancy that little questions will pose themselves in his mind about Kurt. A vile conspiracy to rape and murder, what unspeakable monsters the human race spews out. I don't wonder you bore a haunted look on arrival. The might-have-been is such a living horror. But you seem more cheerful this afternoon."

"Thanks to Diana."

"Ah, yes," he said. "Now, since the robber baronet has

confided his infamy to me, perhaps I may ask him a personal question — your relations with Diana are, how shall I put it, not entirely secretarial?"

"Correct, sir. Passionate, friendly, not in the least romantic. You see, Mr. Gilpin, it happened that before I met Diana, I was almost totally inexperienced in such matters. And so during these weeks I have had a liberal education not only in the realms of crime."

"And with what a schoolmistress, lucky fellow. Such women may be unusual, but less so than one might think. You know, Dougal, the Duncattos gave me to feel that you were a shy and diffident fellow, sheltered from the ways of this wicked world. But it would seem to me that you have made a rake's progress."

"Thanks to Diana. Everything thanks to Diana. I still don't understand why she did all this, took all those risks."

"She likes you. And I imagine that the benefits have not been utterly one-sided. You have most candidly confided in this old scoundrel. Permit one more question: Do you share Diana's philosophy, belief, disbelief about romantic love?"

"No, Mr. Gilpin, I do not."

"I see," he said. "I see."

The wind had changed. There was a light onshore breeze, and low on the horizon a white rim of cloud. "The fog is coming," he said. "But good weather fog. It will burn off early.

"As I see it, Dougal, you want two things. First, to have this money edged back into circulation. If the bills are forgeries, you can put them in the fire, rotten luck. But if they are genuine, it is easy enough. The second thing may require some legal expertise. You want your ill-gotten gains to be wafted across the Atlantic in such a manner that to the British authorities they will seem to be a legitimate inheritance."

"That would be perfect, but . . ."

"The perfect ending to the perfect crime. But what?"

"But I don't want to involve you in the smallest risk."

"There is no risk. It is not a crime of any kind to speculate

196

in the comparative values of U.S. and Canadian dollars. My people deal daily in far larger sums, not cashwise, of course, but that doesn't matter. The second aspect, the transfer of funds to the United Kingdom, does require some legerdemain, but I shall not be remotely involved. Shall we proceed, then?"

Why so little surprise? Why the willingness to help? "If you're sure," I said.

"My toy," he said, taking a miniature transceiver from his pocket. "Carpenter!"

"Yes, Mr. Gilpin?"

"Get on to Lindsell and Cowan, would you please? Arrange for the Galaxy to pick up Lindsell tomorrow morning at ten, and fly him back to New York by one-thirty. Ask him to bring a Canadian thousand-dollar bill. Then Cowan is to be fetched from La Guardia at two o'clock, returning later. And please see that they are not informed of each other's visit, a word to the pilots about that."

"Very well, Mr. Gilpin."

He put the walkie-talkie away. "Carpenter is my invaluable secretary, and his wife helps to look after young Harry, a handy arrangement. Cowan is a lawyer of some imaginative competence. Lindsell deals with money matters."

"I'm most grateful, Mr. Gilpin, and I have no right to ask about all this, but . . ."

"Your face bears honest puzzlement," he said. "A more upright crook I never did encounter. Let me explain a little: In the first instance, I rather wondered why Lois and Tarquie should both give me to think that I might be of service to you beyond the great pleasure of playing host. Next, I telephoned to find you ensconced in a suite at an excellent hotel, with a vibrant-voiced secretary on duty at seven A.M. Incidentally, no word about the secretary has passed my lips. Next, it happens that I have some interests in Scotland, and so I asked our man there to make quiet inquiries about Drin, as a prospective purchaser himself, and he saw your lawyer, who said that you were away, that he had no instructions to negotiate a sale, but certainly authority to show him round. So the report came back of some decrepitude. That was skullduggery on my part, Dougal, sorry. All these things led me to a hunch that just possibly two and two added up to rather more than four, and when the jewel robbery occurred, I thought: *You foxy old rascal, Gilpin, you were right.*

"An outrageous deed one cannot but admire. Tell me, Dougal, will your share be enough to rescue Drin?"

"Just enough, I think. Diana flatly declines to take more than ten per cent, plus wages at a dollar an hour, plus overtime. It's very bothersome."

Harry Gilpin shook with mirth. But he turned to me, serious again. "Don't you think that, if based on Montreal, she may be in some danger?"

"I said that to her, and she told me not to be absurd, one chance in a million of being seen by them."

"H'mm," he said, and stood. "By the way, Dougal, I have not mentioned my suspicions to Gloria. Be Sir Galahad, my boy."

"Right, sir."

"I hardly presume to mention it, but my wife does have jewelry of some value. May I suggest that it be off limits to your gang."

"Lois made me promise that before I left."

"Ah, Lois, what a woman. What a transplanted jewel from my native land. Tell me, Dougal, do you suffer pangs of regret at having strayed from the paths of virtue?"

"None about the theft. I had to jump that bridge at the beginning and nobody suffered. The bloody ending is another matter, not that I regret what we did to those creatures. But it made a decent job dirty, if you see what I mean."

"I see much better what you mean than I see what Tirene meant when she called you a stuffy old seven-letter prig."

"I was, and I will be again, if I ever see her."

"Physician, heal thyself," he said obscurely. "As to tomorrow, Dougal, I suggest that you ask Diana what she wants done with her share. That agreed upon, and provided you hold my credit rating to be adequate, I propose to hand the money to Lindsell myself. He will not know of your presence here.

"But in the afternoon, you should deal alone with Cowan after I have had a word or two to pave the way. In the meanwhile, think of a relative who emigrated to the United States at about the turn of the century. And if there wasn't one, invent one. But don't tell me anything about it. You may even stretch the truth a little — and I know how painfully difficult that will be for you — by hinting to Cowan that your fictional inheritance serves to cloak another munificent gift to the underdog, or in this case, the trusty but penurious laird, by that bashful, self-effacing philanthropist, Harry Zanzibar Gilpin. Good for Drin, good for my Cowan image, still more important, a beautiful loophole of confusion should questions ever be asked."

"I can't thank you enough. But may I ask one more favor?"

"Please."

"It's only that I would like to give Diana a present, but she won't wear any jewelry, stones, I mean. She has one or two plain, modern brooches, metal, not even all silver, I think. I wondered about a brooch in gold or platinum."

"That's easy. Carpenter!"

"Yes, Mr. Gilpin?"

"Would you get on to Lindsell again, and ask him to pick up half a dozen plain, modern, dashing pins in gold or platinum, without any precious stones (without, I say), from Cartier. One or two could be by the designer, Paul Morin. Quite clear?"

"Quite clear, Mr. Gilpin."

Now a cabin cruiser swung, moving very fast, at thirty or forty knots, to run quite close along the north shore of the island. There were two men in the wheelhouse, one astern. A radar antenna was spinning slowly. It looked more like an MTB than a pleasure craft, for a moment a qualm; then I remembered. "That's a hot boat," I said. "It looks like the one I saw tied at your wharf."

"It is," he said. "Captain Tom Camber patrols his island."

ⅺ 25 ⅺ

THE FOG WAS not thick. We would call it a mist or a haar in
Scotland. How peaceful it was, how intimate the world in fog,
and Diana lay asleep.

I went to make us a cup of tea. "Angel man," she said.

"Have you decided about the money?"

"I think I'd better take it to New York. Donna Andrews has
an account with the Chase Manhattan. So if you keep back
twenty-seven, that will more than cover my ten per cent plus
wages and overtime, and we can balance it up before I leave."

"So tomorrow?"

"Tomorrow, New York; Montreal, Saturday; back to work
Monday, my month's leave over."

As swiftly as Diana moved from slumber to full wakefulness,
she moved from business mood to mood of pleasure. But there
the swiftness ceased, and slow delight began, and grew, and
faster grew. Soon we listened to the rhythm of breakers at the
shore. "Every time now we are one wave breaking. Thank
you, Dougal."

"Thank you, Diana."

"It's been the loveliest, wackiest month to remember
always, and good-bye, no soppy regrets."

The fog burned off as Harry Gilpin had foreseen. I gave him
the two hundred and thirty-five bills remaining after Diana's
share, and one in reserve for the brooch. "You might just drop
over to the office after Lindsell leaves," he said.

Diana went swimming with young Harry, and I wrote letters to the Farrows and Merriwells, my chief Canadian benefactors. The helicopter came, and went quite soon, and I walked over. I met Mr. Carpenter the Secretary, a studious type, and then went in to Gilpin's office.

"That's all arranged. And Lindsell is virtually sure your bills are genuine. Now, here is the parcel from Cartier."

I opened the six small boxes. They were all bold, modern designs, but one took my eye, a flowing ellipse of platinum, a lovely curve, and it was the most expensive, eight hundred and sixty dollars. "This one, I think, don't you?"

"Yes, much the best. One has to pay for a Morin design, and rightly too. He will be ranked with Fabergé."

"I kept one bill back. Would it be possible to settle up with that?"

"Certainly, and I can pay them. Would you come in, Carpenter?"

"Yes, Mr. Gilpin?"

". . . You might find out the buying rate for Canadian dollars, and then give the requisite change to Sir Dougal."

He was back in a minute. "It's at a premium of one and one-eighth, Sir Dougal. That makes your one thousand Canadian worth one thousand and eleven twenty-five American. Deduct eight hundred and sixty. Herewith one hundred and fifty-one twenty-five in U.S. funds. We have no Canadian, sir, I'm sorry."

"American is simply fine, Mr. Carpenter, thank you."

"Cowan can take the others back this afternoon, and you might as well send a check along too."

"Very well, Mr. Gilpin."

"You people work so fast, you make my head reel."

"That is Carpenter. He has every quality, ability, but one: He cannot stand alone. And yet that makes him all the more valuable." Harry Gilpin, user of people, it was another side.

"So Diana leaves tomorrow."

"It's very good of you to fly her to New York."

"Not at all. The plane brings up my correspondence and so

on, and goes back daily. But you are such good friends. Won't it be something of a wrench to you both?"

"She said this morning: *It's been the loveliest, wackiest month to remember always.* I feel the same, and as mystified as ever. I don't think that she has once thought of herself."

"A mutual blessing, I would say. Now, about your own plans, Dougal, I need hardly tell you that the longer you stay, the better for us, and for young Harry too, especially for him."

"I hope he will come to Drin later on."

"He mentioned that in his prayers last night. *And please God let me go and see Dougal in his kilt in Scotland.* Which brings me to ask a small favor of you, one might just possibly call it a reciprocal favor."

"One might, indeed."

"Will you don your finery tonight for the Camber Island Gala Dinner? As Gloria intimated soon after your arrival, she has a penchant for lairds, Sir Galahads one and all. So do please give her a thrill."

"Well, okay," I said.

"But in the matter of your plans, do I detect a certain restiveness? Does home beckon?"

"Yes, more and more." And where was Tirene, damn her?

"The harvest of wickedness reaped, the good task to be undertaken. I can very well understand that you are hotching to start work. Besides, a journey in mind is a journey begun. What I suggest, then, is that we fly you across tomorrow night direct to that air force station near Crummock, if permission can be obtained."

"But I have a return ticket with Global Airlines."

"My dear fellow, ask your gifted secretary to arrange for a refund. The Jet Galaxy has transatlantic capability and to spare, although with a full load of fuel we have to use the long runways at Bangor International. You helicopter to there. You are deposited ten miles from home, thus avoiding the long drive across Scotland. In fact, it would be a service to us, Dougal. The pilots have not been getting enough transatlantic work lately, and they like it, need it. Is that settled, then?

"Carpenter, please see if you can get through to Lord or Lady Duncatto."

"Very well, Mr. Gilpin."

"Half an hour from here to Bangor. Five and a half or a little more for the crossing. Shall we aim to have you at Crummock by about ten on Saturday morning?"

"That would be fine, sir."

"They're just calling back, Mr. Gilpin."

"Duncatto here." I heard that, terse and resonant, from ten feet away, and Gilpin winced.

"Ah, Tarquie, this is Harry Gilpin, a good day to you. I have a friend of yours with me, and a very welcome guest he is."

"Hullo, Tarquie, Dougal speaking."

"Oh, hullo, you all right?"

"I'm fine, Tarquie. Could you speak more quietly?"

"Ocean between us, got to make myself heard. Is that better?"

"Much better, positively dulcet."

"How did you get on, a successful holiday?"

"A bonanza holiday, thank you, Tarquie."

"We read about Trocher to the rescue. None the worse?"

"None the worse. How are things at home?"

"Things at home are bloody awful. Gouts of rain and gales of wind for weeks, and I had to go to London."

He hated leaving his bailiwick. "On business, I suppose."

"Searching vainly for m'daughter, if that's business. I went to the publishers, saw Radclyffe himself, the sort of smooth type I can't abide. Well, we knew she'd been sacked, but I asked why, and it was about that manuscript she was reading here. She took it to him, slammed it on his desk and said: *If you publish this perverted tripe, you're no better than a mercenary pederast yourself.* He gave me chapter and verse, smoothness gone, eyes poppin' with indignation. So I lost my temper and told him that the bogus bugger had sponged lunch off me, and I agreed with Tirene hook, line and sinker, and I said a few more things about pornography in the sacred cloak of art, and left. Then I traced down the flat which she and some other female shared, but they had no new address, so I came home, none the wiser. If we don't hear anything by the weekend, I'll go to the police. The girl may be havin' a gigantic trip on LSD or worse, I wouldn't put it past her."

"Surely not drugs, Tarquie. That wouldn't be like Tirene at all."

"What the hell do you know about it?" He was shouting again, and I had to hold the receiver away, and what the hell did I know about it, terrifying thought? "Sorry, Dougal, I'm a bit worried. Well, what's your news? Coming home?"

"On Saturday morning, ten A.M. in Mr. Gilpin's jet, if you can get permission for us to land at Crummock."

"I'll see to it, and we'll meet you."

"Many thanks, Tarquie. How is Lois?"

"In sound health but we're not speakin' at the moment because of London. She didn't like what I told her I said to that twerp. Bernardo's here with me. Want a word?"

"Hullo, Bernardo, big boy, how are you?"

I heard that small whine of love that children and dogs make, a sweeter sound there may not be.

"Well, that's about it. I'm glad it's been a wow, and I hope you bring a bit of sanity to this place. My respects to Harry, oh, and love to Gloria."

"And to Lois from here when you patch it up. Don't worry about Tirene. I'm sure she'll be all right."

A pause. "I wish I was. Well, good-bye."

I vacated Gilpin's chair. "Did you hear some of that?"

"Every word, Dougal, I could not but. Surely the absence of news from one's daughter of twenty-one is not so much out of the ordinary these days?"

"No. But lately Tirene has been so unhappy in herself."

"It is not in oneself alone that happiness may be." Those were almost the words that Ida Peebles had used.

"And there's another thing: Tarquie is not just the matter-of-fact Scotsman he seems. Sometimes he knows things he doesn't know."

"I remember that very well," Harry Gilpin said. "Let us

hope for a happy issue. And now an apéritif and luncheon. Cowan should be here by three."

". . . The only close relation of mine who emigrated to the United States was my great-grandfather's youngest brother, Neil Trocher. He ran off with the coachman's daughter, a charming girl, so the story has it.

"But such unions were, to say the least, frowned upon in those days, and so, in nineteen hundred and two, my great-great-grandfather paid their passages to America, and thereafter sent a small monthly remittance to San Francisco where Neil Trocher settled, not much of a man, not as much of a man as his wife was, they said."

Mr. Cowan smiled. "Go on, Sir Dougal."

"The checks were cashed until April nineteen hundred and six when the San Francisco earthquake happened. After that no word was ever heard of them. My great-grandfather had inherited by then. He noted in his diary in nineteen hundred and four: *The émigré writes with pride that he has spawned a daughter.* And in nineteen hundred and six he wrote: *The remittance man has vanished.* My great-grandfather was a mealy-minded prude. Grandfather loathed him."

"And there was no word of the daughter?"

"None."

"Then an authentic beginning, a disappearance. Now we must fabricate. We need a married name for the daughter, lately deceased, and we need a place of residence. The former you might care to provide, the latter may be easier for me."

We agreed upon my great aunt, Mrs. Marion B. Carlisle, widow, childless, of 1176 Alhama Road, Palo Alto, California.

"In due course you will receive a letter from Montague, Schreiber and Gerhardt, Attorneys-at-law, San Francisco, informing you of the bequest. I understand that the machinery of transfer will be arranged by Mr. Gilpin's office. What a wonderful man HZG is. His services to mankind are legion." Mr. Cowan's eyes glowed with admiration.

"I hear that he has done untold good, ever by stealth. You will send me your account of course, Mr. Cowan."

"A modest account for a modest service. Now good-bye, Sir Dougal, and God speed you home to that land of wonder."

The helicopter spun to life, and I walked back. It was a glorious afternoon, with a few white clouds sailing from the west, the sun stronger, the light harder than in that land of bloody wonder. I walked on my rubber soles and turned the corner to the guest cottage to hear from the verandah:

"It worries me so much, Mr. Gilpin. What do you advise?"

"My considered opinion, dear young lady, is that you should spill the beans — Oh, hullo, Dougal. I was just venturing to advise Diana in financial matters. Cut the cackle and come clean to our Internal Revenue sleuths is my guiding rule." At times he could be quite racy in his speech.

✵ 26 ✵

DOLLED UP TO GIVE Gloria Gilpin her thrill, a displaced
popinjay, I was summoned to zip Diana.

"It's a tricky one," she said. "It catches." But I zipped her
smoothly (another recently acquired skill), and I hooked her,
and I turned her round for a frontal look.

"That's a smashing rig," I said in the lingo she encouraged.
Smashing it was: black buckled shoes, Italian; pipestem
pantaloons, white linen; a high-necked blouse with sleeves,
blue silk, that loveliest blue which is a shade, a fade, from navy
— Diana concealed, delineated and untrammeled. "Lor love a
duck," I said, and went to get her present, but with
apprehension; she was so choosy. "Here," I said. "For you."

Diana took the Cartier box and opened it and looked, and
she was crying, twin rivulets of tears. "Hankie," she said in
her soft sobless voice, and I provided that, having a painful
thought: that *Good-bye and no soppy regrets*, true for me,
might not be true for dear Diana.

Tears over, she took the brooch from its velvet bed. "Paul
Morin too," and then she held it against her in the looking
glass. "Put it on me, Dougal."

"Where?"

"Hereabouts." She touched the blouse below her shoulder.
"Slanting, don't you think?"

"Yes, slanting up. Lovely needle speed, it says for me."

"I thought just that."

She did her face again. "Angel man," she said for the second time, and we walked across to attend the Camber Island Gala Dinner.

Harry Gilpin awaited us, ineffably distinguished in a plum smoking jacket. "Ah," he said. "What a sight for ancient eyes, the scarred chieftain victorious from battle, and proud Diana trousered from the treasure hunt. Diana, you are exquisite. May this gaffer kiss your hand?"

He did so, and Diana blushed. Harry Gilpin, Machiavellian diplomat, super-goon, had her measure, and she loved it.

"Now, what shall it be? Champagne cocktail, daiquiri, martini, or Negroni, bloody mary, even that quintessential elixir of the kola nut. Pray name your tipple."

We had Negronis, and young Harry arrived in his dressing gown. "It's funny," he said. "Diana's wearing pants tonight, and Dougal has a skirt on. That's sort of different."

"Just sort of, Harry," I said.

He inspected me. "What's this?"

"It's a thing called a skean d'hu, a hunting knife." I took it from my hose, and half drew the blade. "Don't touch. It's very sharp."

"Do you use it for people too?" he asked with that endearing gravity of manner.

"Not often, Harry." And there was a silence at twenty minutes to eight o'clock. Silence at twenty past, or at twenty to the hour, we used to call it the silence of an angel passing.

The angel passed, and Mrs. Carpenter came to fetch young Harry. He kissed his father and Diana, and shook hands with me. "Did you mean it about me coming hunting with you with your hunting knife, not for people? Did you mean that Dougal?"

"Yes, I meant it, Harry, not for people."

The son departed, and the mother came. She wore a short black evening dress of chiffon, opaquely tunicked here and there. The neckline dove below *la belle poitrine*, which it manifestly was, barely concealed, one might aver; and at the termination of her diamond necklace sparkled a colossal stone.

The women, so different, accorded one another similar sugar-icing glances, and Gloria turned to me. "I put on my best bib and tucker in your honor," she said, with a certain archness, and curtseyed with a certain grace, the diamond swaying out and home again. "You Highland laddies send a woman," she said frankly, and Diana turned away.

"Och, Gloria, you're bonny," I said, not to be outdone.

"I only wear it on the specialest occasions." She made reproachful moue. "My pride and joy, and you don't even notice."

Thus invited or commanded, I gave attention to her pride and joy. The sparkle of the diamond was not colorless, but distinctly washed with blue. It was pear-shaped, at least an inch and a half on the longer side, and the smaller stones that formed the necklace had the same hint of blue. "Gloria, it's fabulous." But I could do better than that. "As the star shines brightly in the velvet night, so does the great jewel coruscate in beauty's arbor."

"Oh, Dougal, you're a poet. No one else ever said it so divinely. As for Tarquie, he didn't utter a single word. He simply stared that time in London, hypnotized by my Koala until Lois asked him if he would know the Koala diamond next time they met. That Lois is plain jealous of it."

"Come, come, my love, I don't think you're being fair to Lois. Koalas or no Koalas, it is a wife's prerogative to ask her husband whether he will know a diamond next time."

"It's not a wife's prerogative to boss poor Tarquie's kilt off, which is what that Lois does."

Detecting no love lost, I said: "It must be one of the biggest stones alive, I mean extant."

"So it is, Dougal. Big Harry gave me my Koala as a thank offering for baby Harry."

"A most handsome quid pro quo. But why Koala? Isn't that a small, cuddlesome creature which feeds on eucalyptus?"

"Correct, Dougal, and a key to its rather improbable name. You see, this diamond, and the baguettes which were cut from it, was the first great stone discovered in Australia, acquired by a good friend of mine named Conrad Brock, later sold to one Max Vyan, somewhat turbulently deceased. After which it passed into my possession through the good offices of a bold, swashbuckling type called Harry Ambler."

Diana drew breath, a hiss of air sharply and involuntarily taken in, and I looked at her to see the color draining. I had often been charmed by the blush, so becoming, so surprising in her. I had never seen her go pale before. What causes one to blanch? Fear, dizziness, intense emotion.

But that silence of the second angel passed, and Diana was her cheerful self again, exchanging devious badinage with Harry Gilpin. Gloria was my task and portion. Her topics of conversation were Big Harry, whom she worshipped, and who waited on her hand and foot — young Harry, to whom she was a sensible, firm mother — clothes and adornment — people, that is, men. I did my manly best through dinner but, as I have before remarked, it is not much hardship to play the decent chap when one is warmly admired as such.

Dinner was the exception to Harry Gilpin's rule of plain fare at Camber Island. It began with lashions of caviar, continued likewise, and ended with Napoleon brandy.

We were back at the cottage by ten o'clock.

"She really is the end," Diana said. "Totally bone from the bosom up."

"I wouldn't be entirely sure. There may be even more to Gloria than meets the eye. She has Harry Gilpin buttoned."

"Which comes first," Diana said. "The chicken or the egg?" She went to the long mirror. "I love you," she said to the brooch. "I love you just as much as I loathe great vulgar diamonds. You zipped me, Dougal, would you like to un——?"

"Very much, Diana," and I did, bare brown Diana in her pipestem pantaloons. "Your tiger stripes began it, your pantaloons to end it."

"No, Dougal, later. I must pack."

I went to bed and was soon asleep. But something woke me

in the night. It was an owl, *hoo-hoo-hoo,* sonorous and slow, a deeper sound than the hooting of our tawny owl, the owl that guided Trocher of Drin in fourteen hundred and seventy-six, that had hooted for me in the gloaming of this very summer. Three more times the triple hoot, and then it stopped. "Please, Harry, may I?" Diana said beside me, and I wondered.

She made the tea that morning. "Angel woman," I said to her, and we drank our tea before making love. I felt a melancholy afterwards. In more things than love there had been so many first times for me that month, but only this one last time seemed to matter.

"May I ask you a question?"

Diana's body tensed. "Well, what?"

"When Gilpin said that he got the necklace from a man called Harry Ambler, you looked totally shattered, ashen. I believe Ambler is a friend of the Duncattos. Curiosity, but . . ."

"I wish you'd mind your own damned business."

"Okay, chum. And talking of my own damned business, let's settle that account."

Diana sprang from my annoying arms, and soon returned in her dressing gown with account book and some bank notes. Business was brisk, as ever. "You gave me twenty-seven yesterday. You owed me twenty-six three hundred. Add to that twenty-five days, eight hours at a dollar, makes two hundred, plus fifty-eight hours overtime meticulously recorded, that's a hundred and sixteen, your change is three hundred and eighty-four, herewith, Sir Dougal. Please check my figures and the money."

"Duly checked, Miss Arden. Thank you very much."

"You made a tart of me," she said. "I've never been a tart before. It's rather fun."

"Sweet harlot mine," I said, and we were friends again.

"Dougal, sorry I was rude."

"Sorry I was inquisitive."

"But you weren't, not between real pals you weren't." She went to the window, her back to me. "I'll tell you about Harry Ambler. I met him in Queensland. I was eighteen then, and on the drift, actually working on a station. He was flying charter for an exploration company based at a place called Wirriwara, taking prospecting teams all around the bush.

"Well, Harry was twenty years older than me, a soldier of fortune — I don't mean a crook, he wasn't that — and the most glamorous happy-go-lucky type, or happy-go-lucky in everything except flying, a super-duper pilot. So for a month he flew all day, and I jillaroed all day, and we got some sleep at night. He was good to me, and such fun always, and he didn't pretend undying passion; he simply needed the right kind of woman in his pad. I knew that, but it didn't stop me from falling desperately, until one night I asked him . . ."

Diana stood still, her back to me. I waited.

"I didn't ask him to marry me. I knew he wouldn't. I asked him if I could stop taking the Pill."

"Oh, I see."

"He didn't answer, just held me quietly, and next morning he said: *I've finished my charter here. I must push on. Thank you, Love. Anything I can ever do.* I know he made it hard for my sake, but it was pretty rough.

"So that was that," Diana said. "That was how I scared Harry Ambler off, and that was how I learned my lesson."

"Have you seen him since?"

"Only once, on the Australian run last year. He had a girl with him, a marvelous looking *jolie laide* with hair as black as yours. They were traveling first class. I suppose he was still rich because of that Koala thing, but Harry Ambler would splurge his last bean for comfort, or thrive on hardtack if he had to, that kind of man. Cool, kind beast, he said: *Hullo, Diana, nice to see you. This is Mary Dunn.* I liked her at once, and it hadn't changed."

Thus were some things explained about Diana Arden. She came now to sit at the foot of the bed, looking bothered, started to speak and stopped, bit her lip. "What is it, Diana?"

"Harry Gilpin told me about your telephone conversation yesterday, and Lord Duncatto's visit to that publisher."

"Gilpin told *you*. What the hell did he mean by doing that?"

"The reason he told me was that I had just told him I shared a flat with Tirene."

"Go away. For Christ's sake, go away."

"Please let me explain. It isn't at all what you think."

"Get out," I said. I shaved and dressed. Duped, led up the garden path, the whole month a lie, but I had to hear it. She was sitting on the sofa.

"Well?"

"I wasn't going to tell you, but Harry Ambler, oh goddammit, Harry Gilpin said I must. He said that if I didn't tell you, I would have cheated you and Tirene, both. And anyway, one of you would be sure to find out. If you found out, you would think it was a put-up job, and would hold that against Tirene. But Tirene doesn't know a thing."

"Tirene couldn't care less whether she knows or not. Get on with it. Let's have the whole sordid story."

"We shared a flat for a year. Of course I was away a lot, but we had terrific fun, laughed at the same things, liked the same sort of people. Well, latterly, when you were back at Drin and Tirene would go home for the weekend every month or so, I began to hear occasional remarks about Dougal Trocher, how fond she used to be of him when she was young, but what a pedantic bore he had become, although she had to admit that the old stick could still be quite human on occasion, even funny when he wasn't delivering sermons or being utterly speechless. *The old stick* became a sort of joke. *What was the old stick like this time?*

"Well then, I was being transferred to Montreal, so I had to opt out of the flat, and a week before I was due to leave, she arrived on the morning train from Scotland. A sleepless night, a towering rage and floods of tears. The old stick had ceased to be a joke, and had become the enemy, insulted her, called her a phony. Tirene gave me chapter and verse, incoherent

213

and all jumbled, and what's more she was sure the old stick and Daddy were in cahoots about something, and you were off to Canada by Global first class when everyone knew you were stony-broke, and the bloody bastard had called her phony because she said sleepers were phony-bourgeois. Well, she told him to fuck off, the stuffy old fucking prig, and she would never forgive him, never.

"All that's the truth, Dougal."

"Yes," I said.

"And so is the rest. I didn't mention you again, and nor did she. Poor Tirene kept saying that the manuscript by that phony queer wasn't any more phony than she was herself. Well, I thought: I'm going to have a look at this bumbling old stick who suddenly turns out to be so hateful. So I found out what flight you were on, and I told Tirene I was making one last flight on the Australian run, and I left the flat two days early, and that was that."

"But why?"

"Oh, Dougal, you old stick, don't be so clueless."

Diana Arden flew away in the helicopter. I spent part of that last day with young Harry, part of it with Gilpin in his garden. I could not help him over the bones of landscaping, but had ideas about shrubs for color at this season.

Then I went down to meet Tom Camber at the wharf. He showed me round the cruiser, omitting explanation of some esoteric-looking tarpaulined items on deck and below, a rakish gray vessel, sixty feet overall. I was not shown the engine room. "How fast is she?" I asked.

"Well, fast enough," he said amiably, and took me to his own fishing boat for a cup of coffee. He was about my age, and had served ten years in the U.S. Coast Guard before coming back to take over the island from his father. I felt at home with Tom Camber, in his dry way so much like the people I lived with at Drin. It was great fun; you could call it a half hour of preparation for reality again.

"I hear Mr. Gilpin's giving you the treatment, flyin' you all the way home. We get rich guys mostly. You don't act too much like a rich guy."

"It wouldn't be too easy an act," I said. "I'm struggling to keep some land I happen to be fond of."

"Your folks bin there long?"

"About seven hundred years."

"Quite a little spell, makes our two hundred Johnny-come-lately, and we lost it. Y'know that's a decent thing about Mr. Gilpin, he makes us feel it's still Camber Island, well, next best thing. I don't hold with this rich guys all being sons of bitches. What I say is they ain't quite real-like. Know what I mean?"

"I was thinking that just a minute ago. Well, thanks for the coffee, I must go. Good-bye."

"Happy landings. Come again."

Harry Gilpin and I had a drink together at the cottage. "It may take Cowan a month or more to negotiate your inheritance. Can you make do in the meanwhile?"

"Yes, even if the Drin coffers aren't exactly brimming." I was longing to be home and down to work, and I was dreading home. I had regrets, and I had no regrets. I had much reason to be grateful, and I felt resentment.

"You look troubled, Dougal. Is it about what Diana told you? She said that she had followed my advice, and that you at first were very angry. But only yesterday you told me that in this month she had never put her own interest first."

"Why couldn't she have told me long ago about Tirene?"

"Because if she had, you would have fired her on the spot. Then your ventures would have come to naught, and the old stick would not have come to know himself for what he is or can be — a tough go-getter, and an accomplished lover. In that respect, Diana certainly thought of her own interest, and told me so. And besides, young man . . ."

"Besides what?"

"In your present frame of mind, which seems to me to be an amalgam of arrogance and self-pity, you fail to note that Diana

Arden's prime or primary concern was not Dougal Trocher's interest, but that of a very unhappy girl named Tirene Duncatto."

"I told you. Tirene thinks I'm a crashing bore."

"Then un-bore yourself. I find you a crashing bore only when you so describe yourself."

"But I am, with her. I was before, and I will be again. And I insulted her. Duncattos don't forgive."

"Not lightly, I agree. But you did not cheat Tirene. You lost your temper and told the poor girl something that in a part of her troubled self she knew for a home truth." He looked at me with those pale eyes, infinitely shrewd and rather small. "The Duncattos are a warlike breed. They do not respect poltroons. Are you the Dougal who took on two armed men with one hunting knife? Or are you the Trocher who cringes before stripling beauty's wrath?"

"I'm both," I said.

"I do not advocate the skean d'hu. I suggest that you be bold, indulgent, keep the girl guessing, even be a little vulgar."

"But that's another trouble. Diana kept prodding me in Montreal to get with it in my speech, and so I wrote Tirene a truly ghastly letter, boastful, corny beyond belief."

"But she hasn't been home. She left no address. Her parents could have held it for you."

"I hadn't thought of that."

"What a besotted nincompoop you are. And, may I add before you knife me, a knight *sans peur et sans reproche,* as my darling Gloria would agree, with, I have to say, a touch of Don Quixote added, not to mention despairing Hamlet."

"Must you be sarcastic?"

"It is my besetting sin, or one of them. I am also trying to provoke you into being the man you are."

Tarquie had done that one evening at Drin. Now Harry Gilpin did that one evening at Camber Island. "Do you suffer remorse about the robbery?"

"Yes, sir," I said.

216

"Would you do it again?"

"Betcher life, I would."

"Then batten down that questionable conscience. Lock away your one and only crime. Confess it to no man more, nor woman. Let me stress: *Nor woman.*"

"Sound advice. Talking of locking things away, my recent experience leads me to think that you might be vulnerable here to much the same kind of robbery as we seemed to engineer."

"You have seen Tom Camber's vessel, if not its teeth. We have a vault and various electronic gadgets, and directed to the sky if necessary are interesting developments of the laser beam; and there are a few trusted unobtrusive people here. Nevertheless, and comprehensive as these precautions may be, they are defensive, and the best of defenses are vulnerable to offense. That is one reason why I made a suggestion to Diana yesterday. Did she tell you?"

"No."

"What a sphinx that girl is. I suggested that if she should weary of being an airline hostess, she might consider taking on the security aspect of all my operations."

"And what did she say?"

"She said: *Mr. Gilpin, may I think?* I do hope she thinks positively, because in all my experience I never encountered a man or woman with better resource, acumen and cool-headed balance. Our operations are fairly widespread, Dougal, and some are highly secret. There are many aspects to that, but most important always must be the safety of Gloria and young Harry wherever they may be."

"You offered her that on two days' acquaintance?"

"After a few inquiries," he said. "The ogre has his ways and means. Don't you think Diana would do it well?"

"Superbly, but . . ."

"Please say what is in your mind. I detect a doubt."

"Some doubt as to whether Diana would take it on. But I also wondered whether Gloria would entirely approve of so devastating a girl being about the place from time to time."

"Gloria knows that I am her husband, and hers alone. Just as your wife . . ." But he let it go at that.

I remember much about a brief acquaintance with Harry Zanzibar Gilpin, kindly pirate, plutocrat.

✳ 27 ·⋆

A NIGHTCAP, four hours sleep in pajamas on a bunk, the steward with a cup of tea, shave and dress, scrambled eggs and sausages and bacon, one could call it my swansong to the gilded life, the gilded dream that had not happened. Nor was Scotland particularly real below a cloudless sky, bell heather just in bloom, lochs smooth as glass, the greens bright emerald after rain. It was picture-postcard weather, never never, hardly ever.

The cabin altimeter dropped past nine thousand, home must be coming up to meet us somewhere round about. But the captain's voice: "Out of the starboard window should be familiar country in about a minute."

And it was: Ben Drin standing out, the glen, the river, and far ahead the woods that cloaked the Fall of Drin. I crossed to port for a quick look at my neighbor's land: Ben Tarquin, mate to our big hill, the cliffs of Glenauchart, and the two rivers, Tigg and Auchart, meeting to flow past Duncatto.

Our domains swam past us in a minute or less, but I crossed again to see the doll's house of Drin. And now rich lowlands and the North Sea gray against the sun, changing to blue as we swung into our approach.

"Local time is nine fifty-eight, temperature at Crummock seventy-two degrees Fahrenheit, wind northwest negligible. We shall be landing in two minutes."

You flew three thousand miles or so to meet precisely an ETA of 10 A.M., at which hour the temperature was seventy-two — unheard of. My watch was five hours slow, but I would not change it until we had positively, actually stopped. We trundled past a ready line of uncouth, angular, supersonic monsters that played some sort of jolly tag and gamesmanship with the Russian boys in Bears or something.

We had positively, actually stopped, so I changed my watch, muttered: "Thank God that's all over," and descended. The Guard of Honor, Royal Salute, reporters, flashing cameras were strangely absent, but the Lord Lieutenant was there in person.

He nodded, no vestige of a smile. "Morning. So you got back. Customs inside." And he stumped off, tattered kilt and ancient jacket. One hardly expected effusiveness in Tarquie, but he was my staunch and amiable old friend. I knew then, just as I had felt in my Celtic bones these last few days, that something terrible would happen, was happening, had happened.

But one must pull oneself together. One must declare the costume brooches for Ida and for Lois, reminded that one had not dared to tempt providence by buying anything for the other one, the lost and hating only one.

The crew were to rest some hours at Crummock, and fly back to be in New York before day ended. I suppose that, to one another, jet pilots seem ordinary chaps. But to humdrum me, they are supermen. I had that thought, supermen superimposed upon foreboding. "Good-bye, and many thanks, thank you very much, a good flight back, good luck, and thank you." So many goods and thanks, I sounded like a lunatic. The steward was in his own way also a superman, first flew with Imperial Airways in the thirties, and how many pilots had he entrusted his life to since, and how many smuggling rackets had he worked, urbane sardonic super-Jeeves?

So that was that, the baggage piled into the scarlet Mini, and we were off. "What a fabulous day," I said.

Tarquie grunted. I glanced round at him. His square face was expressionless, not quite, the left jaw muscle pulsed, the eyes were sunken worried. We joined the purgatory of the Crummock by-pass, a long load truck before us, another monster on our tail. "Goddam and blast your bloody eyes," he said to a Jaguar that hooted rudely, shot past, tucked in.

Tarquie usually drove well, but that day he was a menace, passed the long load on a bend, and the truck's air brakes gasped to give us space, almost none to spare; and I was afraid for me, Dougal Trocher, not for anybody else, whatever trouble and disaster. "Steady, Tarquie. That was damned dangerous."

"Oh, shut up."

But we escaped to the quiet sideroad. "Bad trouble?"

"Yes," he said. "Bad trouble."

"Is it Tirene?"

"Yes." There was flat finality. He sighed.

I had known it all along. "You'd better tell me."

"The gel's bin hiding in the old bothy-hut up Glenauchart for a week." He turned into the broken gates of Drin.

"Stop!" I said. He stopped. "Get out!"

Tarquie obeyed me. I faced him across his diminutive vehicle. The jaw muscles no longer pulsed. The jaw was slack. "Now take a pull on yourself. You say *bad trouble*. Then you say Tirene's been hiding in a bothy. Is that bad trouble?"

"M'daughter's gone stark staring mad," he said. "Isn't that bad trouble for you?"

He stressed the *for*, not the *you*, meaning bad trouble, not for me personally. Tarquie, unflappable rock of ages, his mouth was trembling. "Please tell me," I said.

Fergus (Fergus McDownie, his stalker) always came to see him on Friday evenings to discuss affairs. Well, last night Fergus did not come alone, but with his wife.

". . . I took one look at them, and I knew something was wrong, but I thought it must be about one of their boys, Duncan, who's been beating it up a bit, so I rallied myself to deal with someone else's worries, always easier, and I drew up a chair for Margaret, but she ignored me, said: *Get on with you, McDownie. Tell His Lordship.*

"Well, what he had to tell was that a week ago he took a walk by the Auchart just to keep an eye on things. I haven't been up myself for ages, the river was far too high to fish." Tarquie paced to and fro in agitation, his head downcast.

"Could you come to the point?"

"The point is that at the head of the glen he saw smoke, a wisp of it, and he went to investigate, and what he found, who he found was Tirene, boiling a kettle outside the bothy, and she said: *Hullo, Fergus, I was afraid you'd come.*

"He didn't understand about her being afraid he would come or how she had got there or why or when, so he sat down and waited, and when she had made them tea, she said that she had walked over the hill from Glentigg, and she had a sleeping bag and all she needed with her, and would he make her a promise: Not to tell a living soul, not even Margaret, that she was there, and not to come back?

"Well, the McDownies have always been her best friends about the place, first thing home from school or wherever, up to see Fergus and Margaret. Fergus said she seemed quiet, *a wee thing trachled*, but all right really. So when he had made sure that she did have pots and pans and food and so on, he gave the promise, although he knew we were worried about her.

"Actually, up to that point I don't see what else Fergus could have done, always been stout allies, protected the children a hundred times from us; I remember just the same when I was a boy, sort of antiparents, antilairds league, everybody in it. So he kept his promise, but he went every day to check on her by telescope, reading outside one decent afternoon, fishing another, but mostly writing at the table, he spied her from half a mile off through the open window.

"Wednesday morning I got back from London, saw Fergus, told him about my vain search for Tirene — he tutted in dismay, I well remember — and I said what about trying for a

222

fish in the Auchart if I could spare an hour, surely the river must be in ploy again. But he said no, still far too high. That seemed a bit odd because the Tigg had dropped three feet. However, Fergus knows the Auchart backwards.

"But last evening I remembered that conversation, and I began to get a bit hot under the collar. He had kept his promise to Tirene, one thing; he had more or less tricked me, quite another. So I slightly shouted: *Stop beatin' about the bush. Come to the point.*

"At that, Margaret McDownie gave me a dirty look, and Fergus came to the point. He decided yesterday afternoon that this could not go on, so he went up to tell Tirene, approaching cautiously in case she was sunbathing or something, a grand day, not so hot as this. She was lying face down in the heather, her head pillowed on one arm, the other out straight, having a snooze, he thought at first, looking through the glass. But then he saw her lift her free arm and smack the ground, thump it again and again, that wasn't snoozing.

So he ran down the gully, and crawled until he was close and looked again. Tirene was standing now, with her back to him, arms waving about, and she was shouting, and the echoes came back from the cliffs round about, it was skeery. She was crying: *I thought I could find it alone. I thought I could write alone. But I can't write alone. I can't be alone. And I hate people. I hate the world and me and everything.* That kind of rant. And then she began to laugh. *Poor Miss Tirene laughing to the tears,* he said.

"So Fergus ran the whole way home, two miles at least, and he poured it out to Margaret, and she said: *You did wrong, McDownie. You did wrong with the good intention. Go you at once and tell the Laird.* So he said he would tell the Laird, but the Laird would have the hide off of him, so he would tell the Laird that he just came on the poor lassie for the first time this afternoon. *You will tell the Laird the truth, McDownie, and I'll put my bonnet on to see you do it.* Fergus came quite clean, even quoting Margaret.

"So then I blew my top at him, and said who the hell did he

think he was to take it on himself, and he had pulled the wool over my eyes about the river to keep me out of Glenauchart, and had I not confided our worries to him? I was a bit beside myself, even called it disloyalty, bloody fool I am, it was misguided loyalty, and at that point, Margaret drew herself up in majesty, all six foot of her, and said: *His Lordship is not the only fly in the ointment.*"

Tarquie smiled faintly. "Perhaps she meant the only pebble on the beach, and she continued: *His Lordship should be ashamed of himself for calling McDownie disloyal when McDownie was doing his very best. And His Lordship is thinking of His Lordship not of Miss Tirene.*

"*Goddammit, Mistress McDownie,* I protested.

"*His Lordshp should not be taking the good Lord's name in vain.* At that point Fergus, who had been hangdog, went purple in the face and counterattacked. *His Lordship says I was disloyal. His Lordship has my notice.*

"Lois had arrived to hear the end of the shouting match. *Stop, you fool!* she said, but I was off to save m'daughter, picked up a sheaf of letters for her on the hall table as an excuse for going, got in the Mini and drove like hell up the hill and along Glenauchart. Instead of having the sense to stop short and walk the last bit, I drove right on until the bothy was in sight across the river. And as I was crossing the bridge of poles, I saw Tirene take off. Well, she can climb like a Highland pony, and I couldn't catch her up Ben Tarquin. So I went to the bothy to find a penciled instruction: *Go to hell!* She must be raving, Dougal. Never in her life told me to go to hell."

"She's told me a helluva lot worse than go to hell."

"Has she now?" he said without interest. "So I left the letters on the bothy table."

"Would there have been one from me?"

"Dunno, and don't interrupt. When I came out, I looked up and she was standing on the edge of the cliff, actually it's the only cliff on that side of the glen, and she called down: *If you don't go away, I'll jump.*

224

"So I went away, and I passed a sleepless night in the dressing room, locked out by Lois, and that is the situation. My daughter's suicidal; my wife's threatening divorce; my stalker's given notice, and my stalker's wife says I'm only thinking of myself. Only thinking of myself, good God!"

I had seen Tarquie angry on rare occasion, he could explode in awe-inspiring fashion. I had never seen him in a helpless hopeless tizzie. He wiped his sweat-smarting eyes, and muttered: "They're all mad, the whole damned lot of them."

"*The whole world's mad but me.* Come off it, Tarquie." I was quite stern with him.

He drew gusty breath. "Yes," he said. "Yes, that is a point. But what can I do? What *can* I do?"

"Drive me up to the house, and we'll decide."

"Well, thank God you're home," he said, negotiating potholes in second gear. "Did you pull it off?"

"Yes."

"Good." It was not much of a *well-done* from the man who had put me up to it, but that man was not quite himself. Strangely, or not strangely, Tarquie's unprecedented *crise de nerfs* gave me a measure of strength.

Drin looked more than ever unkempt, weeds rampant, hay longer on the lawns and gone to seed. What could you do with one and a half gardeners growing four acres of vegetables for sale? All the problems that had lain fallow for a month.

It was cool in the house, and here came Ida, the same ample Ida to enfold me and inspect me. "You're thinner," she said. "And yon's terrible scratches you got yourself."

"I fell into brambles, Ida, in the woods in Canada."

"It was the woods in Canada where I had an awfy dream about you. But home safe and sound, may the Lord be thankit." She looked at Tarquie, at me, at him again. "What is it, Your Lordship?"

He shook his head, and I said for him: "Tirene's been hiding at the bothy up Glenauchart for a week. It seems as if she's having a nervous breakdown, Ida."

"Och, the poor bairn, poor Miss Tirene, I was feared for that. Will Your Lordship take the doctor to her?"

"Hopeless," he said. "She would only jump. What do you say, Dougal?"

"It's a grim place, that, so lonely and away alone. The first thing would be to entice her out, and I can't do it, you know the effect I have on Tirene."

"Entice Miss Tirene out with something Miss Tirene loves the best. And what's that, Dougal?"

"I don't know, Ida."

"The motorbike. Miss Tirene's aye been daft about yon motorbike. If you could leave it where she'd find it, Miss Tirene would go riding, mebbe."

"That *is* worth a try," Tarquie said. "Yes, I really think so." He was rallying.

"I'll have to get it there. Where's McIntoon?"

"Dunno. Could find him through Police HQ in Crummock on the blower."

"Do so, then. Divert him. You know where the telephone is. Get going, Tarquie."

"What shall I say?"

"Say anything. Say you saw a suspicious character on your way to the air station, near the big transformer at Lower Camsie. Drop the word sabotage."

"Right," Tarquie said.

"It's a long journey you've been making, Dougal."

"Yes, Ida." It had been a long, long journey.

"And braw deeds I was reading about, and a puckle mischief too by the looks in your eye. But, Dougal!"

"Yes, Ida?"

"Isn't Miss Tirene the only lassie there ever was for you?"

"Yes, Ida."

"Then away and get her, you muckle lump."

"But, Ida, she's having a nervous breakdown."

"Och, nervous breakdown! Yon's fancy words for being unhappy in herself too long alone. It's no a motorbike she needs for to cure her nervous breakdown."

226

"But I'm afraid of her, Ida. She ties me up in knots."

"A wee joke, a wee wheedle, a wee memory from long ago, a wee enticement to the motorbike, a wee bit hug. Just away and try it."

"Och, you and yer wees," I said. "Ida, have you been all right?"

"I canna grumble," Ida said. "Here comes His Lordship."

"That's all fixed," he said. "My God, Dougal, you should see your library floor."

"I will sometime. Just a minute, I must change into civilized clothes." I left them, opened a suitcase in the hall, retired to the cloakroom, and put on the kilt, the khaki shirt, the very garments that I had worn for my testing by some people called the Dagoes. Old civilized clothes, and new binoculars. "I'm ready, Tarquie. You'd better lead the way just in case McIntoon is not diverted."

"Okay. I'll go slowly. Keep in sight. If I stop, withdraw." Tarquie seemed restored in spirit. "Thank God he's home again, eh Ida?"

"Ay," she said. "Black Dougal's hame, if he'll just bide here."

But as I followed Tarquie on the old motorbike, doubts grew. For one thing, the steering seemed much more peculiar. For another, I was not the new man that they thought I was. We went by the steep byways and the winding lanes on that rare hot morning, and the nearer we came to Duncatto, the more I feared Tirene, the more I feared what I might do to her, the more I feared for her, alone and distraught at the old bothy up Glenauchart, grim valley of haunt, of somber legend.

⚒ 28 ⚒

I FOLLOWED TARQUIE through the Duncatto gates, and then he shot ahead. The speedometer on Grandfather's Combopede was broken, but we chugged along fast enough to make a pleasant coolness in the wind of passage, at twenty-five perhaps, with incipient front-wheel wobble.

I stopped below the cedar of Lebanon, and I was having second thoughts, back where I came from, second thoughts. Supposing Tirene could be tempted out of her melancholia to go for a ride on the motor bicycle she loved so much, would she not be riding into mortal danger down that tortuous hill road? I heard the front door open, heard a single *wowf*, and there was my true good friend about whom I had quite forgotten.

He came at a burly gallop. I had time to dismount, lest he take the machine apart, but because I did not crouch in the way one should, he tackled me low and knocked me down. "Steady, Big Boy." I hugged him to prevent further canine kisses, enough of which can be enough.

At least someone loved me. It was soon evident, however, that Bernardo would not love me so much, loved he not the sidecar more. He leapt aboard and looked round at me, head cocked. The message was clear: *What are we waiting for?*

Tarquie's Mini was there, but no Tarquie. No Lois to say: *Welcome home.* No one to advise me, give me courage.

Bernardo voiced impatience, and I yielded, as I would yield

to any stronger will, and we went by the placid River Tigg to its confluence with the stormy Auchart, which now tumbled past us. If one stalled on a corner going up, one would come to a stop; one could at least get off. But if one lost control coming down . . . The danger was not a product of my feverish imagination. It could be, would be, very real, more real than anything so far this day.

It was hot, and Bernardo hated heat. He sat up beside me, panting, enduring for the sake of, no, actually enjoying.

The road became level again as we passed the McDownies' cottage, but no McDownies were in evidence. I gave a thought to Tarquie's troubles there. Long before Lordship days, he and Fergus had fought all through North Africa together. And since Lordship days, he and Margaret McDownie had shared a gift: They were both dowsers, water diviners, a mysterious bond between human beings. To lose the company of the McDownies was going to be a bitter wrench.

Now we came to the forbidding Gates of Auchart, where river and road wound through a narrow gorge. Glenauchart itself was almost flat, a deep world of its own. The road ran along the west side of the valley, by the right bank of the river. There was steep scree above us. Ahead to the north, two miles away, the cliffs rose sheer. Only the eastern slopes of the glen were for the most part fairly gradual, steepening to the summit of Ben Tarquin. It was over a shoulder of Ben Tarquin that Tirene would have climbed.

The bothy had a stable and a small paddock where the hill pony was kept in the stalking season. At this time of year the deer were high, but they wintered in Glenauchart, sometimes two or three hundred beasts found shelter in this lonely place where the sun did not strike from late November until February. But the summer sun was roasting high.

I stopped for a moment to put my binoculars on the northeast corner where the bothy lay, tucked back into the hillside, out of sight. I saw no smoke. Eleven-thirty was not cooking time, and the temperature must be eighty.

An hour and a half ago I had set foot on Scottish soil, and

here I was in the storied glen, seeking the damsel in distress, and what to do, and what to say?

Not far ahead was Tarquin's Cave. The old tale said that the damsel's first-known ancestor, Tarquin the Centurion, had deserted at the time of the Roman withdrawal, about A.D. 180, and had gone into hiding here with his savage love. But after a year the natives hunted them down and put them to the sword, sparing the infant Tarquin. The damsel was of ancient lineage, a rootless, mixed-up kid, I feared her.

There was a disused quarry short of the cave. I turned into that, and found shade for Bernardo who yawned, grown torpid in the unwelcome heat, lay down in the sidecar and closed his eyes. "Bernardo, don't you want to come and see Tirene?" He growled, and went to sleep.

I spied again, no movement. A hill burn ran down that gully, by the small stone cottage, less than half a mile from me, still out of sight. I was fairly sure that the near rush of water would drown the far pop of motorbike for Tirene's ears. Or had she decamped? Had worse happened?

I tucked the binoculars inside my shirt and ran across the valley bottom, in clear view of any watchers anywhere, waded the Auchart, cold water to my knees, and climbed. I would stalk the bothy, just as Fergus McDownie had, down that steep gully. I looked between heather clumps, seeing the south wall and the east wall of the cottage, not the west and north.

I climbed out of it, and crawled — was that a voice? — crawled further, stopped. It was a voice, not of despair but of irascible impatience, painfully familiar, yet better than despair. Belly flat, I crawled until I could look down upon her. She lay in the shade of the northern wall, elbows on grass and chin in hands, and she was reading. The hair, the pink and gray smudged semmit, the blue jeans, shapely backside patched with red and black. There lay my love, and I lay panting.

"My God, Aggie, what a maudlin slut you are. *I laze away my days alone. Such a blessed thing aloneness is, the mind at peace, the body resting, thinking, yes, the body thinking, and*

230

*he comes back from his twenty-seven holes of golf to swim
with me as nature made us in the azure sea, apart all through
the torrid day, together all the coolness of the velvet night,
love's sweet stern togetherness.* God, what twaddle!"

Tirene cast that letter among others in a pile, and she took
up a last unopened. It was bland, shattering coincidence. It
was the irrational, authentic tap of fate.

"More drooling pomposity, I'll bet. *My dear Tirene, once
again I beg you to accept my apology for a gross breach of taste
and manners at the railway station.* Crummy old pettifogging
stick, I suppose I'd better read it."

Tirene tore open the airmail envelope in slapdash fashion,
and she read. She read my effusion through in silence. And
then she read it aloud, quite slowly, word for awful word, lying
on her stomach by that old bothy in that forbidding glen. As
she read, small echoes rang about, dying as they were
renewed:

"HI, TIRENE, DEAR OLE GORGEOUS,

"I'm writing this in my slap-up suite at the Ritz, which is a swell
joint in both meanings, and the varlets look after me just like it
was feudal home. Well today I played golf with my third cousin
Claud Merriwell, Captain of Industry. I allowed him to cream me
on the last hole less out of my familiar will to lose than out of my
jolly decent wish to please. Claud lusts to win at work and play,
typical plutobourgeois, but I'm very grateful to him for the loan of
a humdinger of a *char*, a BMW Bavaria hot job (just your cup of
tea), hence defeat.

Talking of hot and job the weather is the former and I have the
latter. I'm judging a garden competition getting a smashing wad
of lolly for it and will be busier than a bird dog for the next two
weeks so busy ackshly with "Meet the Celebrities" on TV,
interviews, Highland Society Banquet (that's tomorrow), lectures
on my own green thumb line, and this and that and so on around
and around the goddam mulberry bush that I have had to engage a
secretary who is as plainly competent as her years are uncertain.

But all is not nose to grindstone and I'm following your
instructions to the letter: *Live and learn, live it up a bit.* In fact
this male chauvinist reactionary dodo and stuffy old adjectival prig

is getting himself into a buncha capers that would make your tangled locks stand right up from the comb.

Letter from your mum saying Garry and Bernardo naughty, roughed up a pregnant sow but no harm done except to the Lord Lieutenant's apoplexy. That's a rib tickler, eh? Also worried at no word from you. You're a meany Tirene, bad baby, ring them right away reversing charges as per usual. Hope you're enjoying your job and have novels to read about the honest self-respecting fornication you enjoy, not that Californian sod's perversion. Heard from Ida too, says library floor sagged six inches — good old dry rot. Drin kin buckle for all I care.

Canadians are real decent folks, more matey than us stuffed shirts, less cunning hypocrites that's my sage opinion.

Hoping this finds you as it leaves me, happily in the whisky bottle.

SWAK"

I awaited the purple language that would be my due desert, but none came. "First he insults me," she said quietly. "And then he makes boozy fun of me. First I have to read that moron Aggie's treacle. And then I have to read this, all alone in this horrible place, alone, so hateful and so cruel, hating everything, alone."

Tirene put her hands to her face and cried, lying on the green grass in the shade, a light breeze stirring now, the white wild cotton dancing in the bog. Bereft, alone, and hating me, she cried, and all my sins accused me.

But that dreadful letter was not my fault. Who had encouraged me to with-it-ness? Who was the instigator but Diana Arden, damn her! *Damn her?*

Tirene drew a sobbing breath, and cried no more, and I remembered it. Raising my head a few inches from the purple heather, I loudly quoted:

> *"It is so hard to be alone*
> *Continually, watching the great stars march*
> *Their circular unending route."*

My voice was strong, and the echoes spoke again from this cliff and from that: *to be alone, the great stars march, continually, unending route.* There was wild beauty in the echoes flying, booming, dying, and, most-eerily, the last far words were still the first: *It is so hard to be alone.* And silence.

Tirene stood. She circled slowly, seeking, and I buried my head in the warm, sweet-smelling heather, and she said: "It sounds like him."

I stood and looked at her, and, fear-possessed, I said: "Yes, Tirene, it is I."

"Who bloody else. *Would that be Dougal Trocher speaking? It is he.*"

"Tirene, do please accept my apologies for writing that lamentable missive. I was intoxicated."

"You said you were happily in the whisky bottle, that makes much better sense."

Try to fight it, try, now try: "Sure, Honey, I was looped." If looped, it had been soberly.

She looked up at me, and gave a residual shudder after crying. "Oh, damnation!" Blotched with tears, she was so lovely. "That thing you said — did you make it up?"

"No, Tirene. It was written by a man named Sidney Keyes, killed in North Africa before he was twenty-one, before he was your own age even."

"It says everything I've been feeling here alone this week, the stars and everything alone. Could you say it again for me?"

I said it again for her, and once again the echoes spoke in multiple reply. Her friend had also asked me to say the lines a second time. Diana was my friend too. For her I had deep affection. And yet not this. It was a mystery, a truth. "It is the truth of life," I said to my love below me at the bothy.

"Yes," she said. "So hard to be alone."

That also was a truth, but not what I had meant, and I could not tell her. I was not less afraid, but more. There was not much of me, not much. I went down slowly. The honey bees were busy in the heather.

"What happened to your face? Did some female scratch you?"

"No, Tirene. I had an encounter with a clump of brambles."

"Well, that sounds like a clump of capers too," she said.
The briefest of smiles came and went in her unhappy face. "I
hate everything," Tirene said.

A wee memory from long ago. "Do you remember that time
when you were twelve, and we were stalking, and you said the
stag was bonny, and you tried to stop me firing, but too late,
and you cried: *so cruel,* and you ran away?"

"Yes," she said. "I do remember."

And I remembered much more recently, not more immediately, the buck with horns in velvet in the forest in Quebec. It
was a recollection of Tuesday in this week.

A wee wheedle, Ida said. *A wee enticement to the
motorbike.* But how?

"Please go away. I want to be alone." And Tirene gave a
small snort, perhaps from crying, perhaps about Greta Garbo,
mocking herself even in despair.

I turned to face down the glen. She was not hostile at this
moment. It might be best to go. "Oh, look!" I said.

The eagle glided fast. It came from Ben Tarquin, steeply
across the valley. I pulled the binoculars from inside my shirt,
muzzy, wiped them, put them up in time to see that the eagle
had something in its talons, braking now, arching back against
the air, the wing tips spread like fingers.

"I've seen it twice," Tirene said. "And I know where it goes
— to that favorite ledge above Tarquin's Cave. But I never
can get close enough."

"You might this time, Tirene. It has a ptarmigan. Take the
glasses, quick!"

Tirene ran, and she could run, not floppily legged. She ran
as firmly and freely as any boy.

If she had run left, she would almost at once have been in
view from the eagle's perch and feeding ground. But Tirene
knew this primeval haunt. She splashed through shallow
spawning beds of the Auchart, running then in broken ground
below the black northern cliffs, running south now, never in

234

sight of Tarquin's Cave. I followed her, marveling at the sure-footed grace, the speed.

But speed gave way to stealth. She stopped, looked up at a bare rock in the scree, took her bearings from that known object. It was a walk, a crouch, a crawl on hands and knees, a belly crawl with toes and elbows, worming her way to the crest of a hummock, the stalk accomplished. I had simply stalked the stalker.

"Golly," she whispered. "I've never been so close before. You should see his fierce eye. You should see that beak tear at the ptarmigan's breast, white feathers float away, pluck at the flesh, so merciless, so beautiful, the golden eagle. The eagle kills and feeds and dies alone. That's what it's all about."

"That's what what is all about?" It must have been the intolerable stress and strain that caused my whisper to crack into a loud squeak behind her.

"Idiot!" she said, and stood, and so did I, to see the golden eagle spiral up and up, the broad wings slowly stroking, swiftly climbing, dwindling, the eagle flew back to the summit of Ben Tarquin.

"Trust you to squeak," she said.

"Tirene, our meeting has been so traumatic."

"Oh, God!" she said. There had been a softer moment, remembering lost friendship. Now it was hate again, and I was worse than ever.

Or was I? "You and your father share a tiresome habit, a juvenile trick. You invoke the Deity far too much."

"God's there, isn't He?"

"Yes, Tirene."

"Then what's wrong with Daddy and me invoking Him?"

"Methinks you make a telling point, Tirene."

We were some fifty yards from Tarquin's Cave, and close beyond that was the quarry. How could I entice her thither?

"You see the road? Well, take it. Tergiversate on me, for God's sake. Let me have a bit of peace."

"A bit of peace, Tirene, all alone in this lonely place?"

"Do you want it in four letters off?"

I held up my hand like a policeman stopping traffic, stopping those four letters off. But I had a thought to a stratagem of last resort. "Please, Tirene!" I pleaded loudly. "Please don't make me leave, Tirene! Please, Tirene!"

From down the glen of fabled story, there came a sound. My true friend growled. It was a long loud grumble from his boots.

"That slothful oaf! What's he doing here?"

"He's been asleep, Tirene, in Grandfather's Combopede."

"Lazy bum, I'll fix him." And she strode to do so.

Bernardo was sitting up. He yawned largely; then considered the lovely object of his sole displeasure.

"Say Hullo!" Bernardo shook his head. "Say Hullo, I tell you." And he said it.

"Tirene, would you like to have a ride, just a little one, to this side of the Gates of Auchart, say, but not beyond, that's much too dangerous. It's a lovely day for riding, and the wind of passage makes a welcome coolness. Would you enjoy a little ride, Tirene?"

"Would I ever! Start it for me."

I obeyed. "She's all yours now," I said. "Your very own."

≈ 29 ≈

I BESTRODE THE PILLION seat, and hung on as I had once been privileged to hang before, twice actually, my thumbs and second fingers questing to meet round Tirene's slender middle. The combination lurched to and fro. "It doesn't much like this kind of road."

"I see what you mean," she said, continuing without pause: "That secretary of yours, were you shacked up?"

Having been subjected to other lightning switches of topic lately, I had armed myself to cope with this one: "I told you, Tirene. I said that she was as plainly competent as her years were uncertain, and by that I mean a homely bag of fifty."

"They say some homely bags of fifty are real slick to shack with in the sack."

"That I wouldn't know, Tirene."

"Well, if it wasn't her, it was someone else."

"Really, Tirene!"

"Well, wasn't it?"

I longed to know why she thought she knew, but I said: "Tell me, Tirene, what has been your own recent shacking program?"

"No program. And mind your own damned business."

"Mind yours, then," I said, not afraid at all.

"Please don't be beastly to me." The deep after-sob shook her waist within my hands. I nearly, so nearly, put my lips to the pale valley of her neck, but then I did not dare.

The valley closed to the Gates of Auchart. In front of me Tirene rode; beside me Bernardo sat in episcopal dignity, motionless but for his black nose twitching. "Please stop, Tirene, and let me take the thing through here. It really is a frightful risk."

"What's bloody life without a risk?"

Almost the words of Mildred Farrow. And I thought, as I have often thought, of the linked disparate parallels along one's way. Tirene engaged low gear. To our left, the Auchart tumbled through its gorge. One wheel beyond the lip would mean a ten-foot drop into the torrent. To our right was the inhospitable wall of the ravine.

Tirene rode with caution, her reflex or reaction swift against each wayward swing, but the play was too much. This time we headed inevitably for the brink. "No brakes," she said, and I jumped off and hauled on the handlebars with all my strength, and we were safely through. She stopped on level ground. "On you hop," she said. "It's better with you on. You and your alter ego balance one another."

I hopped on. There was bad to come, although the worst to come might be less bad. Back there, but for my swift herculean action, it would have been sure death for all, and she was not grateful, not one whit.

We turned the bend to the McDownies' cottage. They stood in the rustic porch, broad Fergus topped by majestic Margaret, roughly the size of Mildred Farrow, the thought occurred, two parallels.

"Hi, Fergus! Hi, Margaret!" Tirene screamed above the coughing of our single cylinder. The McDownies blankly stared. "They do look rather glum, and I can't stop."

"Low gear, Tirene, quickly!"

"I suppose Daddy and Fergus had a bust-up."

"Yes, Tirene, I'm afraid they did."

"It's all my fault. Everything is all my fault."

"No, no, Tirene."

"Hang on tight. This is the worst bit." I hung on tight as

we corkscrewed down a last steep pitch, and onto tarmac, safe, or safer.

"You did very well, Tirene." There was no need now to hang on for dear life. My hands decided for themselves, slipped down a little, rested between waist and hipbone. Tirene sighed. She sighed sadly for everything her fault alone, and put on speed, wheel-wobble, slowed again.

"It wasn't like this last time. I think something's loose in the underpinnings."

"Yes, Tirene."

"*Yes, Tirene. No, no, Tirene. Yes, Tirene.* Can't you say anything except my stupid name?"

"I'm afraid of being a bore again."

"Tell me about Canada, then. That doesn't sound so boring."

"I worked long and hard, judging the garden competition."

"That sounds infinitely boring."

"Any more boring than judging dirty books, Tirene?"

"Oh, shut up!"

I shut up, and we continued in silence until she said: "You sounded almost human in your letter, not the same virtuous old stick at all."

"I'm sorry to disappoint you, Tirene. Funny, isn't it? Bernardo doesn't growl now when he hears your name."

"He's as bored as I am. So you made that up when you were pie-eyed. No parties, no dames, no fun at all. How typical!"

It was remarkable, amazing, wonderful. I took my hands from Tirene's lower waist, and I parted her hair, and I put my lips to the soft valley of her neck, and I kissed her and I kissed her and she shivered. "Take that," I said.

There was a surge of speed, but I saved myself, hanging on to her shoulders now. "I knew it from the moment we began this ride."

"Knew what, Tirene?"

"Before you went to Canada, you hung on like a drowning sailor. But today your hands keep talking just a little. That's what Diana said. She said a man's hands tell you about him first thing off."

"Who is Diana?" I inquired with care.

"The girl I shared the flat with. She's my best friend ever."

"Oh, yes." My hands cupped bare silken shoulders. Perhaps she was right; perhaps my hands did talk a little. "I say, Tirene!"

"Well, what is it?"

"I'm not afraid of you."

"Same here, not."

"Tirene, have you had a nervous breakdown?"

"Sort of, but it begins to sort of feel like breaking up."

"Aren't you going to turn into the house?"

"No, I'm not. I'm riding right on to the end of the road."

"What road?"

"Your road, unless this thing has a breakdown too."

"Your father diverted McIntoon, but one never knows. That McIntoon is a frightful risk."

"You said the Gates of Auchart were a frightful risk, and I brought you safe through that one."

"Who brought who through safe is a moot or valid question."

"*Who brought who,* you're coming on."

As we passed Duncatto, the front door opened, and her parents stood there. Tirene did not see them, but I looked back to observe that Lord and Lady Duncatto seemed to be patching their differences up. They were locked in clinch embrace.

And so out of the gates, and along the winding lanes of our native Crummock, which is both a highland and a lowland county, and we rode steep byways where the one merged with the other.

"It's bonny," she said.

"Ay, it's bonny."

"A wee thing hot."

"Ay, a wee thing hot."

"A grand day fer a swim."

"Ay, a grand day fer a swim."

"Did you really make a wad of lolly over there?"

"I made a bit, Tirene."

"Were they kind to you?"

"Yes, Tirene, they were very kind."

"When you wrote *Drin kin buckle for all I care,* did you mean it?"

"It was a tipsy joke, Tirene."

"I do love Drin," she said.

"I'm glad," I said.

It is not possible for me to tell you of my gladness as we approached the gates of Drin. But we had not reached them when, from the smallest of sideroads a white Minivan edged out, the blue light flashing, and from it stepped that puristical pest, Constable McIntoon. He raised his right arm much as I had done in grim Glenauchart.

"Och, four-letter it," she said. "Shall I jink past him? Only fifty yards to go."

"No, Tirene, stop!" In rural Scotland the law is still the law. It pays neither to jink past the law's arresting arm, nor to argy-bargy with it. Our policemen are not cops to cop us, but Bobbies to look after us while copping. Let other less civilized societies take note. There are Bobbies and Bobbies, however, and Constable McIntoon was the latter.

"Names please, Miss?" he said, notebook at the ready.

Tirene hissed with displeasure, having been known to him all her life. But she gave her names.

"Are you the driver of this vehicle?"

"What does it look like, Officer? Of course I am."

"It does look like that, Officer," I said. "But not so. I am driving from the pillion seat, and Miss Duncatto is my passenger. Dismount please, passenger." Tirene got off, scowling. "See, Officer, every control is at my command, and my name is Dougal Trocher, the owner of this vehicle, which has not been licensed since the year nineteen forty-two, bears no insurance, has no roadworthiness certificate. Furthermore, my license does not permit me to ride a motorbike. Would you care to note all that down?"

Constable McIntoon did. He was a conscientious officer, and he linked my numerous confessions to the Vehicles (excise) Act, to the motor vehicles regulations, to the Road Traffic Act, mentioning with some relish that the most serious of these grave offenses was lack of insurance, the penalty for which could be imprisonment.

"Best thing is to own up, plead guilty," I remarked aside. "Get off more lightly."

"Listen, idiot! You said: *She's all yours now, your very own.* Remember? Okay, you own and drive. I own and drive. Got it?"

But he had finished. "How many charges would that be, Constable McIntoon?"

"That would be five, Sir Dougal — Firrst, driving an unlicensed vehicle, the said combination. Second, driving said vehicle without being in proper control, i.e., from the said pillion seat. Thirrd, driving a vehicle inadequate. Fourth, driving said vehicle without insurance. Fifth, driving said vehicle without having a driving license valid for said class of vehicle."

"Don't you need a witness to these offenses, Officer?"

"That's right," he said. "And Miss Duncatto here's the witness, to be subpoenaed, should the court require."

"I won't need to be subpoenaed. I'll be a very willing, hostile witness to the effect that Dougal's told you a pack of lies. I was riding the bike, Officer, not him. And it's my bike, not his. *She's all yours now, your very own,* he said, and so it's mine."

"That is a total fabrication, Officer. The said vehicle is my property, and I monitored the driving every inch, in sole charge, captain of the ship."

There was a dawning puzzlement, if such may dawn, on Constable McIntoon's hatchet face. "You see, Officer," Tirene continued sweetly. "If you prefer these grave charges against

Dougal, I say it was me not him. And if you prefer these grave charges against me, Dougal says it was him not me. So whoever is charged, the other will be the guilty party to every crime. Don't you think that in the eyes of the Bench, the Crummockshire Constabulary might look a wee thing daft or silly?"

Constable McIntoon shook his head and scratched his ear and mopped his brow. "Serious offenses have been committed," he said. "And this is not denied. But the case is vexing, verra vexing. The law will take its proper course."

"I am at your disposal any time, Officer."

"Same here," Tirene said. "And I hope I can help to unvex the case."

"May we proceed, then, Constable McIntoon?"

"It is an offense to push said vehicle on the public thoroughfare . . ." McIntoon caught his breath, sighed long and deep. "Och, well," he said.

"Out, Bernardo!" But he yawned.

So we pushed, and Constable McIntoon was decent enough to lend a hand as far as the broken gates of Drin, where we took leave of him, and proceeded legitimately under power.

"He'll get us, Tirene. Sure as hell he'll get one of us or both."

"No, he won't, you stupid. Think a bit."

"I think thus a bit: 'Thy neck is as a tower of ivory; thine eyes like the fishponds of Heshbron; thy nose is as the tower of Lebanon which looketh toward Damascas. Oh, Duncatto's daughter, the joints of thy thighs are like jewels.' "

We came to the House of Drin, where Tirene and I dismounted with some reluctance and relief, and Bernardo dismounted with alacrity, glad to be home again. He bounded out, but the thrust for the leap was too much for the underpinnings of Grandfather's Combopede, and motorbike and sidecar fell apart to lie on their sides in weeds and gravel.

We walked under the beech trees and up the Den where one day I might make a shrub garden to end all shrub gardens, and it was very hot, no breeze at all at the loud Fall of Drin except the immediate wind of cataract, the sun on ferns that clung to rock, the rainbows in the spray, wet boulders in white water. My trouble had been that I loved the place. My blessing was that I loved the place.

Now it chanced that in my sporran pocket there had remained from last time a small object bearing our coat of arms, once carried in some Trocher woman's reticule.

"May I ask a favor, Tirene?"

"Well, it depends. Well, I suppose so. What?"

"Your hair is such a ghastly tangle."

I drew that comb through that matchless hair with many a tangled tug and some forthright protest from the owner. I combed the hair until it fell in glossiness, smooth order, black touched with smoky tints of deepest red. "That's it," I said.

"You wasted your time. I'm for that swim."

"But, Tirene!"

"Look away, then, if you don't like my looks."

"I'm looking away because I love your looks."

"No one ever said that to me before."

I heard her dive. "Gosh, it's cold. Turn round."

I turned to see her standing shoulder deep, her hair sleek and wet and black with smoky tints. "May I ask a favor, Dougal?"

"Well, it depends. Well, I suppose so. What?"

"Ever since I was small, Ida's told me her favorite story about wee Black Dougal jumping at the Fall of Drin. Please!"

"But, Tirene, well, you know, Tirene."

"Yes, I know. What's there to be coy about, for God's sake?"

Coy, a provoking word, I climbed round to stand on the rock beside the Fall of Drin, above the deep dark pool. It was a long way down. I admired my courage at the age of eight, and steeled myself at the age of thirty-four, made a mammoth splash, and paddled back. It was most refreshing.

We used our upper garments as towels, not that dampness mattered much on that day of unwonted heat. Nothing seemed to matter much.

Bernardo had been ambling after interesting smells, but he arrived now for a cooling dip, and then walked down between us.

"I love you, Bernardo," Tirene said, her hand on his collar.

Bernardo wagged and rumbled.

"I love you, Bernardo," I said, my hand on his collar.

Bernardo wagged and rumbled.

"It's quite okay . . ." I said.

"I know," she said. "To love the dog."

We were happy going down the Den and through beech trees to the House of Drin to take our happiness to Ida Peebles.

Extraordinary things, women. No sooner had we finished lunch than they banished me. "What you're needin', Dougal, is a nice wee snooze."

"Yes, go and indulge your soporific."

The sleep was lovely, dreamless, deep, and my awakening slow. "I brought you a cup of tea."

"Oh, lovely."

"Shall I open up?"

"Well, half." Tirene let some light in, not the sun. "Lovely cup of tea," I said, sitting up. "Everything in the garden's lovely. Did you have a lovely gas with Ida?"

"Lovely."

"What about?"

"Oh, this and that and lovely everything. And then I read the news. I was a bit out of date because they didn't deliver morning papers to the bothy."

"Yes, of course, I mean, no, I see."

"I read about braw laddie to the rescue."

"Did you, now, Tirene?"

"Was she the one you were shacked up with?"

"Not so that you would notice, no, Tirene."

"I smell funny business."

"Why, Tirene, how?"

"Because nobody could change as much as you have in one single month without some funny business."

"A change for the better, I hope, Tirene."

"You're sort of self-satisfied."

"Tirene, darling, why would that be?"

"It is so lovely, isn't it?" She was sitting on my bed, away from me, and I watched her while we talked, but Tirene did not look at me. She looked at my grandmother's ring on her wedding finger. It was an old-fashioned setting, gold with three diamonds, the largest of about one carat, my recent training told me. I had sold almost everything but that. "How soon?" Tirene said.

"I don't know what the rules are. If he published them tomorrow, perhaps next week."

"It must be soon, because not until."

"Tirene, only three months ago you preached Free Love with quite unmitigated passion. Surely . . ."

"That's fun and games, old stupid. That's not marriage."

"Very well, then. Shall we make a solemn pact?"

"That's what I mean."

"Miss Tirene!"

"Yes, Ida?"

"His Lordship's just been on the line, and His Lordship sounds real vexed with you and Dougal. *Where are they, dammit?* His Lordship says. So I says they're away out for a dander in the arboretum, and His Lordship growls he's coming over."

"What's Daddy in a stew about?"

"I dinna ken, Miss Tirene. Come downstairs, though, is my advice. His Lordship's no in any frame of mind to catch you there in Dougal's bedroom."

"Okay, Ida." Tirene stood. "What's our solemn pact?"

"I promise not to delve into the gone-before, Free Love for instance. And I promise to do my best not to annoy you or provoke you about women's lib and so on, even Chairman Mao."

"Oh, him. And what do I promise?"

"You promise not to ask idiotic questions about funny shacking business. Is that a deal?"

"Darling Dougal, it's a lovely deal." She kissed me, and she went away.

The pajamas off, the kilt on again, the hairbrush applied, I was about to follow her to meet her father's wrath about whatever it was, not a light matter — but who could care less? — when I heard the souped-up Mini's snarl, and I went to watch from the upstairs window.

"Now, look here, Tirene, what's this you and that fella have been up to?"

"Keep your hair on, Daddy. What?"

"Carmichael, the Chief Constable, telephoned me, spitting mad. How dare the Lord Lieutenant's daughter set such an example in the county. So I said: *What's m'daughter done, Chief Constable?* I'm a bit afraid of Carmichael, actually, formidable type. So he said that one of his most valued officers had arrived at headquarters in a state of shock, *a very vexing case* was all McIntoon could say at first, poor chap. But eventually he poured out his story, which was that you and Dougal both had pleaded guilty to numerous offenses, you riding your motorbike and that bloody fool Dougal riding his motorbike, which was what sent the bobby bonkers: Could two separate and distinct citizens be charged with the one offense, or series of offenses? So I said: *Stuff and nonsense, Chief Constable. It's Dougal's motorbike. Everyone knows that.* So he said, more cold spitting mad than ever: *The Honorable Tirene Duncatto is prepared to testify that the former owner, Sir Dougal Trocher, formally passed ownership and possession in the vehicle to her.* What's the meaning of it?"

Father and daughter faced one another, and in the background Mother stood. There were times, what Tarquie called his blue-moon days, when his women yielded to his warpath, and this might be one.

"Hang on a minute. I'm coming down."

". . . And Carmichael finished up: *Am I to understand,*

Lord Duncatto, that you personally asked Constable McIntoon to investigate a suspicious character at the transformer at Lower Camsie, which just happens to be the point in his rural charge that is furthest removed from Drin?"

"Well, didn't you, Tarquie?"

"Innocently, yes, an honest ruse to save my daughter, and look what you let me in for. Don't you know you've done the one thing no self-respecting police force ever does forgive? That was another raving of McIntoon's: *Wouldn't in the eyes of the Bench the Crummockshire Constabulary look a wee thing daft or silly?* The Chief Constable means business. He's going to get one of you or both. And if you stick to your damned stupid stories, they'll add perjury."

Tirene had stood before her irate father, hands behind her back. But now she held her left hand out. "Daddy dear," she said, "don't you see that we only have to add one to that to make it impossible for us to bear false witness?"

"You little devil," Tarquie said.

"Darling!" Lois and Tirene bounded into one another's arms, and there were floods of happiness. "What we always longed for, oh how marvelous, it's happened."

"You haven't asked me for m'daughter's hand in marriage."

"Well, I'm asking."

"That's okay," he said, and led me over to the wreck of Grandfather's Combopede. "You could have killed the girl."

"She insisted. It seemed the only hope. It worked."

He lowered his voice. "And you got away with the needful over there?"

"Yes, Tarquie."

"Those helicopter chaps, tried to welch on you and kill you into the bargain, eh?"

"Yes, Tarquie."

"What did you do, have to shoot 'em to get back the swag?"

"In a manner of speaking, Tarquie."

"Serve 'em right. Listen, young fella — Lois is hotching to hear all, but I would say: Don't tell us anything about it, not a word. Damn well do penance for your sins alone."

"Right, Tarquie."

"Aren't we going to celebrate?"

"It'll have to be in whisky. Grandfather drank the last of the champagne."

"I brought a bottle as insurance," Lois said, and the four of us walked across weeds and gravel to the House of Drin, where they and Ida drank to us, and we to them.

"Tarquie," I said later. "Would you telephone the Chief Constable and tell him that McIntoon won't need a witness? I shall plead guilty and take what's coming to me."

"That's sensible of you," Tarquie said.

"I don't think it's sensible at all. I think it's daft. The very first time in all your life you ever committed even a few picayune small offenses, and you can get away with them, but you have to be a big Boy Scout!"

"It's true that this is my first brush ever with the law. But I don't want to get away with it. I want to count the many blessings that my crimes have brought me. Now, be nice, Tirene love."

"Oh well, I suppose so, darling, yes, I'll try."

"Wonder of all wonders," Lois said, and Bernardo wowfed his stout approval on that happy day.

Thus ends my cautionary tale.

But over, if you please:

Postscript

THE OLD SAYING IS that crime never pays. But, as I have indicated, crime did pay for me. It steeled a timid soul to win a smashing wife. It has enabled the two of us to dwell and labor together for the sake of ourselves, of our children, and of Drin. Nor am I such a softy as to regret those misdeeds with a fair accomplice in the sovereign land of Canada.

There is, however, a debit side that plagues. Grandfather wrote in his journal once: *Paul told the Romans that the wages of sin is death. In an ultimate sense no doubt the saintly man was right. In terms of lesser, undiscovered wickedness my experience has been, and is, that the wages of sin are twofold: First, we find ourselves preaching to the little ones what we ourselves have not invariably practiced. And that is genuinely bothersome. Second, our peccadilloes nag us each day that we must walk alone with them. And that is mildly bothersome. Vanity, vanity — hypocrisy.*

I have no other secrets from Tirene, and how often I long to confess to her. But would it be wise to spill the beans to salve a questionable conscience? She would be astonished and enchanted to learn how the old stick plundered the transatlantic rich. But what about the old stick's friendship with her best friend ever? Tirene is nothing if not all wondrous woman, so I wonder.

Thus ends my cautionary postscript.